Ⅲ Ⅲ ⅢⅢⅢⅢ ⅢⅢ ⅢⅢⅢⅢⅢⅢ ⅢⅢ

S67 **W9-AUX-390**

Would you like a FREE e-BOOK?

Download your **FREE** copy of *Skins Game, and other short fiction*

A baker's dozen of Phil Truman's short stories in a range of genres from humor to horror. Guaranteed to deliver a laugh and make you shed a tear.

A no-obligation, FREE offer at author's website:
www.PhilTruman.com

Also by Phil Truman:

GAME,
an American Novel

Treasure Kills,
Legends of Tsalagee

Red Lands Outlaw,
the Ballad of Henry Starr

West of the Dead Line,
Tales of an Indian Territory Lawman

Dire Wolf of the Quapaw

a Jubal Smoak Mystery

by Phil Truman

PTI

Publishing

PTI Publishing
Broken Arrow, OK 74012

© 2018 by Phil Truman and PTI Publishing
All Rights Reserved.

This book is a work of fiction. All characters, organizations, and events portrayed in this novel are either products of the author's imagination or are used fictitiously.

No part of this publication may be reproduced, stored in a retrieval system, or transmitted in any form or by any means, electronic, mechanical, recording or otherwise, without written permission, except in the case of brief quotations embodied in critical articles and reviews.

To Darlene ...

for all the good years

CHAPTER 1

C row Redhand shot me in the back.

Felt like a blacksmith had whacked my right shoulder blade with a hot iron. The impact spun me around, knocking me to the ground.

Wasn't the first time. He'd shot me in July of aught-eight. Shot me from the back then, too, but the slug from his rifle only creased my neck and lower jaw. Left me with a dandy scab and a bit tongue. Hurt like hell; otherwise, hadn't harmed me much. That first time, I'd followed Redhand into Liberal, Kansas where he and his bunch had gone to deposit two hundred head of stolen cattle. They'd cut the animals from a bigger herd off the Burnett outfit up out of North Texas on the trail crossing the Comanche reservation land they called Big Pasture. Also shot up the ramrod and four other drovers in the process, killing one. Don't know if Redhand had done the killing, but as the leader, he'd still hang for murder. I'd been sent to arrest Crow, along with as many of his gang as I could, and bring them back to stand trial in Guthrie, the capital city of the brand-new state of Oklahoma.

The incident in Liberal was the first time I'd come to meet Redhand. Although I'd been told by several people what a ruthless and cold-blooded sumbitch he was, I was still not prepared for his out and out meanness.

The outlaw – a member of the Quapaw tribe – and his boys got away after he shot me in Liberal. Shot his way through my possemen, too, and on out of town.

This second time, he was closer and took better aim. Expect he meant to kill me, but I moved sideways the instant he pulled the trigger. Some folks would call that blind luck. I can't say it wasn't. Things like that happen to me.

1

Seems I tend to have that kind of instinct in critical situations—the ability to escape death, if not personal injury. It has happened often enough to where I can't lay it all on plain luck. Don't really know how to explain it. Tried in my own mind, thinking on it long and hard at times, like when I was laid up in that Army hospital in Denver. Just seems like I know to make some move when calamity is about to strike. Move enough to perhaps keep disaster from becoming fatal. My momma told me it's a guardian angel. Suppose it could be. Although, I never really held to that sort of thing. Besides, I figure any guardian angel worth her salt would be able to move me more than just partly out of harm's way. I just think a person sometimes has extra-sense glimpses that affect his actions. Some more than others like me. The closest I can come to describing it is like having one of those déjà vu things before it even happens . . . like a déjà vu of a déjà vu. Hell, I don't know.

Take that polo accident. Before it occurred, I knew it was going to happen. Also knew that a thousand pounds of horse would crush me, so I made a move to dismount. Didn't really foresee it so much as just sense it. Had to be . . . *un-thought out,* because no rational mind would consider getting off a galloping horse amid others doing the same. This all took place in fractions of a second, and the movement my body made to get off the horse probably saved my life. Anyhow, that's the way I considered it later with all that time I had to lay in that hospital bed and think about it.

We were up around Fairland, Oklahoma when I took that second bullet from Crow. Been about a year after the first. Three weeks earlier I just started work out of the U.S. Marshal's office in Tulsa when word came in him and his gang had robbed a bank in the town of Picher, killing a man in the process. I was still on his trail for that cattle stealing, plus the charges added after him shooting me in Liberal—assault on a

Federal officer, attempted murder, that sort of thing—when his latest escapade came across the wire.

He also became a suspect for multiple homicides that'd taken place near the town of Miami a day after the Picher robbery. Three people named Jakes—two brothers and a woman, the wife of one of them—brutally murdered, and there was a good chance that number could rise to four. The fourth victim, a twelve-year-old blind boy, survived the attack but was critically injured with several slashing animal bites. Not sure he could identify Redhand as the killer, the kid being blind and all, but maybe he could tell us something if he survived. He was in a coma at the hospital in Miami where they took him.

It took me a day to ride up there. I went to Freeman's Mortuary first to see the victims.

Crow Redhand was a Quapaw. The Jakes were Quapaw. He grew up in that area, the sheriff in town told me Redhand knew the victims. Despite his reputation, most around there didn't think him capable of committing such a crime. Wasn't so sure based on my own experience. Crow was a mean and ruthless cuss, and fact is, most killings come by the hand of relatives or acquaintances. On the other hand, after seeing the bodies, I did start to wonder. He, sure enough, put a bullet in my back and was a part of two other killings, but the bodies were so mangled it could only have been done by a madman. Not that Crow was sane, just not that insane.

The undertaker, man named Ted Freeman, said he'd seen a lot, but nothing like this, not from the hand of a human, anyway.

"When I first started out up in Montana, a man was once brought in mauled by a grizzly. That was the worst condition I ever saw in a killed human body . . . up 'til now," he told me.

3

My reservations about Crow as the killer were further reinforced after I interviewed the person who discovered the dead Jakes.

A neighbor to the slain family – an old Quapaw man called Long Walker – and the Jakes brothers were supposed to go hunting that morning. But the men didn't show at the agreed-upon spot and time, so Long Walker returned to his cabin. Said sometimes that happened. He didn't think anything about it. Along about noon, a loud bang rattled his door. He went to investigate and found a big rock thrown against it, but no one was around. Thought maybe it was one of the Jakes. A bad feeling came over him, so he went to their cabin. Found a grisly scene: the men's bodies ripped to shreds, the woman eviscerated, the walls and furniture awash with blood. It filled him with terror.

I went to the crime scene after the bodies were removed, but I could still envision the horror of it. The remains of the carnage made me swallow my gorge more than once.

A raging snowstorm swept through the bitter winter night of the killings. The four Jakes were viciously attacked in their beds. Anyway, that's where the boy and his mother were found. It looked like the two men put up a fight, but it didn't appear they had much of a chance. Long Walker found the boy, but he wasn't slashed like the others. He was bitten savagely. The old shaman carried him into town to the hospital.

All the violence and mayhem turned the inside of that little cabin into a slaughterhouse. The door was smashed in, kicked from the outside. The cabin was half-filled and drifted with snow from the blizzard, the bodies frozen where they died. The crime scene was badly corrupted by all the coming in and taking out of the bodies, but I found bloody tracks on the floor. I brushed away some of the trampled snow to find more—one human, several animal. Hard to tell how many, but all canine.

4

I didn't know enough about tracking to know if they were dogs or wolves. One set was particularly big.

At Freeman's make-shift morgue, I saw the horror-stricken expressions of the victims still preserved from their freshly murdered state. Long Walker said the boy was under a buffalo robe, the body of his ma laying atop it. A curious thing, he said. It looked like someone placed the boy on the bed and covered him with the robe. Maybe the last act of his dying mother to try to save him? Long Walker didn't think so. The woman was too mangled to do that. Said more likely her body was put atop the robe to keep it from blowing off. Hard to imagine such a violent and cruel killer taking time to do that. The doctor said the cold probably kept him from bleeding to death, but the body of his mother and the buffalo robe stayed him from freezing. It was a miracle he survived either, bleeding or freezing to death.

Evidence showed the Jakes brother named Elam fired shots from his pistol, a Schofield .45, which was still in his stiff hand when the undertaker came to gather what was left of the bodies. I found two shell casings from .50-70 cartridges on the cabin floor, but the rifle from which they came, was nowhere to be found. My guess, the killer took it with him, along with the ammunition for it. In all the blood, it was hard to tell if any shots hit the assailant or assailants, but no blood trail led from the cabin.

With the boy's bite marks, the undertaker's killing by animal theory was likely. However, I found part of a snow-covered handprint on the tabletop, a bloody human handprint. I brushed away the snow to reveal all of it. A large handprint, the left one. It was too big to be the print of any of the deceased, even that of old Long Walker. There were triangular-shaped dots of blood an inch or two beyond the fingertips, like the tips you'd see in a bear track left by claws or that of a wolf. A damn big wolf. Only the print wasn't a bear or wolf track, or that from any other animal. It was distinctly human. There were plenty of horse and boot tracks outside and inside the cabin, but they were from the men who came to remove the bodies and those of the undertaker. Impossible to determine if any were the killer's. Although the inside of the small cabin was wrecked, it didn't appear anything else had been taken . . . besides the rifle, I mean.

Redhand was still a suspect, but only by reputation. He was Quapaw by blood, but no evidence came up to suggest he or his men had been there. No immediate discernment as to motive.

"What do you know about these killings?" I asked Long Walker. "You see or hear anything?" His shack, where he lived alone, stood about a half mile from the Jakes's in amongst a throng of willows that crackled against the outsides of the hovel in the winter wind. The man was on my initial list of suspects, but not likely. He was ancient and . . . you couldn't say frail-looking, but boney and bent. Even with tools, I didn't see him generating enough force to cause the damage I saw. Plus, he was visibly shaken, truly frightened.

Long Walker didn't answer, only stared into the flames in his fireplace.

"Did the Jakes own a rifle?" I held out the brass I'd found at the scene. "I found these, but not the rifle."

"Sam has a Spencer," the old man said.

"You didn't by chance take it when you were over there, did ya?"

He looked at me with astonishment and shook his head.

"You know a man named Crow Redhand?" I asked the old man.

Long Walker nodded.

"You seen him around here?"

"Crow Redhand did not do this thing," he quietly said to me.

"No? You know who did?"

He held his stare into the flames for some time before he answered. "It was the wolf of the ancients." He turned his black eyes to me. Cold fear flickered there when he said it. He stared back into the fire again, seeking comfort and refuge in its light and warmth.

What he said confused me. "Beg pardon?"

He studied the flames. It took him a few seconds to respond.

"The Dire Wolf killed the Jakes," he said.

"Who's this Dire Wolf?" I asked. Figured he was talking about someone he knew.

He spoke in a whisper, almost reverently. "The Dire Wolf is the curse of the Downstream People, the Arkansa. He is an evil spirit of the Quapaw."

I sighed and shook my head, knowing how these old Indians liked to throw in a bunch of mythical tribal mumbo-jumbo and superstition to deflect blame from someone they knew. "Well, you know where I can find this Dire Wolf fella?" I asked.

"He cannot be found," the old man said.

"Really. You have reason to believe he's taken off to other parts?"

He said nothing for a full quarter minute, his black eyes intently on mine, searching. I could see contempt in them and a sadness. Made me nervous.

"No," old Long Walker answered at last. "He has not departed. Now that he has awakened, he will kill again."

7

tracked Redhand to a line house up near the Neosho River where he was said to be holed up. The morning air hung thick and bitter cold, and eight or so inches of snow still covered the ground. My four possemen – recruited from town – and I surrounded the house. The four horses outside the cabin said we outnumbered Crow and his boys by one. Didn't seem right. I knew Crow and his gang totaled seven. Maybe the other three rode off somewhere to get provisions, or maybe the gang split up. Didn't know how many were inside the cabin. It worried me.

Lewis Elliot squatted behind a pine twenty yards off to my left. I chirped a low whistle in his direction, motioned him over. "Lewis, you and Bill go scout the woods and road. Don't think they're all in that cabin."

He nodded and crouch-walked over to Bill, passed on his instructions. They silently moved into the brush. Not five minutes passed till Bill returned. "Rider comin," he said.

I looked toward the narrow trail leading to the cabin. A big man with a thick black beard came riding up to the cabin with two horses in tow. Didn't know what that meant: Maybe they'd lost a couple horses in that shoot-out riding out of Picher. Six in the cabin?

Not sure I actually heard the cocking of the hammer, but that's when that instinct thing of mine kicked in. I moved sideways to my left and started to stand. Had I not, that bullet would've gone through the back of my head, instead of my shoulder. The thick pile of my heavy sheepskin coat barely slowed the slug as it burrowed through the back and out the front.

I fell over the wide trunk of a storm-downed sycamore just as Redhand got off his second shot. The slug splintered the top edge of the tree trunk sending out a spray of wood chips and snow. My right arm went numb, but fortunately, I'm left-handed and had my piece in hand. I fired through the gap under the sycamore log. Didn't have the best of aim, but the round hit Crow somewhere in the ankle or foot, as he hopped and fell, hollering and cussing going down. With me shooting, most would call it a lucky shot. Hell, even a blind hog finds an acorn every now and then.

"Redhand, it's Deputy Smoak! Give it up!" I yelled from my own prone position. "We've got you outnumbered and surrounded!"

"Piss on you, Smoak!" he responded. "No damn law's takin me in." He fired again, blowing up some snow and frozen dirt in front of me. I returned another shot.

The black-beard man dropped the rope of the horses he had in tow and reined his bay around, spurring it into a gallop back down the road he came in on. Lewis Elliot stepped out from behind a tree at the edge of that road, and using an old wind-fall oak limb, clubbed the rider right off the back of his mount as he came by. The horse galloped on rider-less down the snow-covered trail.

Shouting, cussing, and more shooting erupted from inside the cabin, and my possemen returned fire. One of Redhand's men, a big red-faced red-haired fella, came out a side window of the cabin where they tied their horses. Tried to mount up, but Carroll Moore took him down with a clean shot from his Henry.

I was taking fire from both sides, that from Redhand off in the woods to my right and from the cabin on my left. I was exposed. With slugs slapping and snapping around me, I clawed and crawled my way through the snow to a small stand of scrub oaks gaining some cover from the cabin fire. Redhand hobbled to black beard's riderless bay standing thirty yards down the road. I laid down some ineffective fire toward

Redhand as he shambled away, but he managed to reach the horse, mount it, and ride off.

With my shoulder wound bleeding from two holes and pinned down, I couldn't get up and take off after Redhand.

Old Bill Aspinwall, who'd fought with the Union at Champion Hill and Vicksburg as a sixteen-year-old boy, was a dead aim shot and took out two of the gunmen in the cabin. After about ten minutes of intense gunfire, it ceased. "Hold on, out there!" a voice called from inside. "We got two men shot up in here, and we ain't got no more ammo! We're givin up and comin out!"

"How many are ya?" I called out.

"They's four of us. Only one man's gut-shot, and t'nother'un ain't got use of his gun arm. Me and Dooley ain't shot but is just had enough."

"You bring those two wounded men out first," I told him. "Don't want to see any firearms in your hands, either. Leave 'em in the cabin."

The door of the cabin opened, and one man came out with his hands up, then the one shot in the arm with his good arm raised. The other two followed one supporting the gut-shot man.

"Y'all sit," I said, my Colt pointed as I approached. "Buck, check inside the cabin, and then go see about that fella by the horses."

"Lewis, what about that guy you whacked off his horse?" I yelled back to Elliot.

"Still out cold," he hollered back. "May've broke his neck, but reckon we'll have to wait 'til he comes around to find out for sure."

I turned back to the men on the ground, speaking to the nearest one of the unwounded. "What's your name?"

"Name's Los Gilmore," he answered glumly.

"All you boys been riding with Redhand awhile?"

10

Gilmore looked up at me sideways with squinted eyes. "Been a few months," he said for the group.

"Looks like Crow run off and left you. Doesn't much appear he appreciates your loyalty."

The bunch considered my statement in silence. One of them, the arm-shot one, spit to his left.

"Yep, he left you high and dry, I'd say," I offered. "Sort of hanging, so to speak. Probably in your futures, too."

"I need a doc," the gut-shot one whined.

"Yeah, several of us do, hoss." I winced from my own pain as I stuffed a bandana inside my shirt to plug up the bullet holes in my shoulder. My breathing was heavy. "We'll get you there. But first I'd like to ask you a few questions about Redhand. You cooperate, and I'll tell the judge. Might make things go better for you."

Moore returned with all the mounts in tow. "That big redhaired sumbitch back there looks to be dead," he reported.

"You ain't sure?" I asked.

"Yeah, pretty sure," Buck answered. "I kicked him in the ribs, and he didn't suck in no breath."

"Tell ya what I know about Redhand," said the man sitting next to Gilmore.

"Shut up, Dooley," Gilmore said.

"Why should I?" he returned hotly. "Bastard ain't done me no favors."

"You with him when he rustled those cows last winter down in the Big Pasture?" I asked.

"Yeah, we all was," Dooley said. "'Includin Mick Hallihan back there." He motioned with his head towards the corpse at the side of the house.

"And I guess all of you helped rob that bank in Picher."

"Yup."

"Damn you, Dooley," Gilmore shouted.

I turned my attention fully on Dooley. "There were some people killed north of here a few days back, up on the Neosho near Miamuh. You know anything about that?"

"Heard about it," Dooley said.

"What'd you hear about it?" I asked.

"Crow spoke of it. Said he heard it from an Indin cousin of his over at Blue Jacket when he went over there to get us some grub. Word travels pretty fast in these parts, 'specially among them Indins."

"You reckon Redhand had anything to do with it?"

"Can't say he didn't. He's gone up to Blue Jacket by hisself for a couple days, so I don't know where else he gone. From what I know of it, though, don't seem like somethin he'd do."

"Why not?"

"Crow's a mean sumbitch. He'll kill ya for a plug nickel. But he ain't crazy. Them killins, the way Crow told about how they was done. That was plum crazy."

"You know the name of this cousin of Crow's over in Blue Jacket?"

"Believe it's Redhand, too. I think he said their daddies was brothers. First name of Willard."

"Wilbur," Gilmore said.

I adjusted the blood-soaked bandana on my shoulder wound, removed my hat and wiped the sweat off my brow with my coat sleeve. Sat down on a wood-splitting stump there in the front yard. Began to feel a little puny. "Well, let's start thinking about getting this outfit back to town," I said. Pressed the bandana at my shoulder wound again. "Get those of us who need it to a doc."

"Bill," I said. "Why don't you take those two horses that one fella brought back to that farm we passed a couple miles back. If they're not that farmer's, I expected he'll know whose they are. See if he has a wagon we can borrow. Tell him it's

U.S. Marshal business, and he'll be compensated for it. We'll haul the wounded and dead back to Miamuh in that.

I gestured toward the horses. "We'll get everyone here mounted up and meet you at that farmhouse."

That's when I noticed a rifle tied to the back of the saddle on a chestnut mare, and I got up and walked over to the horse. The rifle was a Spencer. I opened one of the saddlebags and pulled out two boxes of .50-70 cartridges.

"Whose horse is this?" I asked Gilmore.

"That'uns Crow's," he said.

hate hospitals. Lying in that Miami hospital waiting for my shoulder wound to heal some, left me plenty of time to reflect on it; hating hospitals among other things.

It went back to my year-long in and out stays at that Army hospital in Denver. What got me there was a chain of life events I never expected. Always been sort of a "chips fall where they may" kind of guy, never set any well-defined life goals. Still, ten years ago, when I was a young cadet at West Point, I never imagined I'd be a Deputy U.S. Marshal in Indian Territory. Life takes some funny trails.

I was just a young pup, a new deputy assigned to the Marshal out of Pueblo, Colorado. I ended up there by way of the Army, a second lieutenant working in the Adjutant General's Office in Denver. Working as an administrative officer hadn't been my first choice coming out of the Point. Always thought I'd be a cavalry officer, like my great uncle and namesake. But when you graduate last in your class at West Point, a *goat*, you don't get your pick of assignments. My father isn't proud of that. On the other hand, I did manage to graduate. There was another fella there about as bad a student as me, named George Patton. For some reason, as a First Year, I was assigned to tutor the Plebe. Nobody liked him much as he was kind of brash and quarrelsome, but he liked horses and wanted to be in the cavalry, so we got along. He liked to soldier but wasn't much good at anything else. Haven't heard anything about him since I left the Point. If he got his commission, expect he'll need a good war somewhere to amount to anything.

In my romantic visions as a boy, I'd become an Indian fighter out west, but by the time I got my commission and headed west, the Indian Wars had ended. Still were occasional renegade bands out on the plains raping and pillaging, but they existed more as common outlaws of mixed lineage, rather than full-blooded warriors fighting for their sovereignty. The Army gathered up those left of the great warring tribes and moved them off to places in the Dakotas and Wyoming and New Mexico. Plenty of tribes still lived in the land once called the Indian Territory, now Oklahoma. The red people here, once promised that land would be theirs forever, experienced ever-increasing encroachment from American settlers. What small lands they'd been given to call their nations got squeezed smaller by the tyrannical Dawes Act.

Ironically, I did come to serve as an Indian fighter of sorts, only not in the traditional sense. As a lawman in the southwestern plains, a lot of my customers were Indian, either mostly or part, blood-wise. The fact that the territory I worked had a high population of Indians made it so. Crow Redhand was a good example. Still, most bad guys I dealt with were non-Indian, but not by much.

So, I was sent West to ride, but not quite like I thought. Truth is, my old boss in Denver, the AG – Brigadier General Beaumont Davis – had requested me for my riding skills more than my administrative ability. I was no scholar, but I knew horses. The General brought me in for that very reason. He was a polo enthusiast – still is, I guess – with his own team there in Denver.

Davis always stayed on the lookout for skilled horsemen. I believe the duties of his office came in a distant second to beating his main rival in polo matches. That'd be Colonel Ben Rueben, the commandant at Fort Logan, just outside of Denver. Rueben started the whole thing, fielding his own polo team, who usually whipped Davis's team like a rented mule.

Davis's and Ruben's rivalry went back to their post-war West Point days. Davis came from Virginia gentry, swimming in money from tobacco and horse breeding and somehow managed to regain most of that after the war. Politics, it's said. Rueben was an abrasive and hard-charging son of a New York railroad baron. And the two maintained some of those Yankee/Dixie tensions between them.

I'm a Virginian, myself. Named after my great uncle – my dad's mother's brother – that great son of Virginia and Confederate general, Jubal Early. That's my full name: Jubal Early Smoak. No doubt that brought me into General Davis's command as much as my horsemanship and his rivalry with Colonel Rueben.

The general knew my father, of course. Reason I got my appointment to The Point was because of my father. Though loyal to the Southern Cause, and part of General Lee's entourage at Appomattox, he was politician enough after the war to build his influence during the reparations to gain him social and political standing. I never wanted to go to West Point, but what I wanted didn't enter the equation with my father. I was anxious to get as far west of the man as General Davis was to get me out there, even if it was just to play polo.

Started out to be a good appointment, I thought. My disappointment at not getting a cavalry post flew straight out the window the night I met Penelope Davis. The general threw a Fourth of July soiree for the local elite – Denver mayor, Senator Wolcott, Governor Orman, various other politicians, prominent businessmen, and military brass – including Colonel Rueben. Plus, all the wives and grown daughters. It was mandatory attendance for all of us in the general's junior officers' cadre, although in the social order of the night we weren't much above the serving staff. Believe General Davis just wanted to taunt Colonel Rueben some with his riders, like having a stable of fine horses.

The general's daughter swept into the room like an angelic visitation. Never seen such a vision of the feminine in my life. It hit me between the eyes like someone pressed a live telegraph wire to the back of my head. She came amongst us boys so coquettish and alight with laughter that we all took on dumbfounded stupidity, not quite knowing what to say or how to act.

Bob Tregonne became my friend those first few weeks in Denver. He graduated two years before me at the Point, but I hadn't known him, not in a familiar sense. He was a cadet captain and adjutant when I was second year. There in Denver, we were teammates . . . and friends. Friends, that is, until Penelope Davis showed up.

For her own amusement, she played both of us. Somehow, I won out. Not sure why. I fell for her in a big way. The comradeship between Tregonne and me suffered, but he was outwardly noble about the whole thing, as befitting an officer and gentleman. Not resigned, though. The general liked my polo skills and didn't seem to mind too much me courting his daughter. Looking back on it, believe he felt more concern for me than Penelope, as he had foreknowledge of how these things ended up with his daughter. Unfortunately, for both the general and me, it didn't work out.

In my second polo match with Fort Logan, during the first chukker, I had the line of the ball and was charging toward the goal when a Fort Logan rider, an old Buffalo Soldier named Harris, known for his aggressive play, cut across my line, giving my pony a hard bump. My teammates said he clearly fouled me, and that the corporal made no attempt to disguise it. It was even suggested that Harris's move may've been ordered to take me out of the match. In any case, he did just that and more.

My pony stumbled at the collision, falling to the ground in a skidding roll with me still in the saddle. He came up okay, but my left leg was mangled, and the crash knocked me out as cold as a stepmother's kiss. The two bones in my lower leg had poked out through the skin when they snapped, the leather of my high riding boot the only thing that kept them attached to me. Knee was also dislocated and wrecked badly. Had a pretty good concussion, too, but that was the least of my worries.

The upshot of it all: after a year of recuperating, General Davis decided he couldn't keep me on, even as an administrative officer, and strongly recommended I take a medical discharge. Never came right out and said it, but it wasn't hard to figure he wanted a more able-bodied polo player in my slot. I could still ride but wasn't able to bend my leg at the knee more than about forty-five degrees. It stuck out some when I was in the saddle, prevented me from having tight control of the pony I needed in a polo match. And it ached, always ached. I'd taken to rubbing it a lot. Got to be habitual whenever something was on my mind, something bothering me. I'd rub that knee like some men would their chin whiskers or the ends of their mustache. I had neither, so I rubbed my knee instead. Still do.

Early in that rehabilitation year, Penelope decided a crippled-up second lieutenant didn't have much of a future in the military, as well as no longer fitting her criteria for dashing. With encouragement from her, Bob Tregonne saw his opportunity and took it. Poor bastard. Last I heard they married and moved to Washington where Bob got a promotion and a new post. My guess, he won't be the last of the woman's fools, especially in Washington society. Probably be a long list of husbands and lovers in that bucket.

Anyway, I was done as a polo player . . . and an eligible suitor for Miss Penelope. To his credit, though, the general didn't leave me high and dry and was instrumental in getting me the deputy job with the U.S. Marshal's office. Kind of surprised me, as it was well known in the ranks, I was handier with a horse under me and a saber than a gun. Truth was, I couldn't shoot a handgun worth beans, not much better with a rifle. I took the lawman job as much to keep from going back to Virginia and my father more than anything else. That, and starving. Sure couldn't become a buffalo hunter. Even if there were any left to hunt, I probably couldn't hit one. Figured my wits, my military education, and my intuition would have to overcome my lack of shooting skills.

⧗

Doc called me lucky. Crow's bullet went clean through my shoulder without hitting any nerves, or major vessels, then glanced off my right collarbone before exiting. Chipped and cracked the bastard—my collar bone—but it was a pretty clean wound, all-in-all. Doc said *we* needed to give it some rest and keep the wound clean, so it wouldn't infect. Told me a week of bed rest with the proper care would be the right thing to do.

"Doc, I don't have a week," I argued. "There's a murderer and a bank robber on the loose around here. Need to track him down before he strikes again."

Doc gave me a narrow-eyed stare, motioned over his shoulder to his large nurse. "Missus Dromenko here is going to take care of you. Be best if you listen to her."

Zlata Dromenko was a stout Cossack about my height with a thick single eyebrow giving her a serious, severe look. I found out she'd been a mail-order bride who came over from Ukraine to marry a local farmer, a Russian immigrant. He died, though, and now Mrs. Dromenko worked in the hospital bullying patients like me. I called her "Hun," because she made me think of Attila. I was curious as to how Mr. Dromenko died but was afraid to ask.

After the third day imprisoned by Dromenko, my fever broke. They took that blame tube out, and I felt I had enough strength to fight off her browbeating, so I decided to take my stand on getting out of there.

"What you are thinkink to do?" She came up to the end of my bed as I finished getting dressed. Thick clenched fists

19

propped on her broad hips, she got right up in my face, not six inches away. I could smell borscht on her breath—the beets, the onions, the garlic-y kovbasa sausage. Never heard of the stuff until she shared some with me one day, told me the ingredients. Said it would "tack feefer huhvay." Believe it did that. Nearly my height, she looked me eye-level to eye-level, those dark Slavic orbs made even more menacing by her furry eyebrow.

"Look, Missus Dromenko, you can yell at me all you want, but I'm checking out," I told her.

"Nyet, is not possible. You are in weakness. You are well, not yet."

"Maybe not by your gauge, but I got a job to do, a killer to catch, and the longer I lay around here the less likely it'll get done." I set my hat on my head, pinched the front of the brim in a gesture of respect. "Ma'am." I stepped around her. My gait was slow on my stiff and crooked leg, so I couldn't outrun her. She might jump on my back to stop me, but it was a chance I was willing to take.

The Jakes boy, Zeb, was in the same ward as me. His ma and pa and uncle at the undertaker's. Screens were set up around his bed. I stopped to look in on him, Dromenko right on my heels. The boy's chest and neck were heavily bandaged, his face had cuts, his skin looked a pale orange, more than reddish brown. I supposed him asleep, but he more looked dead.

"How's he doing?" I asked.

"Still in coma," Dromenko said. She spoke softly, sadly. "Is go and touch. Is not look good."

I shook my head slightly. "Damn miracle he survived the attack, considering what the others looked like."

"I hop you find pipple doink this," she said.

"Got some suspects. Sure wish I could talk to this kid, though."

Still looking down at the boy, she said to me, "Meester Smock, I tink person you look for is vicious monster, and you still not well. Pliz, you takink care."

It surprised me she'd conceded my leaving. "First thing I always try to do, Missus Dromenko. Appreciate your concern. And thanks again for the borscht."

⏳

Sheriff Chuck Dunbar kept my gear in his office: my Peacemaker, my Winchester. Clyde, my liver chestnut gelding, was in the care of Julio down at the livery. Gilmore and Dooley still sat in the jail, along with that black-beard fella Lewis Elliot waylaid, both his eyes purpled up and his nose smashed. They called him Feeney. The shot men were in the hospital in a room by themselves and under guard. They buried that big Irishman in an unmarked grave up on Tater Mound.

Once I gathered my outfit, I headed out to look for Crow Redhand. My first stop was the town of Blue Jacket about half a day's ride southwest. Took that long because the jostling in the saddle pained me some, so I couldn't trot Clyde. Hated to admit Mrs. Dromenko may've been right, but I didn't have the luxury of time to wait for a proper healing. On the other hand, Redhand's foot wound probably slowed him down, too. Figured with any luck, I'd find him holed up with his cousin Wilbur there in Blue Jacket.

Finding Wilbur's place wasn't a problem. One stop and inquiry at the only business in town—if you wanted to call it that—a general store of sorts, pointed me to his cabin.

An ancient and mostly toothless Indian woman sat in a rocker in one corner of the store, more of a shed, really. An old cast-iron stove next to her belched a wood fire. The tin flue appeared to leak more smoke into the small room than out through the roof. "Where can I find Wilbur Redhand?" I asked.

She eyed me dubiously for several long seconds. I started to turn and walk out, when she said, "Down the road to the creek bridge. Cross it, go off in the woods to the west."

⧖

Took the field glasses out I carried with me, Army issue. General Davis gave them to me as a parting gift when they cashiered me out. Sitting in the woods past the creek bridge, I scanned ahead with them. The shack sat back from the road in a clearing, overgrown with brush and vines, bare in their winter state. One side covered with unpainted and weathered clapboards, the other three only a tarpaper covering. A rope of white smoke curled from the rock chimney. An old lean-to stable stood at the back of the house. Lean-to was a generous word to describe it, seeing as that's what it mostly did. Whole place looked forlorn and starved as if poverty had shrunk away the meat of any prosperity.

I stayed in the woods, some forty to fifty yards off and circled the shack, hoping to gain some concealment, or at least make a harder target. Saw only one horse, a dapple gray, grazing on a broken bale of hay beside the building. Didn't remember it as the one Crow took.

Hanging back in the trees, I brought Clyde back around to the front of the shack. A man now sat in a chair on the small wooden porch, leaning the back of it against the front wall. A smallish, skinny fella in buckskin pants and flannel shirt. Wore a wide-brimmed black hat with two feathers sticking out of the hatband. Black hair braids draped down across his shoulders to his chest. He held a cob pipe between his teeth while he whittled on a piece of wood.

I gently urged Clyde toward a big elm tree standing twenty yards from the front of the cabin and reined him to a stop partially behind the wide trunk. Pulled my rifle out of its boot and rested it across the big gelding's withers. "You Wilbur Redhand?"

He kept whittling without looking up. "Who's askin?"

"I'm Deputy Marshal Jubal Smoak. Looking for an outlaw named Crow Redhand. If you're Wilbur, I was told you're his kin."

He nodded and kept whittling. Presently, he said, "Crow ain't here. He come, but he left. Needed doctoring. Someone shot him in the foot."

"Reckon that'd been me," I said. "Had a shootout down near Fairland. I shot him in the foot. He shot me in the back."

He squinted at me. "Surprised you're alive. Crow usually aims to kill. Never knew him to miss."

"When did he leave?" I asked.

"Day or so ago."

"Mind if I take a look around?"

He shrugged.

I dismounted and approached the shack, keeping my rifle loosely pointed toward the cabin and the man. Stopped at the porch step.

"You're Wilbur, then?" I asked again, looking him in the eye. "You never did say." He had a narrow ruddy-brown face, weathered. Small arroyos fanned out from corners of his eyes toward high cheekbones, suggesting in time they'd spread to the rest of his face. I figured him to be maybe ten, fifteen years older than me. Had what I'd call wise eyes. Looking into them they appeared deep, with something sage looking back like he knew more about most things than you did. Those crow's feet added to the impression.

"Yeah," he said. "Folks mostly just call me Wil, though."

"Well, Wil, I'd be obliged if you'd lead the way inside. If Crow's in there, I'd rather he shot you first, instead of me."

23

He looked at me and his leathery face creased with a grin. He righted his chair to all fours and stood. "Sure, Deputy. But like I said, Crow ain't here."

"Just the same," I said and motioned with the rifle barrel.

Crow wasn't in the shack, but I found a bucket of bloody water and rags next to a bed.

Wil seemed obliged to explain. "I tried to help him as best I could. But I ain't a doc. He needed better'n I could dish out."

"I could arrest you, Wilbur . . . Wil, for harboring a known felon."

"Yeah, I guess," he said. He took the pipe out of his mouth, used the end of the stem to scratch a spot between his shoulders. "I don't usually smoke this," he commented on the pipe. "Tobacco's hard to come by. But it does make a good back scratcher."

He continued his efforts at scratching for some time, ruminating before he continued. "Yeah, Crow come in here on his own. All I did was give him some food and water and treat his wound. Not like I hid him. Don't even like Crow that much. But it's like you said, he's kin."

He had a point. Besides, I didn't have time to mess with Wilbur. And so far, he'd been cooperative.

"Where'd he head off to?"

Wil shrugged. "Don't know that. Just rode off one morning. Didn't tell me where he'd be going, and I didn't ask." He gave me a glancing look with a smirk. "With a man like Crow, best not to ask him too many questions," he said.

"You know about the killings happened near here a week or so ago?" I asked him. His face went cold, and fear rose in his eyes just as it had in old Long Walker. He looked away from me.

"Yeah, I know about 'em," he said. "Knew the Jakes my whole life. Worked with Elam and his brother Sam over on the

Forked S, the Standback Ranch. Sarah was a good woman, a good mother to that boy."

He took off his hat and rubbed the top of his head. His hands looked rough and big, seemed out of proportion to the rest of him. The nails, thick and yellow and chipped, rounded downward almost like claws. "Hard to figure why anyone would do such a thing," he said shaking his head.

"Some think Crow might've had a hand in it," I said.

Wilbur looked at me keenly. "I've known Crow man and boy for over forty years. He's, sure enough, a mean bastard, always been. Once, we were kids, I watched him put an arrow through a dog's neck because he said it barked too much. Another time saw him slap his mother to the ground when she lit into him about his drinking. Hard to say he wouldn't've killed, but I doubt even Crow would've done it the way it was done to the Jakes."

"You say you knew the Jakes? Know any reason why someone would want them dead?"

"Can't imagine. Quiet, hardworking, kept mostly to themselves. Quapaw people like me."

"What about work? They have any run-in with someone there?"

"Yeah." He nodded. "Elam got cross-ways with one of the hands. Man named Gray MacKenzie, a drifter come in one day and hired on. Indian, but not from around here. Said he was Ojibwe from up north. A powerful big fella with a wild look in his eyes, kept his hair long and loose. Not a friendly sort. He was bothering Sarah. She was Elam's wife, you know, and worked at the ranch, too. Good-looking woman, that Sarah. Elam took exception to MacKenzie's advances and went looking for him, but MacKenzie ambushed Elam and commenced to beat him something fierce. Twice as big as Elam. Probably would've killed him if Sam Jakes hadn't stepped up and laid him out from behind with the butt of his rifle. Old man Standback run MacKenzie off after that. All that took place a few weeks back. Ain't seen hide nor hair of the man since. Figure he rode on out of these parts. Like I said, he looked to be a drifter."

"You say Sam Jakes whacked that fella with his rifle? What kind of rifle?"

Wilbur looked at me kind of funny. "A Spencer. Sam had this old Spencer he was real proud of. Took it everywhere he went. Said his daddy gave it to him." He squinted. "That important?"

"Makes a difference," I said to him, "because I found a fifty caliber Spencer rifle tied to the back of Crow's saddle he left behind after we had our shootout. You think you could identify that rifle as Sam Jakes's if you saw it?"

Wilbur nodded. "Believe I could."

I motioned for him to follow.

I pulled the rifle out of a buckskin scabbard lashed to the back of my saddle and handed it to Redhand. He examined it solemnly, nodding. "Yep, this's Sam's rifle," he said. "You say Crow carried it?"

"He did. One of his boys told me he had it with him when he came back from visiting you that first time."

Wil handed the Spencer back to me. He looked surprised, maybe scared. "Not good for Crow," he said.

"No," I said. "Can't help but wonder if maybe the two of you may've gone over to the Jakes place."

"Wasn't here the first time Crow came by," he said. "With the weather coming in, I stayed over at the Standback place, the bunkhouse, night of the storm. Major Standback can vouch for me, as can a couple other fellas who were there, too.

"Crow come by here and broke in. Stole some of my stuff while he was at it. Don't know if that was before or after he'd gone to the Jakes's."

"Maybe you can see now why I need to track him down," I said. "I'm going to need to take you in, Wil."

"Arrest me?" he asked, becoming a little agitated. I put my hand on the butt of my Colt. Seeing my move, he added, "No need to put me in jail, Deputy. I told you all I know."

"Going to have to check out your story with Mister Standback. If he can back you up, I'll let you go. I'll take you to Sheriff Dunbar's jail until I can find out. I need to know where you are until I can bring in Crow."

"Well, now, wait," he said. "Take me along with you to see Standback. You'll see I don't lie. I can help you find Crow. I'm a pretty fair tracker."

"Why would I trust you to do that? He's your kin. Maybe you'd have me chasing rabbits, so he could get further away . . . or you'd look to do me in."

"Yeah, he's kin, not strong kin. If he's the one killed the Jakes, I wouldn't mind seeing him hang for it. Boy's alive. I know for a fact he wouldn't harm that boy. Be glad to do what I can to help you bring him in."

CHAPTER 4

ajor Yancy Justice Standback was a substantial, hardy man, tall and clean-shaven. His physical size pretty much matched his reputation thereabouts. Folks said he was tough, stern, yet well thought of by most, that he cast a big shadow. He went by his middle name to his familiars, but most folks knew him as The Major. Fought with General Blunt's Kansas Volunteers in the Civil War, distinguished himself as a cavalry officer, especially during the Battle of Honey Springs here in Indian Territory. After the war, with the Union's confiscation of some of the Cherokee lands in Indian Territory, Standback saw an opportunity and gained several hundred acres. It was there he built the Y. J. Standback Ranch and Cattle Company. His registered brand is the Forked S.

When Wil and I rode up to the main house that evening, a tall framed structure with an ample porch, Venus shone above it like a lonely beacon in the cold indigo of that twilight sky. Beneath a gun barrel sky, it took us most of the day to ride to the ranch. We bent through a wind that cut through us like shards of ice. It left us nearly numb, the bare parts of our skin stinging, our horses' muzzles white with frost. A half-mile from the ranch, the wind died out, the clouds receded. The deep bowl of frozen air that lay still across the land promised to make the clear night colder than the day. Through the warm glow of the dining room window, we could see Standback and a woman taking their meal. A servant came in to say something to him, and he looked out the window at our approach in the remaining daylight. Standback met us on the porch as we walked our horses up.

"Evening, sir," I said, tipping my hat. "You're Major Standback, I reckon?" I guessed him to be somewhere in his fifties.

"You must be that deputy I been hearin about." Seeing my surprised expression, he pointed to my badge which caught a glint from the window light. "Dead giveaway," he said.

"Yes, sir, I'm Deputy Marshal Smoak." I motioned toward my companion, but before I could introduce him, Wil spoke up.

"Evenin', Major," he said. "It's Wil Redhand." He removed his hat and stepped forward into the light.

Standback nodded. "I recognized you, Wil. What brings you men out here on a night like this?"

"Couple of things," I said. "No doubt, you've heard about the murder of the Jakes brothers and Elam Jakes's wife."

Standback sighed, gave a nod.

"Wil here tells me those folks worked for you," I said.

"Yep. Good hands, both of them. Sarah Jakes was my housekeeper's niece. Worked in my kitchen some."

"You also heard about that bank robbery up in Picher?"

"Yeah, but I heard you caught those men. Had a shootout with them, that the leader got away. It was that damned Crow Redhand." He turned to Wil. "Ain't he your cousin?"

"Yes, sir, he's kin," Wil said. "But I don't claim him."

"That brings us to the other reason we're here, Major. I have reason to believe Crow may have been involved in those murders. Have evidence that puts him at the scene of the crime on or near the night of the murders."

"What evidence?" Standback asked.

"Sam Jakes's Spencer rifle. It was in Crow's possession. If you don't mind, sir, I'd like to ask you a few questions concerning all this."

Standback considered it all for a few seconds. "Hang on," he said and stepped back inside the front door, only to reappear seconds later hatted and pulling on a thick sheepskin coat as he came down off the porch. "Let's go out to the barn, get my livery man Bennie to take care of your horses. Don't want to leave 'em standing out in this damn cold. Once we get 'em settled, you boys come back in and have some coffee, get yourselves warmed back up. We'll talk a bit."

"Bennie!" he called out when we entered the barn. An old black man emerged from a dimly lit tack room at the other end of the stables. His high shiny forehead reached up to a line of white wool where it receded, a matching short beard and mustache covered his jaws and chin and upper lip. He regarded us sleepy-eyed.

"This here's Marshal Smoak," he said to the liveryman. "You know Wil Redhand." The old man nodded. "Want you to take care of their horses, give 'em some oats, water. Get 'em warm."

Bennie nodded, smiled big. "They sho 'nuf looks cold. Yessuh, I takes care of 'em."

We trudged back through the snow toward the house.

"Old Bennie's been with me since the war," Standback said. "I came across him in Kansas. Fort Row in the winter of '62. Up there with the rest of Opothle Yahola's Creeks . . . what was left of them. Most died from hunger and disease and the cold. Ben wasn't far from it when I found him. He was a runaway from Missouri. Creeks adopted him. Had a wife and kids, but they died in that winter. Took pity on him when I found him. Had my surgeon nurse him and some others to health, those we could. Been loyal to me ever since. Prefers to stay here in the barn. Got a cozy little spot in that tack room. Takes some meals with the boys but prefers staying alone with the horses most the time."

He led us through the big front door and into the well-lit dining room—electric lights. A handsome well-dressed woman with an air of elegance still sat at the table. Her luxurious dark hair was coiffed atop her head exposing a pearlesque neck and face. Singular long curls, one in front of each ear, dangled from the woven mound. Her large eyes held such a deep brown they almost faded to black yet flecked with enough gold to keep them piercing. Full brows furrowed like those of a fox on the hunt. Quite a few years younger than her husband, I'd say mid-thirties or younger. She regarded us curiously, waiting for the Major's introduction.

"Emily, these two men have ridden out here to talk to me about . . ." he hesitated, searching for the proper words to say to his genteel wife. "About the Jakes affair."

She folded her hands in her lap and frowned slightly. The Major continued as if he suddenly remembered his manners. "Gentlemen, this is my wife, Missus Standback. Emily, this is Deputy Marshal Smoak, and . . . I believe you know Wil Redhand."

I removed my hat. Wil held his in his hands. "Ma'am," I said.

"Miz Standback," Wil said at the same time.

She smiled back at us cordially. "Have you gentlemen had your dinner?" she asked.

"Thank ya, ma'am," I said. "But we're not here to trouble you with a meal. Just need to talk to your husband a bit, then we'll be on our way back to town. We'll get our supper there."

The sight and smells of the fine table spread was overwhelming—a large chunk of roast beef in a silver pot, a boat of brown gravy, a steaming bowl of boiled potatoes and carrots, a half-sliced loaf of bread sitting on a board, and a couple other covered bowls of hot something or other food.

Had to admit I was about to cave in, and I'd seen half-starved coyotes happier than Wil, but I didn't think it'd be polite to sit at their dinner table to discuss what we needed to discuss.

"Nonsense," the missus said. "You both look famished and half-frozen. You can't ride all the way back to town on a night like this without food in your bellies and hot coffee to thaw you out. Please sit." She turned to the Indian woman standing by the sideboard. "Asmita, set places for our guests."

The Indian woman glared disapprovingly at Wil, seemed not inclined to carry out her mistress's orders.

"Asmita?" the missus queried in a stern quiet voice. The woman moved, pulling two dishes and utensils from the china cabinet and setting them before empty chairs at the table with an unkindly clatter. Wil and I took our seats. The woman Asmita started serving us victuals from the bowls on the table. Wil accepted it all in humble silence, glancing at the Indian woman with trepidation. No mistaking her animosity towards Wil as she plopped food on his plate.

"If you gentlemen will excuse me," the missus said. "I'll leave you to your discussions. If there's anything you need, Asmita will get it for you." With that, she arose from her chair. I stood, too, Wil followed my lead. We re-seated ourselves once she left the room.

"Asmita," the Major said. "Pour these fellas up two mugs of hot coffee. I'll have some more, too."

The woman returned fifteen seconds later with the two large steaming mugs of coffee which she set before us. She held a coffee pot in the other hand, topping off the major's cup. Wil and I dug well into the food on our plates, our ravenous hunger most likely apparent from our wolfish shoveling.

The major let us eat for a minute or so, sipping his coffee. Finally, he asked, "So what questions you got for me, Deputy, about this Jakes incident?"

I chewed on a piece of beef, then popped in a wedge of potato. Chomped that a time or two and washed it down with a swallow of coffee.

"Well sir, the first thing I need to ask is about Wil here. He claims he stayed in your bunkhouse the night of that snow storm . . . the night the Jakes were killed. I'd like to verify that if you can vouch for him."

"You suspect Wil had something to do with those killings?" Standback asked.

"Crow showed up at Wil's place a day or so before the murders. Wil told me he'd been here the night of the storm, but I need to check his alibi, just to get him off my list of suspects."

"Believe I can ease your mind. When the blizzard started moving in that afternoon, I told Wil to bunk here. He'd've froze to death if he tried to make it home that night. Couple of the boys that stay regular in the bunkhouse can probably vouch for him, too. I've known Wil for a lot of years, Deputy. He's an honest hard-worker and a good man. I consider myself a fair judge of character and don't believe Wil here would be involved in any killing, especially those as ugly as the Jakes. Besides, they were his people"

I gave Wil a nod. He grinned back at me around a chaw of food.

"That's good enough for me," I said. "Other thing I'd like to ask you about is that fella the Jakes brothers had a run-in with. Wil said his name is Gray MacKenzie."

Standback's face clouded. He reached inside his suit coat and pulled out a cigar, cut the ends off with a trimmer, then lit it. Drew on it several times, puffing heavy clouds of pungent blue smoke into the room. Asmita brought him an ashtray. I ate, waited for his response.

"Don't know much about MacKenzie," he said. "Been a few weeks back he rode up, asked to hire on. He looked like a drifter. Indian fella, not from Oklahoma, though. Said he's from a northern tribe up in Canada—"

"Ojibwe," Wil said.

"Yeah, that's it," the Major said. "Didn't figure he's the kind would hang around long, but had a couple boys down with the grippe that week, so we were shorthanded. Hired him thinking he could help in the short term.

"Didn't look like a cowhand and proved he didn't much know his way around stock but worked hard. Still, something about the fella I didn't particularly like. Couldn't really put my finger on it, but you know, there are some just look like trouble. He had that. Like I said, he didn't shirk what needed to be done, so I shrugged off my bad feeling.

"It was less than a week when him and Elam got into it. Come to find out MacKenzie had been making advances on Sarah. She worked in the kitchen and helped Wiley serving the hands their meals. MacKenzie stalked Sarah out to the wellhouse one night after supper, and tried tuh . . . well, she got away and ran to find Elam, all hysterical.

"Elam goes to find MacKenzie, but MacKenzie is waiting for him, waiting to attack, crouched behind a rain barrel. Elam didn't have much of a chance. MacKenzie is a big man and strong. He sprang into Elam with the fury of a mad dog. Probably would've killed him if Sam hadn't come up and laid MacKenzie out with his rifle butt.

"I heard the commotion and come out to see what was going on. Sam and Sarah told me, so I told them to haul all of MacKenzie's gear out of the bunkhouse and fetch his horse and tack. I pulled some bills out of my wallet and stuffed 'em in his coat pocket to take care of his wages, then I slapped him awake, and told him to get out. Ain't seen nor heard of him since."

"How long ago was that?" I asked.

"Couple three days before that snowstorm, I reckon." He took a swallow from his coffee mug and puffed up another smoke cloud. "A few days before Elam, Sam, and Sarah were killed."

"Wonder if he and Crow know each other?" I asked.

Wil shrugged. "'Spect they do," he said. "Worked here at the same time, but neither of them's what you call the friendly type."

By then he cleaned off his plate and was eying the meat dish still on the table. "Help yourself to some more, Wil." the Major said

The skinny Indian eagerly forked more beef onto his plate and spooned up another helping of potatoes and carrots, emptying the gravy boat over all of it.

"Crow ever mention this MacKenzie when he was staying with you?" I asked Wil.

He shook his head. "Naw."

"Something else I oughta mention," the Major said. "The day after MacKenzie left, we found three head of cattle killed. Two cows and a steer. Don't know if one had anything to do with the other, but at the time I wondered if it might be some sort of retribution from MacKenzie for me running him off."

"Shot?"

"No, that's kind of the strange part. They weren't together. Found them at separate spots, mutilated. My first thought was an attack by a big predator. A cougar, maybe, or a bear. But sign at the spots showed a pack of wolves. That didn't really make any sense, either."

"What sign?" I asked.

"Well, tracks we saw were wolf. Wrong time of year for a bear, anyway. Cougar could've done it if she was hungry enough, I guess, but no sign of that, either. Definitely wolves. Three, four, it looked like. The cows were flayed open, slashed throat to tail. Wolves coulda come along after the fact, though. A good part of the carcasses was eaten. This time of year, wolves will take a meal any way they can get it. I think they were bystanders because wolves don't kill like that. There were bite marks on the necks, but the major wounds looked to have been done with a knife or some kind of tool. From what I could tell they seemed consistent with what would be done with claws. Thing is, wolves don't kill with claws."

The room got quiet. We all fell into our own thoughts. Even Wil stopped his eating. He and the woman Asmita exchanged glances as if some unspoken words passed between them. I could see fright in her eyes, even terror. Wil's expression was grave.

"Wolf tracks, ya say? Anything else that might indicate who or what was there?" I asked. "Had to be a lot of blood around killings as vicious as you described."

"I did look for sign. Lots of wolf tracks in the blood, all of it frozen when we got there. There was something at one spot, though." Standback grew quiet, studying the ash at the end of his cigar as he scraped it into the ashtray.

"It was kind of smeared, hard to make out. Couldn't be sure it was what I thought. In amongst all the wolf tracks around the carcass of the steer." Again, he stopped and took a draw off his cigar. "There looked to be a footprint, a big bloody human one."

Asmita straightened from gathering dishes at the sideboard and gasped audibly. Then she muttered something I couldn't make out, something in her native tongue, I supposed.

"A boot print?" I asked.

Standback shook his head with a nervous smile as if embarrassed to say it. "Bare," he said.

I snorted. "Awful cold weather for someone to be going around barefoot."

"What I thought, too," the Major said. "Could be I was mistaken. Like I said, kind of hard to make out."

"You think it could've been MacKenzie's?" I asked.

He shrugged. "Don't know. He's a big man, but can't say I ever looked at his feet, leastwise not his bare feet, so I couldn't say for sure. But after what happened with Sarah and Elam, the thought of him did come to mind. If it was a footprint, it was human, not cougar or bear or wolf."

Asmita was whispering something loud by then. Rhythmic, like a chant . . . or a prayer.

"Major," I said. "I'd like to go to the sites where those animals were killed to have a look around. Would you mind taking us out there in the morning? Hope you won't mind if we could camp out in your barn for the night."

"Sure, be glad to take you out there," he said. "And you can stay in the bunkhouse. Wil's already got a bunk there, and the one MacKenzie had ain't in use . . . that is if you don't mind sleeping in it."

"No, sir, I've slept in a lot of spots where other men have slept, and a bed's a bed, I reckon. Especially on a cold night like tonight. We'd be much obliged."

"Well, wouldn't want you camping out with a pack of wolves on the prowl."

The Major wheezed a laugh, trying to ease the tension some. I smiled half-heartedly. Wil didn't smile at all, and Asmita dropped the gravy boat to the floor where it shattered into a thousand pieces.

CHAPTER 5

Whatever bothered Wil the night before at the dinner table, didn't seem to carry over with his appetite at the breakfast table. He scarfed down a goodly portion of scrambled eggs and bacon along with five or so of the bunkhouse cook's buttermilk biscuits. Held myself to three. We saddled up at daybreak and rode north, the clear dawn air icy-sharp and biting at our bare faces, the horses' breath frosting their muzzles. The Major told us the sites of the cattle slaughter lay a couple miles from the house, all within a hundred yards of each other.

"Doubt you'll find much at these spots, Deputy," Standback said as we loped along.

"Wil keeps telling me he's good at finding sign," I replied.

"Still, it's been almost three weeks since those animals were killed," he continued. "We burned the carcasses the same day we found them, and then we had that snow storm. We probably destroyed most the sign."

We headed first to the spot where they found the steer. I was curious about that footprint and wanted to find it. MacKenzie moved to the top of my list of suspects on the Jakes' murders . . . him and Crow Redhand. That footprint would provide more evidence.

We rode along the north side of a squat hill until coming up to a short shelf of limestone, the ground there shaded from the arc of the low winter sun. Most of the snow had melted but still piled beneath the rock shelf in its shade. But the big burn spot, gray and black with ashes was still evident. Standback reined up his big dun mare about twenty yards from the spot. He pointed to that patch of ground. "This's where we found the steer, 'n burned it," he said.

The horses were skittish, not inclined to go near the area. We dismounted a few yards away.

"I'd best stay here with the horses," the Major said. "They don't much like this place. Happened the last time I was here, too. 'Fraid they'll run off if we leave 'em."

"Whereabouts was that footprint you found?" I asked.

He pointed to an area ten feet below the burned patch. "Out'n there. Hard to say with all that snow still on the ground."

I walked over to the spot, pushed crusty snow aside with my boot. Wil went to the bare patch. "This about right?" I hollered back to Standback.

"Yeah, somewhere in there."

I couldn't find the print. "Find anything, Wil?" I called.

"Mebbe," he said. "You might wanna come look." He squatted on his toes near the edge of the patch. I walked over. Couldn't squat next to him with my bum leg, so I bent at the waist.

Wil gathered a wad of dried prairie grass and brushed ashes away from a two-foot spot. The bare ground was covered with paw prints, appeared to be canine. Made when the ground was soft with melted snow but now frozen in place.

"Those wolf prints?" I asked.

"Not likely," he said. "Not big enough, not for wolf. Believe they's dog. By the looks, a whole pack of 'em. Four, maybe five. Had to come along after the fire, a couple days ago."

"Dogs, huh?" Wil nodded.

I turned back to Standback. "Hey, Major, you got any dogs?"

"Dogs?" He sounded surprised. "Why?"

"Got a bunch of paw prints around here, but not wolf. Wil thinks they're from a pack of dogs, come along a couple days ago."

"Only got one dog, but he's too old and lazy to go much beyond the porch and barn." He reached inside his coat and pulled out a cigar. Biting off one end, he spit it to the ground. Took a match from his shirt pocket, snapped it into flame with his left thumbnail and applied it to the cigar. A cloud of blue-white smoke ascended above his head before he continued. He took the cigar out of his mouth. "Tell you who does have a mess of dogs, though."

He squinted into the morning sun. "Neighbor of mine lives about five miles out that way." He pointed in the direction he faced. "A woman. She's got dogs," he said.

"You think those animals of yours could've been set upon by a pack of dogs?" I asked.

The Major drew on his cigar, shrugged. "Possible, I guess. Ain't never had that kind of trouble before, though. But you never know what kind of notion a pack of dogs can get. Still, there were the claw wounds. Dogs wouldn't use claws, either."

Wil stood and walked the edge of the brown patch. At a stand of winter-bare sumac, he stopped and picked something off a branch, then squatted again. "More dog sign?" I asked him.

"Don't think so," he answered. I walked over to him.

He showed me a wad of fur. "Don't believe this's dog hair. Believe it's wolf."

"How do you know?"

"The length of it and the color. Black and coarse, like wolf hair."

I was skeptical. "I've seen dogs with that color hair, too."

"True enough, but there's this." He pointed to a place on the ground. It was a paw print, a big paw print. "That's wolf," Wil said. "Damn big wolf."

I straightened. "Just the one?" I asked.

"So far," he said. "This one was made before the dog tracks, likely before the snow. I'll be looking for more."

I left Wil to his search and tried to find that bloody bare footprint, but nothing turned up. Wil found indications of more wolves, at least three, he said. We rode over to the other spots and got the same results. Lots of dog prints there, too, and some wolf.

"Major, it seems likely your animals were killed by wolves," I said.

"Looks that way," he said. "But it still seems strange. Never known a pack of wolves to kill just for sport."

I nodded. Couldn't argue with that.

"There's some horse tracks over here," Wil called from his spot twenty feet away. "One horse."

"Wonder what those dogs were doing here, and the person who owned that horse?" I asked no one in particular.

"I think I can tell you where you can find the owner of the horse, and the dogs, too," the Major said.

"Your neighbors?" I asked. The Major nodded.

"What can you tell me about those folks? They ranchers?"

He flipped ash off his cigar, put it back in his teeth to chew on. After a few seconds, he took it out again and spit.

"No folks," he started. "Just her. She's a widow woman. Her husband was a man in the oil business down around Tulsa, that Glenn Pool strike. Story has it he was knifed by a drunken roughneck 'n robbed one night there in Tulsa. Left her quite a bit of money, I understand. She kept his interest in the oil business, too, it's said. I sold her husband a parcel of land in those hills yonder. They built a place back in the woods. She moved out here a year or so ago after her husband died. Been over to the house a couple times, not much. Don't think she and Emily hit it off. She stays to herself. Has all those dogs around her which she always takes with her to get supplies and such. They're big, powerful looking dogs, none too friendly. But they don't do anything she doesn't tell them to. Still, folks tend to cut her and them a wide berth when they come around. Her name's Caitlin McDonald.

"How do I find her?"

"Ride east," Standback motioned. "Stay to the right of those two woody hills yonder. When you come to a creek at the foot of those hills, that's the boundary between her land and mine, bear some to the left till you find a road. Follow that up into the hills. It'll lead you to her cabin."

"I'll pay her a visit," I said.

"I'd ride easy, up there," the Major said. "She doesn't seem to cotton much to trespassers. Uses the dogs to protect herself."

We all stood silent for a bit thinking about all that. Never been around dogs much. My mom had a collie when I was a boy, but she was a gentle animal who stayed around the house, mostly. My father, and the men he knew, all had braces of big surly hunting dogs they used for going after wild hogs. The times he took me with him on those hunts, I was more afraid of those dogs than the feral hogs. Think they could sense it. Always felt like they would've taken the least opportunity to sink their teeth into me.

"Well, boys," Standback said. "If you don't need me anymore, I better get back. Wil, you going to ride on with the Deputy, or you coming back to work?"

I spoke up. "If you could spare him, Major, I sure could use his help."

"Work's slow this time of year. Got a few men can handle all needs to be done. I can see where you need him. If he can help you find the Jakes's killers, that's probably more important than cow-handin for me right now.

"You get back to work when you can, Wil. Your job's still here."

Wil nodded.

🗙

Despite the morning daylight, it was dark back in those woods. Heavy clouds started to roll in, adding to the gloom. By the time we rode within sight of the Widow McDonald's cabin, snow started to fall, big silent flakes in a windless descent.

"We're being watched," Wil said.

Couldn't find them at first, swiveling around in my saddle, searching the thick woods. Snow was coming down pretty good by then, eddying in a light wind. Clyde grumbled nervously, as did Wil's dapple. Then I spotted them, following us. They stayed back in the trees and brush maybe twenty-five yards. Dogs. Big black things with square heads, short hair, smallish ears, and stout muzzles. Their blackness in contrast to the swirling snow made them easier to pick out. They encircled us, silently keeping pace as the horses walked.

"I count five of 'em," Wil said.

Clyde danced sideways a bit and snuffled anxiously. I pulled my rifle from its boot, propping the butt of it on my left thigh. We walked the horses slowly, cautiously. The outline of a cabin appeared through the trees and whip of snow. Two hundred yards up the narrow road, a dim light glowing from a couple windows.

A hundred yards from the house, the dogs made a move. They all growled at once, a low menacing rumble, and they tightened their circle, moving within ten or fifteen yards of us. Clyde and the dapple pranced and whinnied. Had to admit I shared their concern. I levered a cartridge into my Winchester.

"What's your business here?" The voice came from behind us, a woman's voice.

I reined Clyde around. The dogs quit growling, but stood tensed, ready to charge. The silent snowfall heavier, the bare

43

trees whispering in the rising wind. She couldn't be very far away, somewhere in the fog and shadows.

"I'm Deputy U.S. Marshal Jubal Smoak," I called out. "We're looking for a fugitive named Crow Redhand. He robbed a bank up in Picher a couple weeks back and is a prime suspect in some recent murders."

A few seconds went by. "Your fugitive is not around here," she said. "If he was, I'd know about it."

One of the dogs, the biggest, emphasized her statement by uttering a low growl and guttural bark.

I pulled my hat brim down to shield my eyes a bit from the snow and wind and squinted into it. From the side of a large oak, the black double barrel of a shotgun pointed in our direction. The bearer wore a long fur coat and cap, the white and gray of them almost indistinguishable in the white air.

"Ma'am, we just came up from the Standback Ranch. Major Standback had some cattle killed by animals, probably wolves. But we also found some dog tracks. And the tracks of a rider."

"My dogs didn't kill those cows," she said.

"Didn't say they did, ma'am, but it does look like they were there. Maybe you, too."

"You need to put that rifle back in its boot," she said. "Then both of you raise your hands."

The alpha growled again, and the dogs closed in a step. Clyde and the dapple danced, gave out high sounds of fear.

"Don't believe we want to do that, ma'am. Wish you'd call those dogs off. They're scaring our horses." I tried to keep my voice from cracking.

"All I gotta do is say the word and my dogs will take you off those horses. They don't take much to strangers, nor do I."

"I believe you," I said. "No reason to be concerned with us, though. Don't mean you any harm. We're just trying to track down some bad guys."

"Put that rifle away," she repeated. The big male increased the intensity of his growl. The wind cranked up to a low moan, and the snowfall thickened.

Wil already had his hands up but fought to control the dapple. I put my Winchester back in its boot and raised my hands.

"Wonder if you'd mind if we went up to your barn. I'd like to ask you a few questions," I said.

"You rode yourselves up here, you can ride yourselves out. Told you I don't take in strangers, don't answer questions."

"Weather's getting kind of heavy out here. Just like some shelter to thaw out a bit before moving on," I countered. "Maybe let this storm pass."

She hesitated some. The dogs yipped and growled with eagerness, agitated about their mistress's indecision. The big male crouched and paced.

She came out from behind the oak tree. "Get down off your horses. Do it real slow and careful. We'll walk to the house."

We took her suggestions. She came closer, the shotgun still pointed. She was a bundle of fur coat down to her knees, ear-flapped cap, and thick pants. A wool scarf wrapped around her neck and face. Her voice the only thing told us she was a woman. Stood taller than Wil, maybe five-eight, nine in her boots.

"You mind callin' off them dogs, ma'am?" Wil pleaded. "They're makin' my horse plum skittish."

"Hector, back!" she commanded. The big male lowered his ears and retreated a few paces. The rest of the pack backed off, too. She motioned with the shotgun. "Let's head to the barn."

We slogged toward the cabin, bent forward into the fierce howl of the wind, the snow-white fog near blinding. A full-blown blizzard was getting there.

"Get the horses in the barn, and out of this. They could freeze in this wind," the woman said.

45

We entered the barn and she lit a lantern. The raging storm brought an early night. She had a mule and a milk cow. A few chickens huddled and clucked in one corner. The dogs all came in the barn with us. The woman hung the lantern on a nail, sat on a hay bale. Four of the dogs settled on the floor in front of her. The big male circled to a stack of hay near a dark corner on the opposite wall and sat on his haunches, vigilant.

"You wanna unsaddle your horses and give them some feed, that'd be okay," she said. "But first, I'd like for you to remove your gun belts."

"Ma'am, I'm a deputy marshal. I can't do that while I'm on duty," I said.

"What proof you got you're who you say you are?" she asked.

"Well, I've got my badge," I reached inside my coat, unpinned the badge from my shirt, pulled it out and held it up.

"Looks authentic enough. How do I know you didn't steal it?"

I was getting exasperated. "I can't prove a negative. You'll just have to believe me."

We stared hard at each other for several long seconds. Her with her shotgun and dogs, me with Wil. The wind howled around the outside walls of the barn, and the old structure groaned.

"Wait a second," I said, suddenly remembering. "I've got a letter of credit in my saddlebag. I carry it, so I can charge hotel rooms and such to the government when I'm out on the road. It's signed by the federal judge back in Tulsa and identifies me as the bearer." I moved to Clyde and started to unbuckle a strap on one of the saddlebags. The woman cocked a hammer on her gun, and the big male stood, growling.

"If you'll just allow me to fetch it," I said.

She thought it over, then said, "Hector, stay. Go ahead." But she didn't lower the shotgun.

I reached in the saddlebag and pulled out the envelope with the letter of credit in it, walked over and handed it to her. "Take it out of the envelope," she said.

I did as commanded. She removed a fur-lined glove, read the letter.

"All right," she said at last. "I guess I believe you." She handed the letter back to me. "But what about him?" She motioned toward Wil. "He doesn't look like a deputy marshal."

"This is Wil Redhand. He's from over around Blue Jacket. He's working for me as a posseman and tracker."

She regarded Wil dubiously. "Do I know you?" she asked.

"Don't believe so, ma'am. But I do work for Major Standback," Wil answered.

She nodded. "Maybe that's where I've seen you. Been over there a time or two. The Major is a good man. Suppose I can believe you."

She un-cocked the hammer on her Greener and set the stock butt on the floor, gripping the barrel in her left hand.

"I'm Caitlin McDonald," she said, loosening the thick wool scarf from around her neck and down off her face, motioning her chin toward the big male. "You've already met Hector and his gang." When Major Standback said *widow* I pictured an older woman. Not this one. She was young, no more than thirty. The cold on the skin of her fine features made her face shine. She had the clean, clear beauty of a china doll. I rubbed my knee.

Her eyes had a question. "Bum leg," I said. "Weather like this sets it to aching, especially when I ride."

"Fall off your horse?" Wil asked.

"More like the horse fell on me." I continued rubbing. "Polo match."

47

"You were a polo player?" Miz McDonald asked. Couldn't tell if she was impressed or doubtful.

"Not for very long. It was when I was in the Army up in Colorado. Crash that wrecked this leg ended all that, polo *and* the Army."

"You were cavalry?"

I removed my gloves to blow on my hands trying to warm them up. The questions made me uncomfortable. "Always wanted to be, but, nah. I worked for the Adjutant General in Denver."

"West Point?" she gestured towards my hands folded around my mouth. My class ring on my right hand was exposed.

That surprised me. I nodded. "Not many people recognize it as such."

"I've seen a few. One of my grandfathers wore one."

"Civil War?"

"Yes, Union Army."

"My dad, too, but in the Confederacy. I'm from Virginia."

Wil spoke up. "While you two are comparing pedigrees, I'd like to build a fire. You got a stove in this barn, ma'am?" He stomped his feet, hugged himself.

She considered the situation. Grabbed up her Greener and stood. The big male came to her side. "Hector and I are going to the house," Miz McDonald said. "I've got some hot coffee and a good fire going there. Tend to your animals, then come on up. But when this storm blows over, you need to head on out."

"We'd be much obliged," I said. Wil nodded enthusiastically.

⧖

Wil sidled up to the fire, removed his gloves, but left on his coat and hat. Wedged his gloves under one arm and held his hands out to the warmth. I accepted the mug of coffee the woman handed me.

Hector wandered over to a spot at one side of the hearth and settled in, keeping himself between us and Miz McDonald. Don't think the woman yet had complete trust in us.

The inside of the house had ample room. Most of the living space a large single room, but a doorway to the left of the kitchen area led off to another room. A bedroom, I supposed. The place didn't have a country feel to it, except for the big stone fireplace. Fancy curtains hung on the windows, a Persian rug covered a good part of the wooden floor: white oak planks, stained and polished. The furniture sitting on the rug were things you'd have in a city house—a settee, two leather winged chairs, some lamp tables, and a coffee table. Only the dining table seemed to fit the cabin. I rubbed a hand across its clean surface.

"Nice table," I said.

"My husband made it. Native oak," she said. I heard a whisper of sadness in her voice.

A china hutch made from the same oak sat against the wall next to it opposite the fireplace. Figured the man made that, too. Two large oil lamps sat on the lamp tables, one at one end of the settee, the other between the two chairs. Didn't appear she had electricity. Not surprising, though. Even as relatively near as she was to town, the place was isolated . . . and backwoods. And the big cast iron cook stove was a wood burner. But the home was clean and smelled good, although with a slight odor of dog.

Caitlin McDonald said she was Cherokee, but I had a hard time believing her. Her dark red hair, and eyes so green they could curl a man's toes spoke more Scotch-Irish to me.

"Nice place you've got here," I said.

49

"My husband had this place built several years ago. Bought these acres of land in the hills and part of the valley from Major Standback. We were going to use it as our summer place . . . but after he was killed, I decided to move out here permanently."

"The Major told me about your loss, ma'am," I said. "I'm real sorry."

She nodded but didn't say anything, stared out the kitchen window at the growing snow storm. "What did he tell you?" she asked after a spell.

"Just that you were widowed, that your husband had been, uh, murdered. But I believe I remember the case," I continued. "Our office was involved in the investigation with the Tulsa police, although I wasn't personally. Last I heard they caught and tried your husband's killer. Sentenced him to hang. A random act of violence, they said. Some street thug stabbed your husband and robbed him of twenty dollars and his watch."

"No, that's not what happened," she said tersely. "That's why I moved out here. That's why . . . I treated you like I did when you came near the house."

"What do you mean?" I asked.

"I mean the drunk sentenced to die for my husband's murder didn't do it."

"As I recall, it was a pretty open and shut case. They had the guy dead to rights. He had your husband's watch on him. They even used this new thing called fingerprinting to show his were on the murder weapon."

She shook her head. "He didn't do it. It was made to look like he'd done it, but the man was set up. A professional killer murdered William, and he wasn't caught."

"You think whoever killed your husband will come after you?" I asked.

"I do," she said. And it froze me.

"You know who it is, don't you?"

"I don't know the specific person, but I know who ordered it done.

"William was in the oil business. a risky business, and expensive to operate. He borrowed a lot of money to get started and keep it going, and some of his lenders were . . . well, unsavory businessmen back in Chicago. When he struck it big, he paid back all the money he borrowed and the outrageous interest they charged. But they wanted more. They wanted his business. That was their plan all along. Part of the deal he agreed to in order to get the loans was to make them partners. When William refused their buyout, actually more of a threat than an offer, they had him killed. Being partners, they figured his majority share of the business would go to them. Only what they didn't know was that William suspected their scheme, and he put all his shares in my name. Long as I'm alive they can't legally control the company. So now they need to get rid of me."

"Do you think you're safe way out here by yourself?" I asked. "If it's like you say, they'll probably find you."

"They haven't yet, but I'll know it if they do. I've got Hector and his gang. I feel safer with them than I would with any police force around. My dogs are a damn sight more loyal and trustworthy." She covered her mouth with one hand, cleared her throat. Maybe a little embarrassed that she said that . . . but not much.

"Can't prove it, but I always suspected some of the higher-ups in the Tulsa police knew the truth about William's murder and were bought off. They're about as corrupt as his partners."

Hector growled, walked to the door, his hackles bristling.

"Wonder what's eatin' him?" Wil asked.

I un-holstered my Colt and moved to the side of one of the front windows, pulling back the curtains. Miz McDonald moved to the table and picked up her Greener.

51

"Can't see anything on the porch," I said. The wind whipped the snow in a whirl across the porch, building a foot-high drift along the breadth of it. "I'll go outside and have a look."

Hector waited for me at the door, his nose at the jamb. When I pulled it back, he pushed out in front of me, sniffed the air, and moved to the right side of the porch. He barked toward the snowy woods. I could see nothing beyond the black timber and churning snow. The big dog bristled and growled again. Nothing moved in the gathering gloom.

Possibly imagined, but I thought a form glided through the veil of snow, moving behind the trees. It seemed big and hulking, perhaps traveling upright, but hunched over. Couldn't be certain. It appeared and disappeared. What little form I glimpsed shifting its shape as my mind tried to claim the identity—a bear? a man? a wolf?

"Who's out there?" I shouted into the wind and immediately felt foolish for doing so. No unfriendly human would answer such a stupid question, and certainly no animal. I guess I thought my voice would scare off any prowling beast. But my question into the wind seemed to embolden Hector. He moved a step or two nearer the edge of the porch and increased the intensity of his growl, baring his teeth.

"Easy, boy," I said to the dog, but he ignored me. He barked once and bounded off the porch, leaping through the snow and into the woods, snarling his challenge as he went.

I followed for a few steps but quickly lost sight of him. I could hear him off in the woods, his bark and raging snarl. He definitely came upon whatever stalked the woods. I judged the dog's sounds to be a ways off, but the echoes were muted in the snowfall. There was enough light to see Hector's trail through the snow. I trotted along following it.

"Hector!" I called walking on into the dark woods with trepidation. I stopped a few times to listen, fear gripping me.

I imagined coming upon an enraged bear or wolf or assassin in that blinding snowstorm, armed only with my .44. Every fiber of me warned to turn back, but I pushed forward looking for the dog.

Somewhere out ahead of me, I heard Hector's growling and barking change to a yelp of pain, and then silence. The woods around me were dark and deep, the wind droning through the trees, but otherwise quiet filled the snowfall.

When I found Hector, he lay crumpled on his side in a drift, the dark pool around him in stark contrast to the snow. I crouched one-legged beside him and cocked my Colt, pivoting on my heels, wary of any attack. A shadow crossed a shelf of rock above us, and a pile of snow slid from a pine limb, thumping onto the rock. I swung the Colt in that direction and fired.

I cocked the pistol and waited, but no further movement came from above. Whatever walloped the big dog apparently took off . . . or so I hoped. Hector was alive but badly slashed across his chest and shoulder and ribs. The cuts were deep and parallel as if from the mauling swipe of bear claws. He panted rapidly.

I un-cock the Colt and re-holstered it. "Take it easy, big fella," I said, tentatively putting a hand on his head and stroking it. His wounds were deep and long, but it didn't appear any organs were damaged, nor arteries cut. Still, he bled a lot. "Hold on, boy," I said to him. "I'll get you back to the cabin."

I slid my forearms under his spine and lifted. I cried out myself when sharp pain leaped from the unhealed gunshot holes in my right shoulder. I released Hector and fell back on my butt in the snow. "Damn you, Crow Redhand," I said.

Hector was a heavy dog, a good eighty pounds. With my bum left leg and wounded right shoulder, wasn't sure I could manage to lift and carry him the quarter mile or so back to the cabin. But I couldn't leave him in the snow, cut open like that. Now an easy kill for some lurking predator, not that I wasn't.

I positioned my arms under the dog again. Getting my good right leg under me, I shifted most of the dog's weight to my left arm. With a bellow of determination and a push with my right leg, I rose to an unsteady stance, staggering backward into the trunk of an oak with a painful thump. My shoulder wound protested, but I remained upright. Hector moaned and went limp.

"Don't give up on my now, you big bastard," I said to him. "Now that I got you up, we're going to make it." I started back down the trail we left in the fresh snow.

After about fifty yards, we came upon a downslope. My feet went out from under me, and I slid on my butt, still holding Hector. "Dammit!" I said, as much in pain as frustration.

A shadow moved in the woods to my left front. I pulled out my Colt and cocked it. A fraction of a second from pulling the trigger, a voice called out.

"Deputy?"

It was Wil.

"Over here," I answered.

Two forms appeared out of the snow and darkness—Wil and Caitlin McDonald, she carried her shotgun.

"Oh, Hector," she moaned. "What happened?" She dropped her shotgun into the snow and knelt beside me holding Hector's head. I still cradled him in my arms.

"He caught up with whatever was out here," I said. "I didn't get a good look at it. Must've been a bear, judging from his wounds."

"A bear! What? Is he dead?" she asked.

"Don't think so. Still breathing, but he's lost a lot of blood."

"We heard a shot," Wil said.

"Doubt I hit anything," I said. "Something spooked me after I found Hector. It was a wild shot."

Wil and Caitlin grabbed up Hector from me. I stood and took the dog's hindquarters from her. "Here, let's both carry him," I said to Wil. "Miz McDonald, you lead the way. I don't know which way to go in the dark. Don't forget your shotgun."

CHAPTER 6

e laid Hector on the table. Miz McDonald ordered Wil to heat some water and me on where to find and fetch bandages, disinfectant, needle and thread. She checked Hector's eyes and his breathing.

"He's still alive, but just barely," she said. "I think the cold kept him from bleeding to death."

She repositioned the dog's torn hide, compressing the open wounds, cleaning them. Once done there, she sewed Hector up with a big curved needle and heavy thread. I stood by, ready to help, fascinated by her know-how and skills.

"Looks like you've done this kind of thing before," I said.

"I'm a surgical nurse, or I was before I married William. Sewed up a lot of cut-up drunk roughnecks who came into the hospital where I worked. When I came out here, I brought medical supplies with me. You never know when you'll need this stuff."

"Yeah," I said. The depth of this woman started to amaze me, not to mention her slender profile against the flames in the fireplace behind her.

She tied off the last stitch in Hector's side. "There," she said, sighed heavily and gently stroked the dog's head. "At least he's put back together. The rest is up to him. I don't know if he'll make it or not. He lost a lot of blood, but he's a tough critter. If he makes it through the next twenty-four hours, he'll have a good chance of surviving."

"Dog seems to mean a lot to you, Miz McDonald?" I said.

"I got him as a pup four years ago. Well, not exactly a pup. He was a little over six months old. Most loyal friend I've ever had." Tears soak her eyelashes as she stroked his head. "Please, call me Caitlin, or Cait."

"Thanks for going after him," she continued. "He surely would've died if you hadn't."

"Crazy dog," I said. "I tried to keep him from going after that bear, but he wouldn't stop."

"You really think it was a bear?" she asked.

"It was big, whatever it was. Looked bigger than a man. What else could it've been?"

She furrowed her brow, puzzled. "I don't know, but a bear . . . just seems unlikely, a bear."

"Not a bear," Wil said. He stood by the front window, one foot on the seat of a dining chair he dragged over, his right hand around a mug of steaming coffee. The wind blasted against the window glass, rattling it.

"What do you think it was?" I asked.

He kept silent, studying the snow storm through the window.

"Wil?"

"Not likely a bear this time of year. It's the same that killed the Jakes," he said. Took a drink of coffee. "Dire Wolf."

I shook my head. "I don't think so, Wil. Whatever did this to Hector was big. No wolf in these parts is big enough to do that kind of damage."

"No ordinary wolf," he said. "Dire Wolf."

I thought about what he was saying. "Old Long Walker talked about this Dire Wolf," I said. "Is that a man or an animal."

"A little of both, I reckon . . . and neither." He got quiet again, sipped his coffee, reading the window glass. The wind screamed and howled beyond it, out in the feral night.

"What's that supposed to mean?" I asked.

"There're stories among my people, the Quapaw, mostly from the old ones now," Wil said. "Long Walker can tell you all this, maybe better'n me. But here's what I learned.

"Many generations past, before even the Spaniards came, hundreds of years ago, maybe even thousands." He shrugged, shook his head. "My ancestors lived along the Mississippi. Back then they were known as the Downstream People. Moundbuilders, it's said. No one knows why they did this, not now, but most tell that the mounds were spiritual, the dwelling places for spirits, good and bad. The spirit of the *Shanka' Tunka* is one kind of spirit that stayed there, an evil one. Legend has it he awakens every hundred years or so, roams the land looking for a likely soul to take, someone who ain't too far from evil himself.

"Used to be a big wolf was on this land, bigger than those you see today, big as a man or bigger. Fiercer, too. It's told they could take down a buffalo or elk and would attack a man on sight. But they all disappeared. No one's rightly sure just why. Called the dire wolf. That's what we call the *Shanka' Tunka*. Eats up a soul and makes that person take on the shape and habits of a wolf, a dire wolf. One that has a bloodlust. He'll go on a killing rampage for a while, then go back to sleep, usually after the person he took over dies. If he ain't ready to sleep, he'll just move on to another."

After that, it got quiet inside the cabin. Caitlin moved around the table fussing with Hector. Wil stared out the dark window, boot on the chair seat, leaning his forearms on his thigh, nursing that mug of coffee. The storm raged even stronger in the night, shrieking and wailing like furious yowls from a pack of frenzied animals. I sat at the table, considered both my companions, then the floor, contemplating what Wil said. Was sometime before I decided to speak.

Although the Indian ways weren't my ways, been among them long enough to respect their beliefs. All the tribes had their legends, the Cherokee their *Ani Tsaguhi*, their bear legend, the Cheyenne their dog soldiers, the Choctaw their little people, their *Kowi Anukasha* or "forest dwellers." Wasn't my place to dispute those tales, but as a federal lawman investigating the murder of human beings, I had to pursue the facts. The suspicions and superstitions surrounding the Dire Wolf of the Quapaw didn't enter the realm of my investigation. But it did spook me a little.

"Wil, don't take this wrong," I said. "But I have my doubts. I'll agree it could've been some animal that attacked Hector and Major Standback's cattle, but I don't think the killer of the Jakes was one and the same. Most likely, what attacked Hector and those cows was a bear."

"You're wrong," Wil said.

"Take a look at the facts, Wil," I said. "Hector was torn into by claws. The way the Major described those cows, they were killed the same way. A wolf wouldn't do that. A bear uses its claws to maul. The main weapon of a wolf ain't its claws, it's his teeth."

"I already told you, this ain't no ordinary wolf," he said quietly.

⧗

The snowstorm abated, and the wind lessened before daylight which crept in slow and dim. Big flakes still came down. A snow drift, coming up over the front steps and spanning the length of the porch, stood a good three feet high at one end, tapering down to a foot at the other.

Hector was still with us, sleeping fitfully on the rug pad by the fire. The cabin was warm and snug. Well after midnight, Caitlin went off into the bedroom to sleep. She took several pieces of firewood with her for the stove in there . . . and her shotgun. When she shut the oak door between the two rooms, we heard a rattle and thud against it. My guess, she propped a chair under the knob. Wil and I took turns stretching out on the settee under a heavy quilt. One of us kept watch at the window, while the other slept. The cabin door was thick oak and snugged firm to the frame with iron bolts top and bottom. Still, I remembered the Jakes' shattered door. Kept my Winchester in my grip.

It was well past the end of my watch at the window when Cait came out of the bedroom. Knew I wouldn't sleep, so I just let Wil snore on the settee. Intermittently, he muttered and tossed. Cait went straight over to check on Hector. "Mornin'," I said to her. "Put a fresh pot of coffee on about a half hour ago."

Without responding, she squatted next to the dog and stroked his head. He opened his eyes but didn't move. "You're going to be okay, boy," she whispered to him. "You're going to be okay."

"I think you saved him," I said, more out of reassurance than certainty.

She went to the coffee pot on the stove. "I need to go see about the animals and other dogs. They're probably starved and half-frozen," she said.

"I'll go with you."

Pulling on my heavy sheepskin and picking up my Winchester, I kicked Wil's socked foot. He half-sat, still mostly asleep. "We're going out to the barn," I said. "Got coffee made on the stove."

He rubbed his jaw and his face, trying to comprehend where he was, what I said. Cait bundled and headed for the door. I pushed my old beaver skin Boss down tight on my head and followed her out.

We tramped across foot-deep snow in the frozen morning, the air as still and silent as a mountain cat. Big snowflakes fell to earth like crystal feathers. The temperature likely at or below zero. Cait froze in her steps. I stopped, too.

"Did we forget to shut the barn doors last night?" I asked

"No, I closed and bolted them," she answered.

One of the doors hung open about two feet, a snowdrift piled up in the opening. A deep red trail of blood in the snow led from it into the trees to our right. Around that trail a heavy trample of prints, some horse, some . . . wolf, and . . . I'm not sure what. As we approached, all was dark and quiet inside the gap and a scent came from it, a scent that made you recoil. I took the lead, jacked a round into the rifle, moved through the open doorway.

Even though the sky was thick with clouds, and the morning light dim, the brightness of the snow made it difficult for my eyes to adjust to the darkness inside the barn. It was as quiet as a crypt in there, the air heavy with that smell that made hair on my neck prickle and my skin shiver—the sickening sweet odor of blood.

Cait came in behind me and gasped. She smelled it, too. Brushing past me, she pulled a lantern from a post by the door and lit it up.

At first, the reach of the lantern light mixed with the shadows made the scene incomprehensible, the sheer horror of it surreal. But bit by bit the reality of it started to step into our minds.

Cait's mule lay in a bloody heap in its stall. The milk cow was ripped apart. The corpses of the dogs were barely recognizable, and it was difficult to tell how many there were. One completely decapitated. The dapple was still alive, but down. He lay on his right side making guttering noises and issuing weak screams. Clyde wasn't in the barn. I couldn't tell if he escaped the carnage or was carried off. Barn things were tossed and torn, scattered. The dogs put up a helluva fight.

At the sight, Cait fell back against a support post and slid to her knees, her eyes wide in horror, her face aghast and pale. "My God," she rasped. Then again, "My God."

I walked over to the dapple and squatted next to him, stroking his neck. "Easy, fella," I said softly "Easy." His left foreleg was broken, the bones sticking out through the hide. His chest and shoulder were flayed open, and his eyes were glazed in pain and shock. He huffed with dying breaths. A sad sigh escaped me as I stood and aimed the rifle between the dapple's eyes. I squeezed, the report amplified in the dead silence of the barn.

Cait waited a quarter minute before she whispered, "What agent of hell could've done this?"

Queasiness roiled my gut at the dreadfulness of the scene. "Had to be whatever we chased last night, whatever got to Hector," I answered.

"The dogs and these other animals had to be making a lot of noise when all of this was going on. Why didn't we hear them?" she said in a plaintive murmur.

"We probably did," I said. "But mixed in with the howl of the storm, we must not've recognized it."

We heard a whimper, the soft fearful moan of a dog. Cait pushed herself to her feet and followed the sound, holding the lantern out in front of her. "It's okay, boy," she said into the darkness beyond the lantern. "It's okay, it's me."

The animal whined then gave out a half-squeak, a half-bark, a terrified keening. Cait found the dog at the back of the barn behind two bales of hay, wedged between the tines of a rusty implement. She kneeled a yard from the dog's hiding place, holding the lantern high.

"It's Athena," she said, more to herself than me.

"Is he hurt?" I asked moving behind Cait. I scanned the shelf of the barn's loft; suddenly fearful the killer might still be near us.

"She. I can't tell. Don't see any wounds," she answered.

"Come on out, girl. Come on," Cait coaxed, but the dog wouldn't move.

"Help me move this garden harrow away from her," she said.

When I moved toward the tool, the dog laid her ears back and bared her teeth, growling at me hysterically. Cait reached through the tines of the harrow and stroked the dog's back. The dog flinched at Cait's touch and snapped backward at Cait's hand, but the tines of the harrow blocked the bite.

Cait laid her hand fully on the dog. "Hey, hey, it's only me," she said soothingly. "Shh. Shh." The dog seemed to calm some at Cait's voice and touch, whining and licking its chops, but still baring its teeth. I grabbed the tongue of the harrow where it leaned against the barn wall and pulled it toward me. The dog half-whined half-growled and scrambled back to the wall.

"I've never seen one of my dogs as frightened as this, especially not Athena," Cait said. "Next to Hector, she's the most aggressive and courageous of them . . . at least, she was."

Cait removed her left glove and extended her hand out to the dog, palm up. After a bit, it licked her fingers and whimpered.

"I need to go look for Clyde," I said. "I guess in this cold all these carcasses will keep, but we'll need to dispose of them. We should probably burn them, in case whatever attacked them is rabid. Won't be easy with all this snow. I'll get Wil to clear some ground and set up a bonfire. If I find Clyde, and he's able, I'll ride him over to the Standback ranch to get help."

Wil came through the barn doors, rifle in hand. "What in the holy hell is goin' on?" Dazed at the sight of all the butchery, he spoke quietly. "I heard a shot." He saw the dapple.

"The dapple was still alive, Wil. I had to destroy him."

He nodded slightly, fear in his eyes.

"Figure it was the same animal we ran into last night," I said. "Looks like Clyde got away. You need to build a fire to get rid of these carcasses."

"Animals," he said. "There's more than one." He squatted. Arose and walked some more, stopped and spoke, still studying the dirt floor. "Pack of wolves, four of them."

I didn't respond, nor did Cait.

"Something else," he said.

I waited.

"Man tracks, too." He pointed to the dirt floor with his rifle barrel. Footprints, bare footprints.

I broke the silence. "I'm gonna go see if I can find Clyde."

"What if your horse is dead, or . . . you can't ride him?" Cait asked.

"Then I guess I'll have to walk to Standback's."

"That's almost ten miles from here."

"Yeah, I know," I said. "Better get started."

ait gave me a cotton sack of bacon and biscuits and I struck out from the cabin with them and my booted Winchester slung over my shoulder. The sky was high and clear, the sun a bright but meager spark in the deep blue. Wasn't sure where my search would take me, or in what condition I'd find Clyde, if at all. Told Cait and Wil, if I hadn't found Clyde by noon, I'd strike out for Standback's afoot with the intent to get there before dark. That seemed optimistic as walking across the snow-drifted prairie would be tough going, especially with my bum leg.

I tracked Clyde to a cave in the hills about two miles from Cait's cabin. He apparently fled the barn in panic, maybe ran out unnoticed while all the other killings were going on. Maybe he got in a few licks of his own. I don't know, but there wasn't a scratch on him . . . not like the others, anyway. Somehow, he got where he did without hurting himself. Must've come upon that cave after daybreak.

He was spent but still full of fear—snorting and grunting and wild-eyed—when I approached him. About half-froze, too, but the shelter of the cave kept him out of the worst part of the wind and snow. I coaxed him into letting me put on a bridle. Think he sensed I'd take him to food and water and shelter. I inspected him for any outward injuries but found none. After walking him around a bit, I decided it'd be better for both of us to ride him back to Cait's cabin. He needed to get warmed up as soon as possible.

Approaching the cabin, a plume of gray smoke rose through the trees. They built a fire in a cleared space in the snow for warmth while Wil hauled in bigger timbers for the pyre. Cait worked around the fire and helped Wil set the wood for the bonfire as he hauled it in. The dog Cait called Athena sat near the fire, watched us as we rode in.

I walked Clyde up next to the fire and dismounted. Cait and Wil stopped their work as we approached, the dog stood. Thought I saw a glimmer of a pleased smile on Cait's face and a trace of gladness in her haunted eyes.

"You found him," she said.

"He doesn't appear to be injured," I said. Clyde was skittish, dancing by the fire, jerking his head and giving out nervous grunts. I suspected he didn't like standing that near the barn again, could smell the death in there. I grabbed the reins, patted his neck. "Easy, boy. Easy," I whispered.

"Not on the outside, anyway," I added. "Not so sure what's happened to him inside his head." Even in the bright daylight, the barn hunkered like a dark tomb. "May be a chore getting him to pull those carcasses out of there."

Cait rubbed her gloved hand across Clyde's back and flank, brushing away some of the ice and frozen mud. "There's a blanket in the barn," she said. "Would you mind getting it? I don't think I can go back in that place right now."

"I'll fetch it," Wil said. He dropped the end of a pine log on the corner of the stack.

"I'll go with you, get Clyde some feed," I said.

Cait rubbed Clyde's side and back. "And a curry comb, bring that, too," she hollered after us. "There's one in Jack's stall."

As we walked to the barn, Wil filled me in. "She did a fair amount of crying after you lit out, but she straightened herself out after a bit. Went to building that fire. Set me to work bringing in the logs. She told me where to find that double-bladed ax and bucksaw in the barn. She wouldn't go back in there. Sorta wish I didn't have to, either.

"I 'spect we can burn up the dogs with the wood we got, but I reckon it's going to take a lot more for the big animals. Fair amount of dead wood out in there." He gestured toward the thick forest. "That's what I looked for to build a good fire. Don't know how much we can cut down and haul in here before dark, even with Clyde's help. Going to take some work to get that cow and mule out here, too . . . and ole Boots."

He took a deep breath and let it out. "Sure gonna miss that dapple."

I cleared my throat and coughed. "Soon as we get Clyde fed, watered, and warmed up, I'll ride him back to the Standback ranch and bring some help. Stay here with Cait, and continue with the wood cutting, do what you can."

Clyde screamed, he was rearing, bucking. Cait strained at the reins trying to hold him, shouting, "Easy boy! Easy!" Athena stood bristled up and growling.

Wil spotted the cause of Clyde's hysteria. "Wolves," he said. "Bastards come back."

I picked them up, back in the trees, grays. Deeper in the woods behind them stood a huge black, most likely the leader. They moved between the trees in a stalking weave, five. Drew my .44 and fired, three, four times, splintering the tree trunks above them, blowing up the snow and dirt beside them. Wil pulled, too. Fired two shots. Dropped one, sent another howling away with the others. The black, disappeared, too.

We went up to the body of the downed wolf, a big gray. Wil nudged it with a boot-toe, his pistol still aimed at the animal's head. A bullet hole replaced one eye. Wil searched the woods for any of the gray's buddies. Satisfied they'd gone, he un-eared his old Scofield and re-holstered it.

"You ain't much of a hand with a gun, are ya?" he said. "Thought lawmen was supposed to be able to shoot."

I put my Colt away. "Where'd you hear that?" I asked. Cait held Clyde's reins, stroked his neck calming him. Athena stood ready, hackles still raised.

Wil sobered. "Deputy," he said, "we're up against something ain't regular on this earth. Looks to me like it's circlin in on Miz Cait. Maybe us, too. Might be best if we all hightail outta here for right now."

"Can't the three of us get out on one horse, Wil. Our best bet, the fastest, is to go get help. I got the Winchester and my Colt. Besides that Greener, Cait's got a Henry .44 in the cabin, too. You two can hold off whatever's out there if it decides to come back. I figure to get to Standback's and back in this snow it'll take three, four hours."

"Provided rest of those wolves don't decide to make you and Clyde a quick lunch," he said. "Better let me go."

"Can't ask you to do that, Wil."

"Why not? Know the land better, I'll make better time. Besides, they take one look at my skinny old hide, they'd decide to stay here, as you'd make a more satisfying meal."

We returned to Cait, Clyde, and the fire, me carrying a bucket of oats and another empty one with the curry comb in it. Wil had the blanket. I handed the empty bucket to Cait. She removed the comb. Her hands shook. Clyde was breathing heavy and snorting but past the worst of it.

"If you can break through the ice in the trough over there, bring some water," she said.

I took the empty pail, picked up the ax. Under the snow cover, the ice in the trough was about an inch thick. Chopped it up and filled the bucket with water and ice. Cait set it next to the fire to melt the ice chunks, let it warm some before she placed it in front of Clyde.

Wil and I set to work building the pyre. I stayed a little longer to help bring in enough wood for the big animals. Most of the logs were four to six inches in diameter and about six or seven feet in length. We raised a rough triangular structure of the logs about six feet on a side, stacked them lengthwise in a pyramid. Clyde didn't like it, but we used him to haul the carcasses from the barn, all but the dogs. A blindfold helped.

We piled them all in one spot, placed the timbers around and atop them.

⏳

I adjusted Clyde's saddle. It was getting on about noon.

"Wil, I expect we've got about five hours of daylight left."

He nodded, understanding what I was saying. "Don't know how rough the going will be," he said, taking the reins and swinging into the saddle. "But I'll try my damnedest to get us back here before dark."

Wil reined Clyde around and spurred him off down the snow-covered road.

I brought out a can of coal oil from the barn and set it by the wood stack. I knew we had a grisly task ahead of us. "I think it best we get started with this business," I said. "I'll get the dogs."

Cait said nothing, threw the end of a log onto the stack. I handed her the Winchester. "Keep an eye peeled," I said. "Athena'll probably alert you."

Found a wheelbarrow on the side of the barn and wheeled it inside to load up the dog remains. I located a couple gunny sacks to cover them up . . . for Cait's sake.

Athena laid her ears back and whined as I rolled up, then quickly rose to her feet and trotted off to the front porch of the cabin where she sat.

"Guess she doesn't want any part of this," I said.

"Can you blame her?" Cait said. "Neither do I."

I moved the dog remains to the top of the log stack, doused them all and the wood with the whole can the coal oil. "You got any more of this?" I asked Cait.

"I usually keep two cans," she said. "I don't know how much is left in the other."

"This'll get us started," I said. "We should have a good bed of coals by the time Wil and the others get back here."

I set the can aside and pulled a flaming stick out of the side fire, tossed it into the center of the pyre. The oil caught quickly and spread across the logs with a rapid *whoosh,* the flames instantly leaping high with yellow-white heat. As the blaze grew, the roar of the inferno and the pop and hiss of the pine logs were the only sounds in the still, cold afternoon air. Athena moved to the far corner of the porch. The sizzle and burning smell of the animal flesh was unsettling.

Cait spoke first. "I got those dogs when I first moved out here. First Athena, then those three."

"Were they pups?"

"No, they were all at least a year old. Got them from the same man my husband got Hector from. He breeds them and trains them . . . for personal protection. They're called Rottweilers. I got Athena shortly after my husband died, then the other three a few months later."

I started to speak but stopped. After a bit, all I could think to say was, "I'm sorry." The fire crackled and roared and sizzled. The flames held us each with our own thoughts.

"I don't think it was just those wolves that attacked the animals," she said.

I waited a few seconds before responding. "You think it was Wil's Dire Wolf?"

"No." She shook her head. "I think it was a man . . . an assassin."

"Assassin?"

"Yes." She nodded. "A sick, crazy one, but an assassin. Someone come to kill me. Someone sent by those who had my husband killed."

"I can't hardly see a hired killer doing all this. I've dealt with some. They're cold-blooded, some vicious, but their killings are just a job to them. They do it with efficiency. Get it done and get out. They don't want to leave a trail or draw undue attention, so they can go on to the next job. Plus, it'd be kind of unlikely a man would lead a pack of wolves." I thought about those footprints Wil found in the barn.

"Wil found footprints," she said like she'd picked up my thoughts.

I had no counter. I saw the prints, but couldn't reconcile a bare-footed man in a blizzard. All my reason said it was an illusion of some sort.

"I don't buy your business-like, dispassionate killing theory. Not with this one," she said. "He likes it too much."

"You talk like you know this person," I said.

"Before Hector, there was another dog. Not a Rottweiler.

"Carmen was a collie, just a family pet. A sweet, affectionate dog. She liked everybody. One morning we found her on the back porch with her throat cut. She'd been executed. This was a couple weeks after William's falling out with his partners. It was like a warning, something to scare us. I think William's enemies, his partners, thought he'd be intimidated and give in. But he didn't. Two months later they killed him. William brought home Hector a couple days after we buried Carmen."

"So, you think whoever killed your collie . . . and your husband, tracked you down out here, and let you know he's here to get you?"

"Yes."

"Seems a little excessive. Don't mean to be insensitive, but why not just kill one dog? Wouldn't that get the message across?"

She shrugged. "I suppose. But it maybe was to even the odds some, get rid of my protection. Maybe all the rest were for your benefit, after last night with Hector. Besides, considering all the carnage it could be more than one killer."

"Yeah, that thought crossed my mind," I said picturing the wolf tracks. "Kind of hard to see one person, even a big bastard, taking on all four of these dogs at once. It'd be their nature to attack. Don't believe one guy could hold off a pack like that."

The back of my neck got a little itchy. "Well, if what you say is true, maybe we should move inside until Wil gets back with the Major. We seem like a couple of easy targets standing out here."

I picked up the Winchester leaning against a log, becoming more uneasy.

"Maybe you're right," Cait said, gathering up her shotgun and heading for the house. I followed her, turned around, almost walking backward as we approached the porch.

"Athena, come!" she called, holding open the door. The dog hesitated, made a move to slide off the end of the porch away from us. "Come on, Athena!" Cait demanded. The dog lowered its ears and head, slinking toward Cait by the open door. She sniffed to where Hector slept by the fireplace, backed to the wall staying there.

"That dog is really spooked," I said.

"I don't know what to make of this," Cait said. "She and Hector are companions, the alpha and beta of the pack.

"Probably still smells Hector's attacker on him," I said.

⧖

We waited out the afternoon, but Wil didn't return. Daylight faded, and still no sight of him. I got uncomfortable, paced between windows. "Something ain't right," I said several times. My fear that Wil ran into trouble increased with every hour.

Cait made us a pot of soup, attended Hector. The big dog slept mostly, but when awake panted rapidly with his head raised. Athena stayed as far away from Hector as she could.

Around midnight I still stood vigilant at the window. Weariness crept into my bones as the mental strain and exertion of the day wore on me. Coals still glowed from the pyre, a few flames licking up from the remaining stumps of logs. It gave off some light in the inky darkness, but not much into the moonless, starlit night.

Cait stirred from the settee where she lay. She sat up and rubbed her face. "Wil ain't here by daylight, I'm going to go look for him," I said.

She came to the window, taking the barrel of my rifle in her right hand. "Go get some rest," she said. "I'll watch for a while." She yawned big.

"I'm okay," I said.

She yanked the rifle from my grip. "Go," she said firmly.

I released my hold on the Winchester. "Awright, but just a short nap. Wake me in about thirty minutes."

I couldn't get up. Clyde lay atop me his neck broken and ripped open, and I was trapped beneath him as his death throes shook me. Cait was backed up against a rock face. A large black beast slowly approached her on all fours, slavering over long, bared white teeth, its coal-red eyes burning with malevolence. She had no way to escape, and she called out my name.

"Deputy," she said. "Jubal wake up." Her hand on my shoulder shook me into consciousness. When I opened my eyes, a shaft of sunlight fell through the front window. Cait stood over me.

"It's Wil, they're coming," she said to me.

I swung my legs off the settee and sat upright, rubbing my eyes and face. "Why didn't you wake me sooner?" I asked with some irritation.

"No need," she said. "Major Standback isn't with them."

Cait walked out onto the porch. I followed. Wil and two men sat a-horse, two of the ranch hands I met at

Standback's—a big fella they called Husker and the top hand, Cole Turnbow. They brought along two extra horses. All the men dismounted at the front of the cabin, cold and grim. "Where's Standback?" I asked Wil.

He mounted the porch steps, stopped when I spoke. "Major's near dead," he said. Kicked his boot toe into the step riser, knocking snow off, raised his hat brim, his eyes rimmed with weariness and fear. "Might be all dead by now. They found him out on the range day before yesterday. Been attacked. Musta happened after we left him to come out here. Hit like the dogs out there, like the Jakeses, only somehow he survived . . . but just barely."

Wil grew silent, waited for the foreman to continue the telling. Turnbow spit some tobacco juice into the snow and wiped his gloved hand across his mustache drooped with brown ice.

"Horse come back to the barn without him, so we went lookin, Husker and me. Thought maybe he took a fall. Horse got spooked and bucked him off or somethin. Anyways, we set out. Felt they was a storm comin and the daylight was fadin. Major's a tough old bird, but we knew even he probly couldn't survive one of these northern blows for very long, especially if'n he's hurt.

"Come upon him only a mile or so from the ranch. Appeared some animal had jumped him, wolf signs all around him, tracks and such, but his wounds didn't look like wolf done it. Throat slashed, front of his coat's tore through with claws. Had some fair-sized cuts on his chest, too, but I s'pect that big leather sheepskin of his may've saved his life. Somethin besides wolves done most the damage.

"Looked like he put up a fight. Found his pistol about twenty feet away like it were knocked outta his hand. But they was two rounds fired. Figger the Major put a slug intuh whatever come at him, and they run off afore finishing him.

"Anyways, he's still alive when we found him, but not by much. Cold probably kept him from bleedin' to death. Got him back to the ranch house alive. Wil come in yestiddy evenin. Too dark to start back, and Wil was half froze, so we waited for first light. That's when we lit out for here."

Cait leaned against the doorjamb, bringing her hand to her mouth.

"Whatever attacked him musta followed us on over here. Did what it did to Miz McDonald's animals . . . and old Boots," Wil said.

All the men nodded but didn't add anything. Finally, I spoke up. "What about Miz Standback? She okay?"

"Well, she ain't been harmed, if'n that's what you're asking," Turnbow said. "Left two hands at the house to guard her, plus there's that old Quapaw woman, Asmita. She's shuck up. More'n the missus, I'd say. Woman may appear delicate, but she kept her wits about her when we brung the Major in, took charge of all of it. Anyways, they's nursin him best they could, but I ain't sure he'll live.

"Sent another'n into town to fetch the doc . . . and sheriff," he added.

"Well," Turnbow surveyed the smoldering pyre. "We best get done what needs to get done here, get headed back over to the ranch house. We need to get back there before dark."

"I can't leave," Cait said.

"That's not an option, ma'am," I said,

"Hector needs me. I can't go off and leave him."

"Can't any of us stay here with you, Cait, and you can't stay by yourself. Too dangerous." I moved closer to her, out of earshot of the others. Spoke in a whisper. "You know yourself, whoever's out there doing this killing is likely after you, too."

She dipped her chin.

75

"So, we gotta go. We'll get back into town where I can get you some more protection. We'll take the dogs, too. Hook one of these horses up to that wagon of yours."

Athena came to stand by her mistress, staying vigilant. "He's not strong enough, yet," Cait said. "The trip could kill him."

"That's a possibility," I said. "But I doubt it. Like the Major, he's a tough sumbitch."

CHAPTER 8

elieve that there's the spot where we found the Major," Turnbow said. He reined up at the top of a knoll, pointed down the south side toward a clump of scrub oaks whose dead brown leaves still clung tenaciously to their limbs, bent low with piled snow. I pulled left on the reins and walked Clyde down to the spot. Turnbow followed; the others stayed with Cait and the wagon.

The disturbed and trampled snow marked where Standback was wounded. Still a few crimson stains on the white, but not much sign of a struggle. Clyde and the other horses snorted and shied.

I dismounted. "When you found the Major, you fellas see anything here to tell you who or what may have tried to kill him?"

"Don't recollect seeing anything," Turnbow said. "It's gettin' kindy dark when we come upon him, and the snow almost covered him."

Moved some of the snow with my boot. "Well, I can't tell anything now. Best get heading back to the ranch house." Finding that MacKenzie fella seemed more and more like what I needed to do.

⧗

Wil tied his horse to the wagon, drove the team the rest of the way for Cait. She wanted to stay in the back to keep an eye on Hector. We tried to get Athena to ride in the wagon, too, but she'd preferred to galumph through the snow drifts. Ice chunks clung to her belly and paws and frosted her muzzle by the time we got to the ranch. She seemed willing to suffer that than be anywhere near her mate. Took us more'n five hours to get to the ranch house, counting our stop at the spot_of the

Major's_attack. Slow going for the horses. We had to circle wide of a few places where the snow drifted deep. Couldn't take a straight line as a person normally would from Cait's place to the Standbacks'.

"You got a warm place we can take Hector?" Cait asked Turnbow. "I need to re-dress his wounds."

The foreman spit to the right. "Reckon we can put him up in the bunkhouse. Got a corner he can lay in." He spit again. "That dog ain't mean, is he?"

Cait smirked. "He's mean, alright. But in his condition, I don't think you've got much to worry about. You leave him alone, he'll leave you alone."

"What about t'other dawg," Turnbow asked.

"She'll want to stay with me," Cait said. "As to her disposition, same applies. If she thinks I'm in danger, she'll react."

Missus Standback opened the front door as I kicked the porch steps to knock the snow off my boots, brushed it off my pant legs.

"Hello, deputy." She spoke in a soft tone, deep. Her eyes had a strain, her face set with anger. "Good to see you folks made it back. Wil said you've had quite a time."

I removed my hat, nodded. "How's the Major?"

"Doctor Riley says he's critical. His survival all depends on the next forty-eight hours. Lost a lot of blood. But . . ." She pushed a loose strand of hair behind her right ear. "He's resting. Fitful, but resting. Hasn't regained consciousness. Asmita is with him every second. Believe she's saying some Indian prayers over him . . . constantly, it seems."

I didn't know exactly what to say. "S'pose it can't hurt," was what I came up with.

"Come in," she said, swinging the door wide and stepping behind it.

The coffee tasted good, felt good going down. Took off my gloves, laid them on the table, and put both hands around the thick clay mug, holding it tight to let its hot penetrate my icicle fingers. My bum leg ached. We sat at the kitchen table, a shaft of sunlight from the south window lay across my half. It felt good. I rubbed my knee.

"Don't mean to seem insensitive, Miz Standback, but I'm gonna need to talk to the Major as soon as I can. Turnbow thinks he fought off his attacker. Could've shot him."

"He's been unconscious since they brought him in. Not sure he'll wake up soon . . . if ever."

I kept quiet, took another sip of coffee.

"Where's Missus McDonald?"

"She's out at the bunkhouse with Wil and your foreman. One of her dogs was badly injured. She's tending to him. I expect she'll be in directly."

"Yes, Wil told us you had quite an ordeal yourselves. Lost some livestock to some predators?"

"Two of her dogs, also. One may die yet. One got away unscratched but seems pretty spooked."

She shook her head. "My, all this is so strange. Do you think the two incidents are related?"

"Well, the method is certainly similar, but I don't know. Hard to say."

"This place can be such a wicked land." I expected there'd be grief in her eyes. It puzzled me there was none. More like anger, I thought.

"You from here in the Territory, Miz Standback? Oklahoma, I mean." I knew she wasn't, just fishing for something to talk about other than the obvious.

"Oh, Lord, no." She coughed into her hand, whispered a small laugh. "I met Justice . . . the Major, at my home in Chicago. He was a handsome war hero, about thirty at the time. I was just a girl, nineteen. My father brought him home

79

for dinner one night. I think he was trying to recruit him to come work for him. He couldn't, though. Justice never wanted to have any boss but himself. Anyway, he carried me off to this ranch. That was before statehood, still Indian Territory, and as wild as I'd imagined. My father wasn't at all happy about it, but he didn't stop us. Think he was more intrigued about getting in on some of the land deals, like Justice, than losing his daughter. Been here ever since." She sighed. "That was twenty years ago."

"What was your daddy's business?" More searching for conversation, wishing Cait would hurry up and come to the house. Rubbed my knee some more at that spot where the bones hadn't gone back together quite right, where it barked as a reminder when the weather changed, where my hand went when something troubled me. The woman made me nervous. Maybe it was her uncommon beauty. Maybe her fathomless dark eyes.

"You know, I never was quite sure about that," she said. "Or even really cared, for that matter. Land speculation, I think. He had various other businesses in Chicago. All I knew for sure was he made a lot of money. He was important. Men came and went around him all the time, some of them kind of scary. I never felt unsafe around them, though. They all seemed to bow down to my father. I grew up a spoiled princess." She smiled at me "Justice kind of picked up my father's lead, as far as that goes. But I've tried not to take too much advantage of it."

Thought I caught a hint of humor in her faint smile. Not sure, though. Whatever it was added to the discomfort I felt sitting there with this lady. I pressed on with things I knew how to talk about. "I've come out here hunting for a man named Crow Redhand. He's wanted for cattle rustling, assault, and murder. Robbed a bank near here, killed a man there, too. Then there're the killings of the Jakes."

"Yes, I heard. Such a horrible thing."

"Your husband knows Redhand. Do you?"

"I know who he is, what he is. Everybody around this area has heard of Crow Redhand."

"Just wondering if the Major might've had some run-in with him."

"I don't know."

"What about Gray MacKenzie?"

"What about him?" The question seemed to startle her.

"The Major told me he had some trouble with him, that he'd gotten in a fight with the Jakes brothers over his advances toward one's wife, Sarah."

"Sarah worked here in the kitchen . . . this very kitchen." She dabbed her eyes with a lace hanky, sniffed.

"Both men are suspects in the murders. The attack on your husband, too. So, if there's anything you can tell me, I mean, other than what we already know, anything at all."

"All I know about MacKenzie is what I heard from Justice. He was a drifter, Justice hired him as a hand, then ran him off after that trouble . . . with Sarah. I never met him, don't believe I ever even saw him.

"Crow Redhand has been around for a long time. The Redhand family is prominent in these parts, that is, in terms of numbers. Known him since he was a boy. Seems like he was always in trouble. He came to work with his cousin Wil a few times. I believe Justice would let him work, try to make something of himself, but he'd never stick around. Justice never ran him off, but after about the third time coming back for work, he didn't take him on, either. The cowhands are a rough bunch, but most of them are dependable."

A knock came at the door. Relief hit me. "Must be Cait— Miz McDonald," I said, rising from my chair. Missus Standback went to the door.

"Oh, my dear, come in. You must be exhausted . . . and frozen." She took her coat from her, ushering her to the parlor fireplace and in front of the crackling fire. "What can I get you, some coffee? I could put a little brandy in it."

"Just coffee would be fine," Caitlin said. Her small smile expressed humble thanks, uncertainty. She removed her gloves and held her hands out to the fire.

"I bet you're hungry, too." Her arm still around Caitlin's shoulders, Missus Standback turned and shouted, "Asmita!"

"Don't go to any trouble, I'm fine," Caitlin said. I could tell she was uncomfortable, more than a little tired.

"Nonsense. It's no trouble. Besides, you look like you're about to faint."

Asmita came down the stairs. "Yes, missus?"

"You can leave Major Standback awhile. Bring Missus McDonald some buttered biscuits and jam, hot coffee, too. Enough for all of us. Put some ham slices on the plates, too."

I held my hat, regarded the women. "All the same, ma'am, I best go see about—"

"Wiley cooks for the men." She cut me off sharply. Smiled curtly. "I'm sure your man will be fed."

Kind of hit me wrong, her saying that, the way she said it. Made me bristle some. "Thanks," I said, putting my hat on. "I'll be back in a bit."

⏳

They had a room off the bunkhouse, part kitchen, part . . . couldn't call it a dining room, that'd be too elegant for this bunch. In the Army, we called it a mess hall. This one was smaller, smokier, maybe a little more pungent with cowhand smells, but that's what it was. I found Wil there chowing down earnestly with Turnbow and Husker. The cook they called Wiley was off in the kitchen part, slamming the oven doors and a big skillet on the stovetop, muttering. Seeing me he scowled. "You'd be wantin a meal, too, I reckon." He swore under his breath, turned angrily back to his fry pan.

"I'd be obliged, if it ain't too much trouble," I said.

He pulled a plate out of the cupboard and smacked it down on the sideboard. "Too much trouble? Aw, hell, it ain't no damn trouble." Ladled up some thick stew from a steaming pot on the stove, gingerly picked a couple of biscuits out of a pan in the oven, all the time muttering things I couldn't make out. I sat down next to Wil.

"Don't mind Wiley," he said, loud enough for all to hear. "He's allus pissed about somethin. Says he don't like late lunchers whilst he's in the middle of cookin supper. Figgers if we miss lunch, oughta have t'wait till supper."

"Sorry," I said to Wiley. He ignored me. Wil snickered into his plate of stew.

"What's the missus say about the Major," Turnbow asked me.

"No better, no worse, I reckon. Still unconscious, she said."

He spooned in a mouthful of stew, took a bite of biscuit.

I turned to Wil. "She told me you brought Crow with you to work here. You never mentioned that."

He barely paused in his eating. "Been a few years back. Tried to get him on to some honest work, but, as you can see, it didn't take. Never mentioned it 'cause it didn't seem important."

"He get along with the Jakes?" I asked.

Wil eyed Turnbow and Husker wondering what they'd say. "Yeah, he did." He leaned against the chair back, moved a stew potato with his spoon. "Crow never caused trouble here, not like that MacKenzie fella. Ain't that right, Turnbow?"

The top hand shook his head. "No, not like MacKenzie. Hard to get any work outta Crow, is all. Didn't take direction good. Has that bad temper. Crow and Sam got into a fist fight one night but believe that was over a hand of cards."

"Hell, we all of us, Redhands and Jakes, known each other since we's kids," Wil added. "Sarah, too. All us went to school together."

"Tell me about MacKenzie," I said to Turnbow and Husker.

"Man was quiet," Turnbow said. "Mostly kept to hisself. Feller's a hard worker, strong as an ox. Never had no trouble with his efforts. Not a good cowhand, though."

"Nobody liked him," Husker said. First time I'd heard him say anything. A big man, wide at the shoulders, thick arms, and neck.

"How come?" I asked.

Husker shrugged. "Just the way he was, way he treated ever'body. Didn't want to make friends." He went back to eating.

Wiley came over to the table, coffee pot in hand, topping off our mugs. "I'll tell ya about MacKenzie. Just a mean bastard. Had that wide dark face, long thick black hair, and them blue eyes cold as winter ice. Looks he'd give ya was scaresome. All the boys just stayed clear of him. Elam and Sam Jakes onliest ones brave enough to go after him, after Sarah told 'em what he's up to."

He set the coffee pot back to the stove, checked the biscuits in the oven. "If you're lookin to figure which of them kilt the Jakes, I'd look to that MacKenzie. What I know of Crow he's maybe nasty an' crazy enough, but I ain't sure he'd done it that way."

"Nope," Husker agreed.

The cook continued. "Believe the Major was right runnin him off. MacKenzie, I mean. Musta had other concerns, too, if you ask me."

"Okay, I'm asking," I said.

He stirred the stew pot. "Well, it mighta been more'n Sarah's skirts he's chasin. One night I's out t'water spigot, seen him and Missus out t'back porch of the big house. She hauled

84

off and slapped him a good one, then turned and went in the house. That was the night before that ruckus with Sarah and the Jakes brothers. Figure she musta said something to the Major."

"Miz Standback don't mix with the ranch hands," Husker said.

"True enough," added Turnbow. "First time I spoke to her in years, or she spoke back, was after we brung the Major in."

"Treats us all like we's beneath her," Husker said.

While I ate, I thought about what Wiley said, and Husker. Recalled that Emily Standback told me she didn't know MacKenzie, never met him. Presently, I got up from the table, my left leg protesting. "You got a bunk I can use tonight?" I asked Turnbow.

"Yeh, there's an exter."

"Gonna go check on my horse, fetch my gear." I grabbed the biscuit on my plate. "Damn good grub, Wiley. Thanks."

The cook snorted something in response, bobbed his chin. I headed for the bunkhouse door, munching the biscuit, glanced over at the corner where they bedded down Hector. He was awake, panting, his yellow eyes steady on me.

I walked over to him. Wouldn't call him friendly, but not hostile either. Squatted in front of him, held out the biscuit. He sniffed it, made a tentative grab at it, took it down in a couple of bites.

"Guess you're ready for a little grub," I said. He laid his head back down. "Well, we'll take it a little easy."

Someone had put a bowl of water next to his pallet. I picked it up and brought it to his mouth. He raised his head again and lapped. Drank the whole bowl. I refilled it, he drank half of it. Laid his head back down and closed his eyes. Didn't even say thanks.

I stepped to the kitchen door. "Hey, Wiley. Bring me a bowl of that stew." Figured if Hector ate that biscuit, he might want something more. It was a good sign.

⧖

Clyde snuffled when I approached. I stroked his neck, scratched his nose. Bennie had thrown a blanket over him to help stave off the cold, but the tight barn with all that hay wasn't too bad. "Hey, big fella," I said to him. "Comfy? Nice to be in a luxury suite for a change, huh?" He grunted. I bucketed up some oats, held it for him as he munched, going over things in my head.

Doubts crept in as to Crow Redhand's part in the Jakes' murders and Standback's assault. More and more, MacKenzie came to the front. Only thing that didn't take Crow off my list was the Spencer rifle. But, hell, he's more a thief than a killer. Possibility he could've gone to the Jakes' cabin after the murders, just taken the rifle. Maybe he was the one covered the boy with the buffalo robe . . . and his mother's body. Maybe he was the one alerted the old shaman Long Walker. Still had lingering suspicions, though. Yet not able to rule out animals for either attack. But my assigned duty was to bring in Redhand. The murders of the Jakes not really in my purview, my authority. Only thing that kept me after it was what happened two nights back at Cait's . . . that and Redhand's possible involvement.

Thought I'd better head back up to the big house to check on Cait. Had a couple more questions to ask Missus Standback, too.

I knocked. Cold porch, probably could've opened the door and gone on in, but my momma had taught me manners. Besides, the Missus was a proper woman, not likely to take kindly to breaches of class protocol.

The Quapaw woman, Asmita, opened the door, gestured for me to come in quickly so as not to let in too much cold. The two women sat in the dining room.

"Deputy Smoak, you're welcome to join us," Missus Standback said.

I removed my hat. "Appreciate it, ma'am, but I ate at the bunkhouse. Wouldn't mind another cup of coffee, though."

She motioned for me to sit. Cait smiled, glad I came back to relieve her from some of the conversation, I think.

"Caitlin has been filling me in on the details of your ordeal. Thank goodness you were with her."

I ran a forefinger under my nostrils and sniffed. "Well, glad I was there, but I believe Miz McDonald could take care of herself, her and those dogs."

I realized what a stupid thing I'd said. "I mean, it's . . . sorry, Cait."

"That animal you brought with you, the one who was injured, how's it doing?" I think the Missus expression meant to show concern, maybe compassion, but her eyes betrayed that.

I directed my answer to Cait. "Believe he's gonna make it. He took some food and water."

"Wonderful," said the Missus. Lines of concern at the corners of Cait's eyes relaxed some.

"Missus Standback, you said you'd never had any dealings with MacKenzie," I said.

"That's right."

"One of the boys said he saw you and him in an encounter one night, out by the back porch. Said you appeared to be in an argument, that you slapped him."

She drew up some, her lips tightened, her eyes hardened. "Yes, that did happen. I didn't mention it because I didn't want to talk about it. He made advances toward me. I reacted the way any woman would. It scared me."

"Did you tell your husband?"

"Of course not. He would've thrashed him . . . or shot him." Her demeanor became angry. She arose from her chair. "It's been a long day. If you'll excuse me, I believe I'll retire. Cait, Asmita will show you to your room, see to your needs. She will draw you a bath if you so desire."

"I would like that," Cait said. "Thank you."

I nodded to the Missus as she walked by me. "Were you able to find accommodations in the bunkhouse?"

"Yes, ma'am."

She turned to me. "I almost forgot. Sheriff Dunbar wanted me to tell you to call him. He has some information on the man you're seeking."

"Crow Redhand?"

"I believe so, yes."

"You have a telephone, then?"

"In the parlor."

CHAPTER 9

C row needed to make distance, but he couldn't keep his left foot in the stirrup the way it was swollen and festered. Every gallop of the horse shot a shaft of fire up his left leg. A time or two he nearly passed out from the fever and pain, desperately gripping the horse to keep from falling off.

He knew a woman who could help him, a Wyandotte woman named Janey Little Mingoes, a healer. She lived with a trader named Doety near the Wyandotte village. If he could keep his pace and not lose his seat, he'd make it down there by sundown.

Delirium swirled his mind with images of the dead: Sam and Elam frozen in their own blood, Sarah ripped open like a summer melon, her back atop the boy, him still alive. Claws swung, beasts lunged and slashed with their teeth all smeared in his vision. How did this happen? What did I do?

Woods surrounded Doety's place, a clapboard building grayed-out by years of weather. Ground fifty yards around it had been cleared over the decades, some of the stumps still spotted the patch. The rough road to the town five miles beyond passed right by the front of the shack.

Despite his plan, the agony slowed Crow. His horse brought him up to the store well past dark. He didn't remember arriving, nor how long he sat there in the saddle going in and out of awareness. No other horses were there to Crow's relief. Didn't need anyone else knowing his whereabouts. Hoped he wouldn't have to kill the Wyandotte woman and Doety. Just wanted Janey Little Mingoes to dig the bullet out that sumbitch deputy put in him, get some rest and food in him and head out again.

89

The store sat dark. Crow, in his saddle, tried to decide whether to bust in or call out for help. Wasn't sure he could dismount and walk.

He called out. "Doety!" His voice a rasp.

A minute went by. Either they's asleep or they's lookin out the window to see who the hell's callin out in the dark. He called again. A glow came through the store's front window. The door cracked, and a shotgun barrel poked out.

"Who ya be?" a man asked. "What's yer business?"

"It's Crow Redhand, I need your woman's help. I been shot."

"Crow Redhand? How is it you been shot?"

"In the foot."

"No, I mean, why'st?"

"Shot m'self, loadin my gun."

Silence from Doety. The door widened a bit more. Doety came out in his long handles, his shotgun still pointed at Redhand. The woman followed him holding a lantern high.

"Git on down and come in. Keep them hands away from yer piece."

"Can't get down on my own. Gonna need a shoulder. Not gonna cause trouble, aim to pay ya."

Doety considered it. "Janey," he said. The woman moved to the horse and rider, let him slide down using her as a crutch. "Git ya inside, I guess. See what Janey can do. Best not try anything."

"Told ya, I ain't gonna. Just need this bullet dug out . . . and some whiskey."

They took him to a table where he sat atop it, propped his shot foot on a chair. When Janey pulled on the boot, Redhand hollered and cussed mightily. She couldn't budge it. Doety tried. The outlaw raised his level of swearing, kicked out at the trader with his good foot.

"Gonna have to cut that boot off," Doety said.

"Bring me whiskey," Redhand said.

Janey went to her cabinet, ground up some white willow bark. Gave it to Crow to wash down with the whiskey.

"What the hell's this?" he asked.

"For pain," she said.

"Aah. All's I need for pain is this whiskey."

"Take," she said, pushed the powder in the cup toward his mouth.

It took twenty minutes and half a jug before Crow became drowsy enough and drunk enough not to give a shit what Janey did to his foot *or* his boot. And that potion did kill the pain. By forty minutes he passed out.

She unwrapped the bloody bandage and examined the wound. Infection hadn't set in too bad, didn't have that smell. She could save the foot. In fifteen minutes, she had the bullet out, most of it. She plastered up the wound in a paste of red onions and honey to draw out the poison, wrapped it all back with clean linen. He'd get well, but not without a permanent limp.

Doety and Janey drug him off the table and laid him on the floor. He didn't awaken. They went back to bed listening to him snore before they could drift off.

Crow awoke in a sweat, disoriented. He reached for his gun in panic, couldn't find it. He lay on a wood floor that smelled of tobacco spit and dirt. He tried to sit, but pain enveloped him centered at his foot. It started coming back: the Wyandotte woman, the trader, that bullet in his foot. He reached down and felt the new bandage. Didn't think it pained as much. A gray sliver of daylight cracked the bottom of the window. His head still swam some from the whiskey.

He needed to get out. Took inventory in the dim light of the store of what he could take with him: a blanket, a ham. He found a pair of boots, one barely big enough to fit over his repaired foot, the other too big, so he found another. Fancier than the other but it fit right. Needed his pistol but couldn't locate it. Damn trader musta took it.

He limped toward the room off the store. Hated it, but gonna have to kill Doety and Janey to get his gun back. At the door, a glint of something silver hanging on the wall caught his eye: a rifle, a big one. He grabbed it up. It was a Sharps buffalo gun. That'd do. He searched a cabinet next to the wall, found boxes of .50 caliber cartridges. Loaded his coat pockets with them.

Aw, hell. Maybe he didn't need to kill 'em. They done him right. He'd just take the rifle and stuff. Maybe any money they had. When he opened the drawer to take the cash, he found a pencil next to a ledger book. Decided to leave them a note. Owed them that much, he reckoned. He ripped a page from the book and started writing.

When they awoke the next morning, Redhand was gone. Doety checked the cash drawer first, knew it'd be empty, though—the whole twenty dollars. He checked the rest of the store to discover what else was missing. The pegs on wall where he hung the Sharps were bare. "And that sumbitch said he'd pay," Doety grumbled to his wife. He found the scribbled note on the counter: "Sorry what I tuk but I well cum bak to pay. I got mony only not on me. I tuk yours as I mite need it for I get bak."

CHAPTER 10

The sheriff in Miami told me he'd gotten a call from the Indian constable in the little village of Wyandotte to the southeast. The constable said he got a call from a trader named Doety, who'd been robbed a couple days back. Identified the robber as Crow Redhand.

Wil and I got to the small settlement called Doetyville a little before noon. Near abandoned now, it was located on Wyandotte tribal land. It wasn't much more than a wide patch in the road, couple of old shacks, and a small shambled store. The store the only occupied building. Only thing that distinguished the store from the other buildings was a weather-worn plank sign nailed over the door with "Doety Store" painted on it. The white letters about as faded as the wood.

Lots of places like this around here. Leftover from the Indian Territory days, some enterprising fella—a white man— would come into the Territory, settle in and start selling merchandise to the Indians, usually hootch. They'd expand their inventory to include dry goods and food to cover their main product, the whiskey. Selling liquor was illegal in Indian Territory, remained so after statehood. Nobody but a few do-gooders in the government and some church ladies wanted it that way. Local authorities could be convinced to ignore the law-breaking, with a few bribes and free samples. After a while, the merchants moved their stores from canvas tents to wooden buildings. Places stayed for decades, sometimes little villages sprouted up around them. Some even became post offices.

Besides the local Indians, a rough crowd hung out in those places. Had to watch what you said, who you met eyes with when you went in, not ask questions about anyone or

93

anything. Also, best not to go in the place unarmed, employee or patron.

Old fella was splitting firewood at the side of the store when we rode up. A double barrel shotgun leaned against the store siding, which he grabbed, held it pointed at the ground, waited for us. "Haddy," he said.

"Morning," I said.

"You boys needin sumpin from the store this morning?"

"Just got some questions. I'm Deputy Marshal Smoak." I pulled my coat aside to show my badge. "Heard there's a robbery here a couple days ago."

"Damn sure were." He leaned the shotgun back against the side of the building. "I'm Sel Doety, own this place. Sumbitch come in here wantin some docterin on a shot foot. My wife give him that—she's a Wyandotte woman, good with that sort of thing—so she dug that bullet out, plastered him up with her medicinal fixin's, and I'll be damn if the bastard didn't rob me in my sleep. Made off with m'rifle and all its cart'iges, too. Left a note he's sorry about it, the stealin. Said he'd pay us back, but I ain't so sure."

"You know him?" I asked.

"Yeh, it were that damn Crow Redhand. He knew about Janey—my woman—about her healer ways. Believe that's why he come here. Guess I oughta be glad sumbitch didn't shoot us." He shook his head and smiled, but not happy. "That's why I called the Marshal intuh Wyandotte. We got us a telephone, had it about ten years. One of the first to get one around here. Us and the marshal in Wyandotte."

I loosened my hat with a gloved hand, set it back on my head. "That rifle he took, what kind?"

"Buffler gun," he said. "Fifty Sharps. Old buffler hunter come through here some years back, said they ain't nothin left to shoot with it. Needin money more'n that rifle. Offered to sell it. I give him ten dollar for it. Took it with me bear huntin.

Cain't shoot nothin else with it. It'd ruin a deer, blow a turkey plum up. Course, I used it to run off a scalawag or two what'd come in drunk, lookin for a fight. Never shot none, though. Pointin it at 'em seemed to convince 'em."

"He give you any indication which way he was headed?"

"Naw. Left while's we's still asleep." He gestured toward the road. "'Spect he headed on to the Wyandotte village, but don't know if he stayed that way. Way he's feelin, don't 'spect he traveled too fer. That's mornin 'fore last."

"Where does that road go?" I asked.

"Wyandotte be the first town you'd come to, 'bout three mile."

He scratched an armpit, waited for us to speak. "Whyn't you fellers git down and come inside? We got some hot coffee on. Could fix y'up with some beans and cornbread, too. Two-bits apiece. An' you'uns warmin by the stove wouldn't be no charge."

"Sounds like a good offer," I said. Figured Crow's trail wouldn't get that much colder in thirty, forty minutes, so we let the steaming coffee and hot potbellied stove help warm our bones, the beans and cornbread fill a void.

We headed west after an hour. The constable in Wyandotte didn't spot Crow in town, I think to his relief. Don't think he looked much. We doubled back along the road. Maybe we missed a camp. Sure enough, we found one back off in the woods some fifty yards. Fresh camp, no evidence of a fire. Probably Crow's. After some searching, Wil picked up an outbound trail.

"That's unusual," He squatted next to a set of horse tracks. "He's headed back up north and east. Stayin off the road."

"Had to figure we were coming after him. Maybe he's trying to throw us off."

"Ain't too old," Wil said of the tracks. "Maybe fresh yesterday morning."

I peered into the woods, then behind us, feeling a little apprehensive. The bullet wound in my shoulder gave me a twinge. Sure as hell didn't want another one from that sneaky bastard Crow.

"Let's get on the trail, Wil. See where he's taking us."

⧗

Been on Crow's trail long enough to know some of his tactics. Almost sure he knew I'd not be far behind him. That time in Liberal, he showed some instincts about being trailed. Made me learn a lesson, pay a price. A person didn't want to take Crow Redhand lightly. Besides his meanness, he was smart as a wolf. Knew what was going on around him. Hell, I don't know, maybe even smelled trouble. He could make quick decisions. As far as preserving his own well-being, they were usually the right ones. Knew when to run, when to attack. I believed he wanted to ambush us. That thought kept me alert.

The land was hilly with thick woods—blackjack oak, hickory, sycamore. some pine—now deep with snow. Air was crisp, clear, and still. Not many sounds in the woods, now and then a crow cawed afar, a hawk screeched. The oak and pine limbs, not given to shedding their leaves and needles in winter, slumped where snow piles clung to them. Blocked the line of sight into the woods. Rock outcroppings sprung from the steeper hillsides, some with overhangs and shallow damp caves. Be easy for him to hide, but also hard for him to get a clear shot. I counted on that.

People in these parts were kinda sparse. Some scrub farms, a few tiny settlements like Doetyville. White and Indian, mostly Indians, all from local tribes lived here— Quapaw, Peoria, Miami, Wyandotte, Seneca. All had been squashed up into this part of Indian Territory back during the removal days. The nations now a part of the great state of Oklahoma, but still their designated lands. Only difference was, anybody could live here if they wanted. Still, no love lost between the white men and Indians. The latter with their prejudices and wariness, the former with their well-earned mistrust and bitterness. Still, most here, Indian and white, were dirt poor. Quite a few back in the woods or otherwise well-hidden were outlaws in one way or another—thieves or murderers or both, like Redhand. Only a few around like Major Standback who grabbed up a lot of cheap land after the war. Stolen it, more like it, but they were considered a higher class thief, respectable.

Crow was wily and crafty in the woods. I was hoping having Wil on my side offset that. Still felt a little nervous about them as cousins. Blood's thicker than water, they say. Especially Indian blood.

He pulled up, searched the ground and out into the shallow water. The trail ended at the edge of a stream running partially unfrozen six inches to a foot over a rocky bed. He scanned the opposite bank.

"He cross here?" I asked. Probably a dumb question, the tracks in the snow led up to the water's edge, hoof prints through the thin ice at the bank.

Wil tolerated my ignorance. "Don't think he crossed." His eyes moved upstream and down. "Believe he followed the creek. Probably upstream so the current would more cover his tracks. That's what I'd do."

"Let's head that way, then." I urged Clyde into the water.

"Hold on," Wil said. "I'll cross on over and head along the bank. See where his tracks come out. Doubt his horse is crazy about walking too far in that cold water and on those rocks. You stay on this side and do the same, case he doubled back."

That thought occurred to me, too. That's why I kept my .44 in hand as I rode along. It gave me false comfort. I knew he'd shoot before I could react if he saw me. Could be lying in wait.

I studied the ground by the creek's edge, but the thought I might be in Crow's sights made it hard to concentrate.

A shot cracked above the sound of the creek rush and echoed through the silent woods and fields. It made a booming sound, not like a Winchester. I ducked reflexively, but it came from the trees some distance off the bank where Wil rode. I wheeled Clyde into the creek and crossed. Another shot popped, this one closer. "Wil!" I called out.

"Over here," he answered. "Git down."

I dismounted into the water, pulling my Winchester from its boot and grabbed my field glasses off the horn. Still had the two-foot high bank and some cottonwoods for cover. "You okay?" I called out to Wil.

"Yeh, but he shot m'damn horse. Threw me off when he's hit. I scrambled over here." The bulk of the horse lay on its side ten or so yards out in the open, still jerking in its death throes. "I ain't havin good luck with horses, lately," Wil said.

I moved in my stiff-legged, semi-crouch toward him. He'd slid behind the frozen creek bank and brush. Raised the glasses to my eyes and searched the line of the trees and hills two hundred yards in front of us. "Know where he is?"

"Didn't see the shot, but I suspect he's up in the trees, yonder." His eyes stayed with the trees. "Need t'git him to shoot again."

"What, you want me to step out and draw his fire?"

"Well, I'm a better shot than you. Just don't show yourself much . . . or very long."

He had a point, but I didn't much like it.

"That blown-down tree." Wil pointed to a storm-toppled oak, the roots and dirt butt-end of it perpendicular to the ground, six feet tall with the snow atop it. "Run to that. That'll draw him out. That Sharps is black powder, so he shouldn't be hard to spot. I'll be ready for him." He brought his Henry up to his shoulder, sighted down the barrel.

I let out a long breath, mentally calculated the distance to the upturned tree base. Said, "Shit!" and took off. My hobbled gait and the snowpack made the going slippery, but the excitement in my blood gave me some added speed. At the fifth stride, the foot of my good leg caught a snow-hidden root and I fell. Saw the flash, heard the crack from the rifle when my shoulder hit the ground. The air snapped above me about where my head had been. Back on my feet with more juice in my muscles, I bounded headlong into the pit the tree roots and dirt had left. Wil's Henry boomed somewhere in there. Another slug tore off a clod of dirt and roots above my right leg. I pulled it in. The two shots fired almost simultaneously.

Wil fired again, then silence. "You see him?" I shout-whispered back to Wil.

He shook his head.

"Think it's Crow?"

He shrugged. "Definitely a Sharps fifty."

"Think you hit him?"

He hoarse-voiced back to me, "Hard to say. I was just aimin at the tree line where I saw the blast. Run back over here, see if he shoots again."

"Like hell."

"Well, he's either shot, took off, or waitin us out. That means you only got a one in three chance of getting shot at again. Not bad odds."

A clump of trees sat off to the left of my position about thirty yards. Past that, the edge of the woods curved toward the clump with only about ten, fifteen yards of open ground between them. "Wil," I said. Pointed to myself, then to the clump of trees and beyond, made running motions with two fingers, and pointed to the big arc of trees. I pointed back at Wil, pantomiming him shooting his rifle at the shooter spot. Hoped like hell he understood my signals.

I broke for the trees and he opened up, firing in rapid succession. Wil received no return fire by the time I reached the clump, so I took a deep gulp of air and headed for the arc of woods.

Still no return shots, only Wil's. I searched again with the glasses, could find no one, only a cluster of cedar around a big rock, a good spot for a sniper. I crouched and moved through the trees and brush coming up behind that rock. No Crow, but beneath it, packed snow and boot prints. Found three shell casings—fifties. I quickly searched the woods left and right. No sign of Crow. No sign of blood, but tracks said he mounted up and rode off, still to the north. I walked out of the woods into the clearing, motioned for Wil to come on over.

He came across the open ground at a trot. I squatted studying the sign. "Whadda you reckon?" I asked Wil after letting him catch his breath some, held up one of the fifty casings.

He took it, squatted to check the boot prints around the rock. "Yep, Crow," he nodded. "Don't believe he meant to miss. Mebbe he decided to take out my horse instead of me, us bein kin and all. But don't believe he meant to miss you. Crow's a good shot, even with a buffalo rifle. You're just lucky."

I squinted below my hat brim. "So, you set me up as a decoy, knowing I'd probably get shot?"

Wil shrugged. "You told me you's always a little lucky. Figured it was worth a try, so I could get a bead on him."

I chewed on my upper lip, picked up the other brass. "This kin thing, maybe you don't want to shoot him either."

"Mebbe," he said. "Come down to him or me, I'd shoot."

"What about him or me?"

He hesitated a little. "I'd shoot."

Have to go with that, I reckon, but I wouldn't count on it.

"Let's get after him," I said.

Wil mashed a foot into one of Crow's horse's tracks in the snow, rubbed it out. "This was a warning. He'll still be layin for us."

I scoffed some. "Not like him. Why would he warn us?"

"Not us," Wil said.

I got his drift. Shifted my eyes out to his dead horse. Clyde had come up out of the creek bank, standing some way off from the carcass. "Better get your gear. Guess we'll have to double up until we can get to where there's another horse."

"I'd rather walk," Wil said. Headed toward his shot horse.

⏳

We rode north—or rather, I did—through scattered woods with open slopes and valleys. Tried to stay mostly in the trees, find the narrowest spot between exposed and forest areas. When we came to a wide spot, I nudged Clyde into a gallop. Wil would trot across, his saddlebags slung over his shoulders. We rigged his saddle behind mine to lighten his load some. Wil took it at his own pace, reading sign as he went. He stayed in the open, exposed, not concerned. Couldn't say the same about myself. I was nervous as fall buck, my head on a swivel, fearing a fifty-caliber bullet coming my way. And I sure didn't want Clyde shot. Slow going, most of the time. Needed to give Wil a breather or two.

Dark came upon us with no sight of our quarry. We made camp for the night. Too damn cold for a cold camp, so we built a fire. Figured Crow knew we were behind him. One of us stood watch throughout the night, not that it would've done much good if Crow took a distant bead on us with that Sharps. But we found a good-sized clump of rocks inside a thicket of trees which felt fairly safe. Still, I kept one eye open after I bedded down. Wil, on the other hand, sawed 'em off good when it was his turn.

I rousted him at daybreak, we took off without coffee or breakfast. After a couple of miles, we came upon a farm. Small place, and poor. A few chickens scattered about scratching bare ground in the snow, a sow and two half-grown piglets rooted through the white. A pregnant Indian woman, bundled against the cold, sat at a fire outside a shack, cooking. She didn't give us much mind as we approached, kept on with her chore.

"Mornin," I said. She didn't respond. Wil said something to her, not in English, she muttered something back. They carried on a terse conversation for about thirty seconds.

"She's Miami. Her man's Wyandotte. Don't speak American."

"You speak her language?"

"Not really. Know enough Wyandotte to get by. She understands some Quapaw. Between the two, we sorta understand each other."

"Ask her if she's seen Crow."

Wil spoke again, went on for some time, making hand motions. When he finished the woman stayed silent, her hands working something doughy. After a bit, she answered quietly, briefly.

"Appears he did come through last night. Stayed long enough to eat something and warm up a bit. Left at dawn."

Crow had a day's lead on us. Hard to figure why he was heading back north again, back like he was returning to the scene of the crime. Something he left undone? It suddenly struck me: the boy.

"I asked her could she spare some breakfast," Wil said. "She seems willin."

"Crow is headed back to Miami. I think that boy who survived is still in danger. We can't stop for breakfast."

Wil shook his head. "Nuh-uh, Crow ain't gonna hurt that boy."

102

"You don't know that. I think he already has. We need to close ground with him as fast as we can."

I rode on. Wil followed reluctantly, still afoot.

row's track took us back to the Forked S, not sure why he'd do that. Wil's best guess, he was a half day ahead of us. About half-past four, we came upon a cabin located at the bottom of a bowl-like valley surrounded by low wooded hills. A barn stood off behind the place with a corral on one side. Several horses in the corral watched us come in, while others munched on scattered hay. It'd been a clear bright day with enough warmth to melt the snow some, but the shadows now stretched and put the air back below freezing. A pumpkin sun gave off a splintered glow through bare limbs of the surrounding trees when we wandered into the cabin clearing. Figured that sun had about three-quarters of an hour before it disappeared for the night.

Nothing palatial about the place, but well kept up. Had a deep and wide porch where a slatted wooden rocker sat. Hanging from the porch eaves, dream-catchers swayed and rattled softly in the slight breeze. Smoke, promising a warm fire within, trailed from a rock chimney.

A man came out, cradling a Springfield carbine in one arm, his right hand around the waist of the stock. Not a young man, but not old. Striking fella, somewhere in his fifties. Could've been younger, could've been older. Wrinkles crowded his eyes and neck, his face a weather-brown red. Kind of the way it was with these people. Aged forty to eighty about the same. Their faces a study of a hard life, yet sturdy. He wore dungarees and a plaid shirt, a flat-brimmed hat with a high crown. Long black hair hung down past his shoulders. Could've been Wil's brother. Hell, I guess he was in most respects.

Still sitting a-saddle, I greeted him. "Evening."

He said nothing.

"You speak English?" I asked.

Was beginning to think he didn't. He turned to Wil. *"Skun'-Sta,"* he said.

Wil answered, *"A-Toh-We Shu-te Nom-Bah. Hah-gee-hikah-naha?"*

"Eh-Pah-Ha-zhe."

They spoke this way for a minute or so.

"He's a brother Quapaw. Wanted to know what we want. Told him we look for Crow. He knows him. He doesn't much trust you, like most white men. That's why he only speaks to me."

"Did you tell him I'm a deputy marshal?"

Wil nodded. "Yep. Don't think that helped, though. Might've made it worse."

"Does he speak English?"

"Probably," Wil said.

"I'm a U.S. Marshal. You understand me, right?"

He didn't answer. I was sure his eyes had pupils but centered in the deep mahogany around them, they were hard to detect. I sensed an edge of animosity in them. "We only wish to find Crow Redhand, who has killed innocent people, Quapaw people."

Nothing.

"What's your name?" I asked him. Then to Wil, "What's his name?"

"Joe Elkfoot," the man answered.

I turned back to him. "Mister Elkfoot, we don't mean to trouble you. We only wish to find this outlaw. He's a very dangerous man."

"To you, maybe," Elkfoot answered.

I adjusted myself in the saddle, acknowledged that with a nod. Dark was coming on, and cold. Knowing the nature of Indian hospitality, I said, "We've been on the trail all day. Wonder if you could give us a place to stay for the night? We've got some food we'd share."

He spoke to Wil. "*Ge'weh*," he said. Then to me, "Come in, but do not insult me. I have food."

He did have food and a fire. No one else appeared in the cabin. In the middle of our elk steak supper, Wil asked him— in English, I supposed in deference to me— "You have no woman?" It was a casual conversation in Indian terms. Apparently, such a question is not considered impolite. Whereas, something like "How many horses do you have?" would be. Be glad to tell us how many if he wanted to brag, but it was rude to ask. You had to pick your personal questions with the Quapaw, as with most Indians. I left all that kind of asking to Wil.

Elkfoot answered in English. "Had two that died. Last one left. She was young and complained a lot. Got her in trade from a Cherokee farmer for two mules. She was here six months, ran off with a Peoria man who came to buy a horse. I didn't mind so much. Got a good price for the horse and now it's quiet."

"You sell horses?" I asked.

His eyes turned to me with admonishment, like an uncle would a child who'd interrupted adult talk. But he answered me. "You want to buy a horse?"

Thought that was obvious after the way we arrived. "Wil has need of one," I said. Didn't want to risk another insult. He let me pass on the food thing because I was a stupid white man. Not sure I'd have a warm place to sleep if I handed out another.

Wil helped me out before I could answer. "Mine was shot out from under me. Crow did it, with a buffalo rifle he stole."

Elkfoot thought it over. "I have many horses, all for sale." To me: "I will sell you one for cash."

"Your price?" I asked.

"Depends on the horse. The best, seventy-five dollars. I have a mule I'll let go for twenty-five."

I opened my mouth to seal the deal, but Wil spoke first. "No horse is worth seventy-five, even though that's what you may get from the Army, because they're foolish with their money. I'll pick my horse but will pay you forty."

"Impossible," Elkfoot snorted. "I could take no less than sixty, even for my worst horse."

Wil sighed, made some guttural noises. "I'll give you fifty, no more."

"Fifty-five," Elkfoot shouted.

"Ach!" Wil paced three steps back and forth. "Fifty-five, then. But that should include breakfast."

Elkfoot laughed. The two Quapaw men grabbed right forearms. They spoke several minutes to one another in their own language, becoming quieter with a sober change in demeanor. They ignored me, except for one or two furtive glances my way. It was my distinct feeling I was the topic of their conversation.

Wil picked a buckskin. He complained it wasn't Elkfoot's best. Elkfoot insisted it was, still appearing irritated that he didn't get full price. But as we left, they were cheerful and full of regard for one another. Elkfoot took my fifty-five dollars, eagerly. Not so much my offered hand.

"What was that conversation about, after you made the deal last night."

Wil hedged. "It was Indian talk. I had to compliment him on his bargaining. He had to compliment me."

"Seemed to get pretty serious for trading compliments."

"We have our ways."

"Anything concerning me in that Indian talk?"

"No. You're not important enough."

"Fair enough. What about your cousin Crow? Did he come up?"

"We're on the trail of Crow." He kicked the buckskin, trotted up ahead to inspect the trail for sign.

CHAPTER 12

His grandmother and the people of the village called him *Myeengun* – little wolf – when he was a boy. He liked the name, felt it in his blood when he ran with the pack, when his blood rose in the hunt, when he ate with the pack at the body of a fresh kill. But he didn't keep the name. He took the one of a white man when he turned fifteen, names whites gave some of the wolves – Gray MacKenzie. He reasoned the name would make it easier for him to live among the whites if they thought he was a part of them.

The elders, the old *Waabanowag* of his Ojibwe people, said they couldn't tell him what to believe, only point him in the right direction using the stories and traditions of the *Waabanoowiwin* lodge. He did believe in *Manitou*, that fundamental life force in everything, everywhere – living things, the non-living, even events. He knew there was the *aashaa monetoo*, the good spirit, as well as *otshee monetoo*, the evil one.

His grandmother taught him that. But they were of the Wolf Clan, whose totem is called *Ma'iingan*. Since the creation, his people and the wolf had a spiritual relationship, a brotherhood. He and they have much in common.

Going back to his grandmother's grandfather it was always about clearing the wilderness of his people and the wolves by the pale-skinned invaders. They came into their land and moved them out, all the *Anishinaabe* and the wolves, killing as many of each as they could when they came, if not by bullets then disease. It fulfilled a prophecy: the people will go the way of the wolf, what happens to one will happen to the other.

He always felt kinship with the wolves. When he was a boy growing up near the Chequamegon Bay, roaming the shores of the great waters of *Gitchi-gami,* wolves were his companions. They never bothered him but welcomed him. Perhaps they felt he was akin to the shape-shifter *Manabozho.*

His grandmother taught him the history of his people and the whites, the constant threat of them, and the hatred. But he also experienced it first-hand: beaten by a man who claimed to be his father, a white man. Some said he was French, a trapper. His mother murdered by the same man. He was small and didn't know him, except when he came around drunk to beat him. But the Frenchman died before he could kill him. The first white man he killed was a trapper who'd captured him in the woods and hauled him off to his cabin where he held him for five days using him for his pleasure. He was seven. It was before he roamed with the wolves.

On the fifth night, he freed himself from the leather fetters the trapper put on him and waited by the cabin door. He found a bear claw mounted on a stick the man kept in his cabin. He didn't know its purpose, but it served him well as an instrument of death. When the man entered the cabin, the boy raked his face and neck with a fury beyond vengeance, a rage born from *otshee monetoo,* the Evil One. Over and over he ripped him and pummeled him until the man was a bloody heap rasping out his dying breath.

He stood over the dead man exhilarated in his heavy breathing, a feeling surged through his veins that transcended pleasure. He threw back his head and howled, a long, ecstatic howl that shattered the night. When he left the cabin, the bear claw still in hand, he found several wolves gathered, watching him from the edge of the woods. They heard his call. He went to them, they welcomed him into the pack.

It was that night he embraced the spirit *otshee monetoo.* His way of the wolf would not be to retreat from the whites but to attack them, to kill as many as he could.

And killing was what he did best as the years increased. The more he did it, the better he got: his method, his style, not so much for its efficiency as the terror it generated. His reputation among the Indian people grew, not just among the Ojibwe, but others. They thought him a spiritual being, the great *Manabozho,* and began coming to him with requests. They would pray to him asking the *otshee monetoo* to have him kill someone they wanted killed. They would leave him gifts even though he would do the killing for the pleasure of it, especially when it was a white man. But sometimes it would be an Indian. Eventually, it got to where it didn't matter to him, and he began to require payment instead of gifts. He became known among the white lawmen because of his killing of the whites, but most of those he killed were undesirable or irreputable, so they didn't pursue him. And his killing of other Indians didn't matter to them. They had little motivation to chase after him into his deep-woods habitat surrounded by wolves.

Most of his hunts took him into towns and cities because that's where his prey lived, also, those who hired him. One man in Chicago sought him out, offered to pay him more than he'd ever made to do a job, but he would have to travel out of his country and away from the company of his brother wolves.

⏳

When he came into the land of the Quapaw, *Makade-ma'iingan* joined him. He didn't need to seek her out, she and her nephews came to him before the night he took his revenge. And it pleased him. She was unlike any wolf he knew: black as midnight and twice as large as her nephews. She spoke to him, "I am the *otshee monatoo.* Our spirits mingle. I will guide you in your killing. You must kill."

And that first night he did kill, the lust of it thrilled him as it had all the others. These were not the ones he'd been sent to kill; nonetheless, he delighted in it. He ripped the men's throats washing the walls of the small cabin with blood, he tore out the woman's belly. *Makade-ma'iingan* was pleased. He started to kill the blind boy, but she pushed ahead of him and attacked the boy herself, biting into his neck and face.

But he failed the next time, the prey for which he'd contracted. He didn't kill the white rancher, and he took a bullet. Neither had ever happened. Nor did he kill the woman. It should've been easy, even with those dogs of hers. *Makade-ma'iingan* and her nephews could handle them while he cut up the woman. But there was interference: two men rode in. One of the men and a dog chased him in the night. He took out the dog, but not the man. The wound slowed him. He'd find another time, another place to kill the woman. At that time, she would have no dogs.

The gunshot wasn't serious, just a hole through the skin on his left side, but it angered him that he let it happen. And it angered him that he didn't finish the job. He killed every man or woman he set out to kill whether hired to or not. He'd finish it, though. That night.

No need for *Makade-ma'iingan* and her pack, they'd cause too much disturbance, so he sent them back to the lair. Two of the woman's dogs survived and came to Standback's house with her. One was already near dead, the other wouldn't be a problem.

He waited near the house and watched. One window alight upstairs. That must be where they put the rancher. He saw movement downstairs through the windows. Two women, one Veneto's daughter, the other the McDonald woman. An hour went by, he moved to the house, searched the outside for an entrance, tried the windows on the side of the porch. The dog inside came to the window raising hell, but it was noise from the bunkhouse that stopped him. He retreated into the darkness beneath the large oak in front. Not long after, a man rode off, then one of the cowhands came to the door of the house and talked to the women. He waited and watched. Two more men rode in. It was the one he encountered at the woman's cabin. The lawman. Perhaps he should attack the upper room from the roof.

CHAPTER 13

C row's trail meandered, not much sense to it unless it was his plan to lead us on a goose chase. Had no further encounters with him, though. Most of the day, Wil stayed out ahead of me a quarter mile or more, reminding me that if Crow lay in wait, I'd be further out of range. He still didn't think his cousin would shoot him. A couple times, Wil waited at spots where it did appear Crow hunkered down, perhaps scouting us, then went on.

Clouds covered the afternoon sky, and darkness came early. Felt like another storm coming: thick and cold. Wil disappeared for a couple hours, and the gathering gloom made me nervous and jumpy. Only comfort was knowing I probably wouldn't take a .50 caliber slug from a long distance shot in that darkness. Not so sure what lay in the shadowy ground around me, though. My Colt was drawn and ready.

Heard horse hooves at a lope coming toward me, and I eared back the .44's hammer. "Wil?" I called into the night.

"Yo," he answered and came out of the dimness, reining up next to me. "Don't need to camp tonight. Can see lights from the Forked S, a couple miles off."

"Figured we had to be close."

A welcome sight, riding up to that big house. Cait came to mind. Hadn't thought outright about her until then, but it niggled in the back of my brain, wondering about her. It came right to the front: I was a little worried about her, wanted to protect her. It all kind of surprised me, thinking about Cait like that. Not that she needed *my* protection, tough woman that she was. Could take care of herself, had and would. Still, something about the situation wasn't right, something about Miz Standback and that Asmita woman bothered me.

A half mile out from the ranch house, the snow came, thick and heavy. The place was fully lit, upstairs and down with the glow of those electric lights, the snow made them brighter. A dimmer light came from the bunkhouse windows. The light reflected off the spread of smoke ascending from the chimney, and patches of old snow still on the ground. Figured the boys had a pot of coffee on the stove. I hoped Wiley wouldn't grumble too much about heating up some victuals.

The foreman Turnbow came outside the bunkhouse door as we rode up, a Winchester hung from his right hand, barrel down. "Turnbow," I greeted him.

He nodded back. "Good to see you boys. Wasn't sure we would."

"Why's that?"

He swung the rifle barrel up, resting it on his right shoulder. "Crow come through carrying a big Sharps. Busted in 'n held us up for some grub 'n coffee. Said he's purty sure he shot ya."

"He damn sure tried," I said. "Got Wil's horse. When'd he leave?"

"Little over an hour ago, I reckon."

The house looked peaceful and secure in its electric glow, but a little shard of panic stabbed me. "What about the women . . . and the major?"

"Just come back from there. Went t'check on 'em the minute Crow rode off. Miz Standback's handy with a gun, so's that McDonald woman. That Indin Asmita is sittin by the major's bed with a double-barrel twelve gauge acrost her lap, and they got that big bitch dog in there with 'em. So, with all that, don't think we need to worry much."

"Major's still alive, then?" Wil said.

"Yeah, he's that, but don't seem to be getting better."

Turnbow pulled out his pocket watch and consulted it in the window light. "It's damn near ten o'clock," he said. "Get them horses to the barn. Looks like y'all could use some food and fire. While you're doin that, I'll get Wiley to stir something up for ya."

True enough, didn't think I could go another step chasing after Redhand. Not that late, not in the dark. A hot stove and warm food sounded too good to pass up. Didn't hear Wil complain, either. After that, I'd go check on Cait.

Hector raised his head when I came into the bunkhouse. He recognized me. Not sure if that was a good sign or bad. He still stretched out on that pallet they made him. Wiley stood in the cook-room door, hands on his hips. "He getting any better?" I asked.

"Seems to be," Wiley said. "Got up a bit wantin to go outside. Wobbly on his feet, but he made it and done his business, then came right back to the bed. Ain't made no friends amongst us. He tolerates me, 'cause I give him food 'n water, let him out t'piss. That McDonald woman comes down ever mornin t'check on him, cleans his wounds and such. Believe Asmita sends some potions out to put on him."

The big brute stared at me for a bit before I headed to the kitchen.

We sat at the long table. Wiley set a bowl of venison stew and a mug of coffee in front of me. "Thanks," I said. "Appreciate it."

"Well, it's like I'm running a damn restaurant here. First, that damn Crow Redhand come in after supper, now you'uns. I ain't put nothin away yet, anyway." He slapped Wil's bowl down in front of him and turned back to the stove, muttering.

"You got any idea why Crow'd come back here?" I asked Turnbow. He sat opposite me, sipping from a mug. Husker walked in, poured himself a cup, leaned against the far wall.

"I ain't," Turnbow said.

"Believe he's lookin for MacKenzie," Husker offered from the corner.

I turned to him. "MacKenzie?" I almost shouted. "Why you say that?"

Husker shrugged, drank from his mug. "When he's here, said so."

I turned to Turnbow. "He said that?"

"Not to me, he didn't."

I turned back to Husker. "When did he tell you this?"

The big cowhand straightened from the wall, put a booted foot on the table bench, leaning forward, forearms on his thigh. Even Wiley stopped his muttering to listen. "I's out at the woodpile when Crow come up. Had that big-assed buffalo gun pointed at me, but I weren't feared. Me 'n Crow allus got along when he's here. I stopped my choppin and asked him, 'What you doin here, Crow?' That's when he told me, he come lookin for MacKenzie. Said he thought MacKenzie's the one kilt the Jakes. Crow figured it'uz him got the Major, too. Meant to come back to finish it. Mebbe the missus, too."

I sat silent, considering. Wil kept his eyes on his stew bowl, shoveling it in. "Why'd Crow care about MacKenzie?" I asked.

"Crow wants revenge, especially for Sarah and boy," Husker said. "Weren't no secret he's sweet on Sarah. Sam and Elam didn't seem to have no problem with him. Treated that boy like his own."

Wil spoke. "Husker's right." He went back to his eating.

"Go on," I said.

He scraped on the bottom of the bowl with his spoon. Asked Wiley, "Got any more?" reaching the bowl back to him. The old cook ladled in another bowlful. Wil set it back on the table, blew away the rising steam.

"All us were kids together; me, Crow, the Jakes boys, Sarah. We's all smitten by Sarah, 'specially Crow 'n Elam. Sam was quite a bit older than Elam, maybe ten years, had other interests, it seemed. Anyway, Elam and Crow got into several fights over her growing up. When we's in our teens, Crow

116

appeared to win out. But then he got that wanderlust and took off, got into his outlawing. Sarah took up with Elam then, had that boy first year they's together. All sorts of speculation that the boy was Crow's."

Husker cleared his throat. "Somethin else, I oughta mention. I's out feedin cows this morning, man rode up to me, told me he's lookin for Redhand, too."

"What?" Turnbow was pissed. "Why didn't you say something when you come in for supper?"

"Told him I hadn't seen him. At the time, it'uz the truth. Didn't seem important."

Wil paused a bit in his eating. "Get the man's name?" I asked.

"It'uz Joe Elkfoot," Husker said.

"What the hell, Wil?" I slapped my hat down onto the tabletop. "Did you know about this, too? All that Indian talk between you and Elkfoot wasn't just Quapaw chitchat, was it?"

"You know Elkfoot?" Turnbow asked.

"We stayed at his place last night. Told us he hadn't seen Crow." Wil ignored my anger.

My posseman, my *trusted* guide sighed, set down his spoon, leaned back in his chair. "Joe is Crow's cousin, too. We's all cousins. His momma was my daddy's and uncle's sister. Just about all us Quapaw are kin nowadays, one way or another. Sarah was a cousin, too, twice removed."

He drank from his coffee mug. "Crow did show up at Joe's place, night before we did. He told Joe we's chasing him, but figured he slowed us down some. Said he's after Gray MacKenzie, gonna kill him for what he done to Sarah and her family. He's the one thought MacKenzie's still lurking about here."

"Why's Elkfoot going after Crow?" I asked.

"Most likely he's going to join up with him." He looked me square in the eyes. "Quapaw blood runs thick. Mostly because ain't that many of us left."

That panic in my gut seized me again, this time stronger. I grabbed up my Winchester. "I'm going up to the house. Figure I'll stand watch there tonight. Come daylight, we'll head out for Crow again, Wil."

⧖

The snow reflected light through the drawn curtains as I walked the distance between the bunkhouse and the big house. Snow on the ground does that even in the gloomiest of nights, almost like it gave off a faint glow of its own. An outside light shined onto the porch and front steps, a single bulb dangling from a porch rafter. Wind blew swirls of new snow across the floorboards with a faint whisper.

As I started up the steps, I heard the dog growl on the other side of the door, and the distinct sound of hammers eared back on a shotgun.

"Best identify yourself," came a female shout from inside. "I've got a hundred-pound dog and a double barrel twelve gauge ready for action."

It was Caitlin.

"Cait, it's Jubal."

The dog didn't care, let out a snarling bark. "Athena, stay," I heard Cait's stern command. The door opened, but she still cradled the shotgun. She un-cocked the hammers and set it against the door jamb. I stepped inside, closed the door against the snowy wind. Thought she was going to hug me, but she didn't. Touched my shoulder, instead.

"I didn't think I'd see you again. Turnbow said . . . he thought that outlaw had shot you."

At the sound of her voice, I felt the winter cold recede some from the back of my neck. "Nope, just Wil's horse."

118

The big dog Athena didn't regard me as tenderly as Cait. Figured my throat in her teeth would be her choice if only her mistress gave the word.

"Had any trouble?" I asked.

"Not really," she said. "Some noises outside. Asmita's in the kitchen, guarding the back door. Emily's upstairs with the Major. Anyway, Athena raised such a row, I think she scared them off."

"What kind of noises?"

"I don't know. Something knocking around outside. Probably just the wind. After Turnbow told us about Crow Redhand . . . and MacKenzie, we've been kind of jumpy. Well, Asmita and I. Emily is such a rock."

"Dogs don't get jumpy unless they hear or smell something they don't like, especially a dog like Athena." I looked down at the tensed beast, wondering if she picked up that I was on her side. Didn't indicate she had.

"I'll go check around the outside of the house," I said. "You stay here and keep that shotgun ready."

"Take Athena with you."

The dog and I stared each other down. I may've blinked. "You think she'll know the difference between some bad guy and me?"

Cait gave me a crooked smile. "That's probably up to you. My dogs can sense good guys from bad."

I raised an eyebrow, coughed a Hmmph. "What's her measures?" I asked.

"Don't make her mad."

"You mean this ain't mad?"

A coal oil lantern sat on a small table by the door. She lit it, handed it to me. The tall clock in the foyer chimed. It showed 10:30.

Athena walked out ahead of me, pausing every few steps to sniff the air, the ground. She glistened in the snowfall, flakes

119

caught up in the slight bristles along her spine. She made no sound other than the whisper of her sniffing. She checked off and on to make sure I was keeping up, still her human backup. The dog was leading this hunt, she'd let me know if she needed my help.

A couple times, she stuck her snout in the snow, raised her head to look about, grumbled low and menacing. Like an idiot, I whispered, "What is it, girl?" She regarded me with contempt, enough to convey what a stupid, noisy critter I was, then went back to her investigation.

The lantern sent a sparkling glow a few feet into the swirling snow around me. I held it low to the ground to find footprints. Held it high to hold off the reflecting glare of the white fog. I walked around the side of the house near the back corner before it occurred to me the lantern was a liability, not only for seeing in those conditions but being seen. If Redhand or MacKenzie were out there in the darkness, I made myself a highly visible target. I set the lantern on the ground, quickly took several steps laterally out of the light's reach. Moved from where I would've last been seen in the sights of that Sharps . . . or whatever it was MacKenzie might hold.

I crouched by the trunk of a big oak, giving my eyes a chance to adjust to the darkness. The snow bit at my neck and face. I raised the collar of my sheepskin coat, set my hat a little lower. Bowed my head and shut my eyes for a few seconds. When I opened them, the snowy night glow gave me a highlighted silhouette of the house. Other shapes loomed out of the churning, foggy darkness: the stacked wood in back, some of the barn and corral, another shed. A dim glow floated from the direction of the bunkhouse, but it could've been wishful imagination as much as real. At the back of the big house, a hazy electric light shone next to the back door.

Apparently, Athena went on without me. Squinting toward that porchlight, I saw her sniffing the ground around a structure leaning diagonally against the house—a ladder. She raised her front paws onto the third rung and rough-barked.

The ranch house was a big structure. Three stories if you counted the attic. At that top story, a window sat in the end, a small gable. My guess, it had a matching one on the other end. An eave ran around the entire house between the first and second story. It curved out some making it almost perpendicular to the pitch of the roof. Four big dormer windows crossed the front of the house, recessed at the base, creating a small ledge in front of them. The roofline angled severely atop the second story ending in a flat crest with what looked like an ornate iron fence around it, maybe three feet high pinned at the corners by lightning rods.

Athena pranced and growled at the base of the ladder, leaped up several rungs frustrated that she couldn't climb it to get to whatever disturbed her. Nothing visible on the fluted eave and dormers that might give rise to her increasing fury. I moved toward Athena. Maybe Crow was right: MacKenzie came back to finish off the Major. One of those dormer windows was that of the bedroom where the rancher lay. Athena's display said somebody had gone up that ladder. Suppose it could've been left leaning there after some hand had gone up earlier to fix something on the roof, but I don't think the dog would carry on like she did if that was the case.

I climbed the ladder. Would've been smarter to run back into the house, go upstairs to the bedroom and check things out from the inside. Less chance of me slipping off the icy roof. At the time, though, I didn't have the luxury of doing the smart thing. Besides, Athena was egging me on, raising enough ruckus to wake the dead.

Just as I reached the top of the ladder to step off, something hit me in the chest with enough force to knock me and the ladder backward. The ladder, with me clinging to the top of it, arched toward the ground. Things slowed down in that interval between the blow and falling. A black shape scrambled up the steep pitch of the roof, over that ornate fence, and out of sight. Thought it was a man, a big man, but it ambulated on all fours, fast and agile. When I hit the ground, I sunk into a crusted snowdrift. It dazed me, knocked the wind out of me. Wasn't sure if I lost consciousness for a few seconds, but the sting of that unhealed bullet hole in my shoulder brought me back around as if someone put a firebrand to me. I reflexively reached for my chest, felt bare skin and something wet, that's when the cold air hit me.

Cait gasped when I came through the door. My sheepskin had a diagonal slash through it. That, my shirt, and the skin beneath it laid open with a twelve-inch gash. The coat and shirt took most of the force of the blow. It was bloody, but I didn't stop to worry about it.

"The Major and Miz Standback!" I said, bounding up the stairs. Cait followed. Asmita, hearing all the commotion inside and out, came right behind her.

We burst through the door to find Emily standing by the bed, her Winchester pointed at the window. "Someone tried to come in through the window," she said. Puzzlement crossed her face. "What happened to you?"

Asmita went to the Major's bedside, found him still breathing.

"Met up with your intruder. Did you get a look at him?"

She shook her head. "You and that dog must've scared him off." She walked over to me, leaned her rifle against the wall, and examined my wound. "Asmita, go fetch some hot water and the rubbing alcohol."

"I'll go get my medical kit," Cait said. "Looks like you'll need a few stitches."

It felt like red hornets attacked my chest. Cait's darning needle piercing my flesh started the hornet stings—eight in, eight out. Asmita rubbed a concoction over the cuts sending in the rest of the swarm. It smelled strongly of horseradish, but it was a pasty mix with something else from her apothecary. In addition to the burn, it made my eyes water.

The women tolerated my screams and swearing during the procedure, but Miz Standback did admonish me to hush a time or two. When I asked Asmita what was in the oil she applied, she held me with those cold brown eyes and said, "Snake." I left it at that. Badly wanted to throw down some of the Major's whiskey Emily offered but thought I'd better stay as alert as I could through the rest of the night. The bite of my freshly stitched flesh helped me in that effort.

"I'll get Wil in the morning," I told the women. "We'll start to track down MacKenzie."

"You think it was MacKenzie last night?" Emily asked.

"Seems the most likely. Believe he was coming for the Major. Can't see Crow doing that."

⧖

"That the Major's coat?" Wil asked. When I'd come into the bunkhouse the next morning at five, the hands were at the table eating breakfast. The thick sheepskin hung a bit big on me.

"One of them," I said. "Met up with MacKenzie last night, I think. He cut my sheepskin to shreds." I took in their startled and puzzled expressions.

"MacKenzie?" Turnbow asked. "How'd you know it'uz MacKenzie."

"Most likely, him," I said. Related the whole episode. Turned to Wil. "Daylight, we'll see if we can pick up his trail if the snow hasn't covered it."

ector was gone. I noticed he wasn't on his pallet when I came in. "Where's the dog?" I asked.

"He seems to've took off," Husker said. "He went to the door last night, sniffin at it n'growlin. Figured he needed to piss, so I turned him out. Didn't want to follow him out into that snowstorm, so I stayed in. Figured he'd do his business and come right back in. Lord knows it weren't a night fit fer man 'r beast. It got to be five, ten minutes. Put on m'coat and went out lookin for him but didn't have no luck. Wandered around out there in the wind 'n snow hollerin and whistling 'til m'nose turned blue. Thought that damn fool dog knew where it's warm if he wanted to come back, so I come on in."

"What time was all this?" I asked.

"Reckon it'uz about eleven or so. I went on t'bed."

The snow dropped down to flurries before daybreak, but a thick layer of iron-gray clouds still hung low in the morning sky, running fast to the south as Wil and I headed out. We found some tracks behind the house that led to the field behind the barn—human tracks—but the snow obliterated any trail from there. When we swung out of the barn, about two hundred yards out, sat a big black animal like it was waiting for us to ride up—Hector.

Been about ten days since the attack on him, and although cut up bad, he healed well and faster than I thought he would. He limped a little, didn't stretch out far when he ran; otherwise, didn't let on the stitched wounds bothered him much. I was hoping whatever Asmita put on him she put on me. Dog was strong as they come, guess he stayed out in the cold and snow all night hunting. Maybe he found something and smart enough to know he couldn't take it on by himself.

That's why he waited for us. Don't know how he knew we'd show up, but he did.

I dismounted when we got close and walked cautiously over to him. He sat in the snow with a disinterested expression. I knelt three feet in front of him. "Damn, boy, how you doin?"

He didn't answer. Didn't appear any of his wounds had re-opened, but something in his eyes told me he wouldn't mind a drink of water, maybe a bite to eat.

"Wil, reach in my left bag and fetch my tinware. Some of that jerky, too. Bring my canteen."

Hector lapped up the water I poured into the tin plate. I poured some more, he drank that, too. Almost took off my fingers when I offered him the jerky. Wasn't apologetic, though. Just looked at me like he wanted more. Had no mind to turn him down. With my left hand, I reached out cautiously and stroked his shoulder. He ignored me, giving most of his attention to chowing down the jerky.

Squatting there, I patted the dog a couple more times. Didn't want to push it, though. A sun glint broke through the clouds. The overcast parted from the horizon as it pushed northeast leaving a blue scar across the southwest. Wil studied the ground around us, his eyes lifted toward the rising sun following sets of partially snow-covered tracks leading away from where Hector sat eating his breakfast.

"One man. Two, maybe three . . . wolves," he said.

He hesitated. "Man tracks show bare feet."

A sudden chill creased my back, despite the frigid morning air. Wil picked up on my concern, turned back to the fresh sun.

"Damn big wolves." The creases at the corners of his eyes deepened, and he set his jaw. "Doesn't appear Hector chased after them. His tracks lead only to this spot, nothing going or coming back. Guess he's smart enough to know not to take them on by himself."

"A bare-footed man running through the snow with wolves?" I tried to reason that out in my head.

Wil sighed, swallowed. "May not be all man. May be the Dire Wolf."

I whistled a breath through my teeth. "I doubt that." Said it, maybe more out of fear than disbelief. Wil walked back to his horse. Hector walked down the trail of tracks, sniffing them. After about ten yards, he stopped.

"Guess you two are ready to go after . . . whatever's waiting for us." I mounted up.

⧖

A couple miles on, the tracks—those of the man and dogs . . . or wolves, as Wil thought—led to a wooded hill. The small mount ascended about three hundred feet, give or take, its incline roughly thirty degrees up to the crest. Its base ran about a half mile either direction from where we sat in our saddles, curving some before merging with another hill about half its size. A forest of trees covered it: blackjack, hickory, some red cedar, a few pine. The trees didn't venture into the valley, choosing to cling to the hillside. Blackjack densely held the majority, stubbornly refusing to give up their dead leaves to the winter wind and cold. Snow clung to them, sagging the limbs, and blocking out most of the daylight beneath them. We stopped at a divergence: two sets of the animal tracks angled off to the left, one to the right. The man's tracks didn't vary from the line we followed.

It was mid-afternoon. We studied the hill a half-mile off— and the tracks—planned our approach, considered the threat hidden there. The sun, bright now in the cold crystal sky, hung low in the southwest. I pulled out my pocket watch: 3:52. Only a couple more hours of daylight on that mid-winter day. Even a bright twilight wouldn't do much good in those thick woods. Hector sat twenty yards off, watching the hill intently.

Wil stood in his stirrups, settled back down. "My guess, MacKenzie wants us to split up, too," he offered. "Either that or figures to flank us if we stay together and come after him."

I leaned a forearm on the horn, furrowed my brow. "Good move, either way."

Wil rubbed a gloved hand across his upper lip and sniffed. "That torn up dog there may not be as big as those wolves. In his condition, not so sure how he'll do fighting."

"I've heard it said, 'Ain't how much dog's in the fight, but how much fight's in the dog.' Reckon ole Hector's pissed, wants a little pay-back for what was done to him and his pack."

"Take more than guts to go up against three grown wolves," Wil said.

"You're probably right. I say we go in together, take them all on as they come. Maybe that'll help even things up for Hector."

"So straight in, or follow the two wolves?" He gestured to the pair of tracks angling left.

"Might as well go straight in. Figure he's watching us anyway, so it doesn't matter which way we go in."

Wil kicked his horse. "Ain't so sure this is smart."

As we spurred the horses forward, Hector followed the man-tracks, nose to the snow, like he understood our strategy. I conceded Wil's point about the smarts of it all. Custer would've been proud.

The woods gloomed deep once we got into them. The snow-laden limbs of the dense forest and the incline made it slow going. Our passing through the low-hanging boughs brushed snow onto us and disturbed enough of those branches above to create a mini-blizzard. Only Hector, out in front of us, remained undusted with snow.

Wil and I drew our pistols, the closeness of the timber making rifles impractical. A hundred yards in, maybe thirty yards up, the trees gave way to a twenty-foot high concave shelf of layered gray stone. The ground leveled off some in front of the shelf, creating a small clearing, Between the top of the rock wall and the trees, a small expanse of sky appeared. It was still bright enough to tell us the sun was still up but didn't illuminate the area around us much.

The first wolf leaped in a white blur from the slight overhang and drifted snow of the shelf. Wil instinctively raised his left arm in defense as the big animal struck him in the chest, its glistening teeth clamping tight on his lifted arm. The blow knocked him off his horse and headfirst into a tree trunk. He slid limp to the ground, either out cold or dead, as the wolf, slavering and growling, slashed and tore at Wil's lifeless arm. Clyde became frantic, turning in circles, rearing, screaming. I fired wildly, the shot going into the trees as the wolf savaged Wil. Before I could ear back the hammer to take another shot, Hector, like an eighty-pound cannonball, plowed into the wolf's side, sending dog and wolf sprawling into the snow beyond Wil's side. They thrashed and snarled and ripped, flinging bloody saliva into the white around them. The big dog fought with ferocity, despite his injuries. With surprising quickness and agility, he rolled atop his adversary, snapped his powerful jaws onto the wolf's throat, and ripped it out.

Just as Hector made his kill, a second wolf sprung from the trees onto his back, chomping its fangs into the back of Hector's neck. He howled and rolled, flinging the wolf off him. They got to their feet and faced one another, slavering, teeth bared, crouching, circling, growling their challenge. I holstered my Colt and yanked out the Winchester. Clyde still in a panic, I flung myself off him. I chambered a round, brought the butt to my shoulder. Hector's hind legs trembled, he slipped some trying to stand. The wolf sensed the dog's weakness and lunged. Hector tried to dodge but didn't have the spring. The wolf bit the dog's left hind leg with a sickening crunch. Hector yowled in pain. From fifteen feet away, I fired. The wolf spun to the ground releasing its grip on Hector's leg. The creature snarled and howled, unable to move its hindquarters. Luck, not skill, had sent the bullet through the gray's spine. Hector surged, dispatching the second wolf. He collapsed into the snow, downed by the exhaustion from his battle and bleeding from his fresh wounds, his hind leg useless.

A ton of fur and teeth hit me in the back. I hit the ground hard on my right shoulder, found myself face-first in the snow, the rifle knocked from my grip, most of the air blown from my lungs. My shoulder was electrified in pain, my arm and hand immediately numb. Somehow my hat stayed on. Hot breath and saliva burned the back of my neck. Growling and snarling so loud and close I could hear no other sound. I gasped, sucked in air. Intense pain seared my right shoulder. Above it, near my neck, pain spiked like a tightened vise. The gripping pressure released and came again higher on the back of my head, hot sharp spikes clamping into my skull down through the beaver skin of my hat and ripping away as the beast bit down. I flailed and kicked, getting some wind back, my right arm a board of pain I couldn't move. Knowing the next bite would kill me, I kicked frantically with my legs, desperately grabbed a wad of fur and hind wolf leg with my left hand, pulling at it with my last ounce of strength.

A menacing guttural sound came from somewhere behind, and the wolf released me, the weight of its huge paws left my back. Still face-down, I turned my head to the left, and with one eye at ground level, just above the top of the trampled snow, I spotted Wil sprawled in an awkward position, one leg turned under him at the knee, the back of his head against the base of a blackjack oak. Snow covered half his head and his body, shaken loose from the limbs above.

Phil Truman

My vision blurred as something wet seeped into my eye. The red tint convinced me it wasn't sweat. Vomit came into my throat. Footsteps approached. Had to be MacKenzie. Didn't figure he called the wolf off to save me. Guess he wanted me for himself.

A barefoot wedged under my left side, flipped me over on my back. I gasped with pain. The indigo patch of sky framed a big man. Well, from where I lay, big. About six feet, but his broadness made him big—huge upper body, stout legs. His head and face were wild with black hair. Even in that dim light, his eyes more yellow than brown, made them appear to shine. He wore a coat of fur that ended just below his mid-section, buffalo maybe, rough texture. Had a strong feral smell to it. The whole thing was an odd garment, but the most curious thing was the right sleeve—it ended at his elbow.

A handgun hung strapped around his waist on the left side, an old Schofield revolver. Big sucker, long-barreled. The pistol not his weapon of choice, though. His right hand was covered by a leather gauntlet that ran up to his elbow. Each of the leather fingers ended in curved claws, like a bear's or a big cat's. They had an ivory patina like bone with the glint of metal on the tips and underside of each.

I coughed, the head-blood running across my lips spaying out above me, falling back on my face in a red mist.

"Shoulda left it alone, lawman." His voice was deep, menacing almost like a growl.

I spat, cleared my throat, raised up on my left elbow. The wolf who attacked sat five yards off, cold blue eyes the color of death. A coal-black beast and huge, twice the size of the dead wolves in the snow. Gray flecked its ebony fur giving the coat a silvery sheen. It waited for further orders.

"How the hell do you train wolves?" I asked.

"I don't. *Nindawemaa* and her nephews go as I go. We speak to one another."

The wolf didn't appear to be particularly angry at me, just cold-blooded, waiting for the kill.

"That's the dominant bitch," MacKenzie said. "Smartest one of the pack. She sent the others in to kill you, only attacked herself when she knew you were beat. Gotta watch the dominant bitches, they're clever."

I thought about my Colt, still holstered on my right hip. "That how you killed the Jakes, let the wolves do it?

"They helped, but this did the killing." He held up the claw gauntlet, admiring it.

My arm was limp, and my fingers tingled, pained at the shoulder when I move it. I clinched and re-clinched my hand to get more feeling into it. Didn't know if my upper arm was broken or dislocated at the shoulder. The pain just didn't feel like a broken bone.

"Why'd you kill those Jakes?" My half-numb fingers touched the butt of my .44. They slid like frozen sticks around the handle. The muscles in my hand and arm didn't cooperate. I couldn't pull the gun free of the holster. The slightest effort made me wince.

"That woman scorned me. Her brothers went where they shouldn't have. Nobody lays a hand on me and lives to tell about it."

"What about that boy? He didn't do anything to you."

"Boy's just in the wrong place at the wrong time."

The gun moved. I had my hand around it but couldn't really feel it.

"Why'd you do that to Cait McDonald, come after her?"

"Business deal," he said.

"Hell of a deal, slaughtering all her animals like that."

MacKenzie shrugged, threw back his head and laughed. "Did that for the nephews. They needed some blood sport."

He looked at Hector, the dog's ribs heaving up and down. "That dog there was the only one put up any real fight. Gritty bastard to come out after us alone that night." He had admiration and respect in his voice. "Didn't figure him to live."

Had the gun, slipped it clear of the holster. I bit down hard on my lip to suppress a scream. "Why the Major?" I shouted.

"He had it coming, but there's other reasons. Never figured him to survive, either."

"That's why you were on the roof the other night? To finish him off. Who hired you, MacKenzie?"

He laughed, more like a snarl. "You would've stayed alive if you stuck to your business, kept after that outlaw. But you kept getting in my way. You were an annoyance, not that it matters. People hired me, all they care about is the job getting done. If you or someone else stopped me, they'd send others. Now I gotta kill you, so I can get on with business. No hard feelings, though, lawman, 'cause I always enjoy it."

I cocked the Colt's hammer, struggled to bring it to bear. His left foot kicked my wrist just as I fired, pinned my arm to the ground. Wouldn't have mattered anyway, my dead-handed shot went well wide of him. The pain nearly blinded me.

He threw his head back and howled like a beast from hell. Swung his gauntlet-ed fist back above him to swing it down across my torso in one powerful and fatal slash.

The instant expanded, the world moved slow. His arm swung toward me, and he shuddered, then blood burst from his chest and he spun, falling to one knee. Almost at the same moment, an explosion erupted somewhere behind me, not particularly close. I had an odd recognition of the sound—the same sound I heard from that creek bed a few days back, something between the firing of a rifle and a mountain howitzer. An explosion of snow and dirt erupted at the feet of the black she-wolf, then another report came, this one from a Winchester. The animal sprung to her left and into the woods on the downhill side of the clearing. MacKenzie arose from his kneel and followed the black beast. A plug of splintered pine burst from a tree next to MacKenzie's head as he, too, plunged into the dark timber.

Footsteps crunched the snow behind me. I was woozy, knew I couldn't get up. The pain had dulled some, I wanted to sleep. A blurred person stood over me. A rifle barrel with a fifty caliber bore, six inches away, pointed at my nose. It was a Sharps, the bearer was Crow Redhand. And here I thought I was saved. "Shit," I said, right before I passed out.

⏳

My own bellow brought me back to the land of the living, although I wasn't entirely sure I wanted to be here. For a minute thought I was in hell. Someone's foot pushed against my ribs, someone pulled on my right arm perpendicular to my body. I felt and heard a pop in my shoulder. I whimpered and swore. The arm-puller laid my hand and forearm across my chest and took a squatted position. The flicker of firelight outlined his form, I felt warmth. Recognized Joe Elkfoot. A swath of stars crossed the open sky patch above me.

"You oughta be okay, now. Gonna be sore for a few days," Joe said.

My head swam, but the pain was less intense. The wolves—at the edge of the firelight—still lay where they fell, pools of blood around them sparkling with frost. Wil was propped up further against the tree, the snow brushed off him. A buffalo robe covered him. I had a blanket under me, the Major's sheepskin my main cover. Hector lay on some fresh-cut pine boughs next to Elkfoot, as beat up as I felt, but alive. He raised his head when I spoke. "Redhand?" I asked.

"Gone. Didn't finish what he came to do, so he took off following MacKenzie's blood trail," Elkfoot said. "He's gonna kill you, too, but I talked him out of it. Took some talking, but I did. This dog here helped with the convincing." He motioned his head in Hector's direction, laughed a little "Appears he had some objection. Me, I didn't think Crow needed a dead lawman on his list, too. Not that it'd matter. On the other hand, he mighta just put it off. He's in a hurry to get after MacKenzie."

I craned my neck. "Wil dead?"

"Nah, just knocked cold, got a couple pretty good wolf bites. But he'll be awright. Wil's a tough bird. 'Spect he'll have a headache when he wakes. Appears this dog put up a good fight. He might have a broken leg, though."

I felt my head, found my hat. Lifted it off to examine it—rips and puncture holes, blood. Been a damn good hat, not sure I could get another one like it, with the scarcity of beaver skins.

"I put that back on you to help stop some of the bleeding. Your head got chewed up good."

I pushed off the ground to get up, my head and shoulder thought better of it. My whole body felt stiff with aches. I slid back to a sit.

Elkfoot didn't try to stop me. Knew he probably didn't need to. "We'll spend the night here," he said. "You're not in much condition to travel. Neither's Wil. Besides, there's only my horse. Yours must've scattered when those wolves came around. We wait, they see the fire, might come back. Plan on feeding this fire all night, in case there's any more wolves out there wanting to make a meal, especially that damn big black one that got away. Hope you don't mind sleeping with the dead."

I pulled the collar of my coat up around my wounded neck, glanced back at the dead hulk of the dead wolves. "Not too crazy about it."

"That black one's the one jumped me," I said. Elkfoot worked the fire, didn't respond. "Wil thinks that animal to be the Quapaw Dire Wolf. You and Crow believe that?"

He took his time answering, stoked the fire. "Not entirely, but I do respect the old traditions. Old man named Long Walker, sort of the tribal shaman, used to keep us boys fascinated with the old stories. Way he told them, you could tell he for sure believed them." He took out a pouch from a pocket inside his sheepskin, shook some of its contents— black, small leaves—into a palm. "Crow, I don't know. Do know one thing, I've never seen a wolf like that around here before."

"I've met Long Walker," I said.

He ground the leaves in his palm with his other thumb and brushed it into a cup of melted snow sitting by the fire. Stirred it with a stick, handed me the cup. "Drink all this. It'll ease the pain, help you sleep. Already gave some to your dog."

"Not my dog," I said, drinking.

Elkhorn nodded, "Umph." He went to his horse. "Got some salt pork and shortbread. It'll tide us over."

Something bothered me, something made me anxious. The threat to Cait was still out there. Couldn't shake the feeling I needed to get back to her, that she was still in danger.

"Crow," I said. "You think he'll catch up with MacKenzie?"

Elkfoot sliced the salt pork in silence.

"You think he's headed back to the Forked S?" I asked.

"Hard to say. Why would he?"

"MacKenzie's out to kill the Major, him and Cait McDonald. Told me he was hired to do that." I pressed my fingers into my shoulder joint, rubbed it some, despite the pain. "I've got this feeling it ain't over. Crow might catch MacKenzie, might not. That black she-wolf of his is still alive. They could ambush Crow like they did Wil and me. Who knows, maybe they've thrown in together. That'd explain why his shot from that Sharps didn't take MacKenzie out."

"Crow?" Elkfoot asked. He smiled, stirred the fire with a stick.

135

"Why not Crow?" I said. "Believe Crow'd just as soon kill somebody for hire as not. He and the Major got some history."

"You're wrong, deputy. Crow's a lot of bad things. Got killings attached to him, but he wouldn't hire out to kill, even a white man."

"Hell, he tried to kill me. Shot me twice. Killed a cowboy out on the Big Pasture and that banker."

"He didn't kill those two men, one of his gang did, said it was a big Irishman. As for you, that's different."

I scoffed. "How'm I different?"

"Well, you're the law. Way Crow thinks he's got the right to shoot the law. It's like you're opposing warriors. Not a crime among the Quapaw to kill an enemy. Besides, he didn't kill you. It's more like he's counting coup."

"Since when does counting coup involve bullets?"

He shrugged.

"It doesn't work that way, Elkfoot. As for those two other men, their killings were during the commission of a crime. Crow's as guilty as the man who pulled the trigger."

Elkfoot poked the fire some more, threw on a couple sticks of wood. "He could've killed you tonight but didn't. If Crow had made up his mind, I couldn't've stopped him. I reminded him he just saved your life. Saving another's life is powerful medicine to an Indian. Means you owe him. Told him maybe he could use it on down the road."

What Elkfoot said, struck me. Redhand did, in fact, save my life, and spare me. Something weighty wedged in my gut. I didn't like the idea of indebtedness to Crow Redhand. "It still remains, he's a criminal," I said. "It's my duty to uphold the law, and bring him in, debt or no debt."

I'm not sure it came out with conviction. Elkfoot said, "Umph,"

"I need to go after both of them, Crow *and* MacKenzie," I said.

"Why?"

"He's a hired killer, admitted to me he killed the Jakes and attacked Major Standback. The murders he committed will most likely involve Federal marshals. Investigations need to be made into who hired him. Might be evidence on him to help with that.

"Besides, every man, even a monster like MacKenzie, deserves a fair trial . . . or a decent burial."

"Maybe in the white man's world," Elkfoot said.

CHAPTER 15

C lyde's every step caused pain to whip from my head down to my bad leg and several points in between. Elkfoot was right about the horses coming back in the night. I awakened predawn with Clyde's muzzle two inches from my nose, snuffling. Behind that immediate horsehead, a couple stars still twinkled in the paling sky patch. Joe was also right by saying none of us, besides him, were fit to travel.

Wil awakened some and sat cross-legged in front of the fire, the buffalo robe wrapped around his shoulders. He loosely held a cup of something steaming, more'n likely some of Elkfoot's chicory brew. I poured some up for myself. Wil's eyes were vacant, his brow rippled in pain.

"How you doin, Wil?" He didn't speak, took a sip. He furrowed his brow trying to figure out the answer inside his scrambled brain. "Who're you?" he asked.

A sense of foreboding came over me. I got up. "We need to head back to the Forked S." On my feet, my vision spun. Wrapped my left arm around a pine, on the verge of throwing up.

"You're right." Elkfoot came out of the trees across the small clearing. "Don't know how you two and that dog are gonna make it, though." He poured a cup, squatted in front of the fire. Thought I detected some anxiety. "I dozed off last night," Elkfoot said. "Don't know how long. Something woke me. A sound, a feeling. Ain't sure. Something big was moving in the woods, circling us. I took up my Winchester, followed the sound. It eventually quit. Didn't realize until daylight that those dead wolves were gone."

"You think wolves carried them off?"

"Don't think so. But I got this nervous thing in my head saying MacKenzie and that she-wolf came back for 'em."

138

"Came back?" I studied on that for a minute, my own mind calling up a primal fear. "So, either MacKenzie took care of Crow, or Crow's his partner."

Elkfoot kicked an unburnt piece of wood into the coals. "Appeared to be one of them. My guess is Crow's dead. I checked the woods. Sign of one man and a big wolf. Matched MacKenzie's bare feet and his girlfriend's. No other tracks; not men, not wolves. Not Crow's."

A chill grabbed me like the cold clutch of death. Took a drink from my cup, tried to swallow some, but retched. Wiped my mouth and nose with a sleeve. "We need to go after him, we need to ride. I can ride."

"Doubt that," Elkfoot said. "For sure not Wil. That dog won't get far, either. I tried to look at his leg, but he'd have none of it. Didn't argue with him about it. I followed the tracks. Went down the hill on into the valley."

"He couldn't have gotten far." I gathered my gear. My head still spun with confusion in the dim morning light. "Trail shouldn't be hard to follow. We can catch up with him."

"Yeah, we can, but we really need to get Wil some doctoring, get him in a warm bed. Way he's acting, he might have a cracked skull. Best bet is to get him back to the Forked S."

"We can't let MacKenzie get away, he's probably headed back to the ranch." I stumbled to Clyde, tried to mount up. "Need to get to him before he gets there."

"Hold on, deputy. He ain't going to outrun us in his condition and a-foot. We need to rig something up to haul our wounded. If MacKenzie is headed for the ranch like you say, we'll track him down before he gets there, if he does. Good chance we'll find him dead in the snow. Took a Sharps fifty slug, remember? A lot of thousand-pound buffalos didn't survive that. Doubt a man can, even MacKenzie."

139

I relented, sat down and threw up again. Elkfoot cut down a couple saplings and made a travois for Wil and Hector, stretched and tied two horse blankets across poles making its base, used the buffalo robe to cover man and dog. We got started about an hour after daybreak, made maybe five, six miles by noon. "How much further, you think?" I lost all track of our location and direction.

"Six, eight miles," Elkfoot said. "Shorter the way we're going than the way you came."

Wil slept on the travois. Hector didn't like sharing it with him. His hurt leg made him short-tempered, growling and snapping at every jolt.

"Maybe we should give Hector some more of that pain medicine of yours," I said.

"Gave him some before we left. Don't want to give a dog too much of that, it'll make him go crazy."

Hector, half-under the buffalo robe, bared his teeth, licked his chops, grumbled. "Maybe you already gave him too much. You think Wil's safe riding back there?"

"Long as he doesn't make any sudden moves, or touch that dog's leg. Anyway, what choice does he have?"

We rode on, mostly in silence, keeping the horses' gaits at a walk. We followed MacKenzie's trail about two miles, but they angled off. We were headed southwest, his tracks turned east.

"Any idea how much of a head start MacKenzie's got?" I asked.

"Hard to say. But he's hurt bad and on foot. Might die before he gets where he's going."

"Back to the ranch," I stated it more than asked.

"Don't think so. Not immediately, anyway. Hurt as he is, he'll want to hole up somewhere and heal a little. I figure he's got someplace around here to do that, that's why he changed direction.

"How you figure MacKenzie's alive?" I asked. "Never seen any living thing survives a shot from a Sharps fifty, not in the chest, anyway. Even a hit in a man's arm would likely take it off."

"Don't think MacKenzie's an ordinary man. Likely the bullet went right through, didn't hit bone or anything vital. Still, must've left a big hole."

"What about Crow?"

"He'll damn sure be disappointed, I mean about not killing MacKenzie with that shot."

"I'm talking about where he's gone. I still need to bring him in . . . if he's alive."

"Crow's alive," he said. "You think I'm gonna tell you where he's at? Not sure I'd do that even if I knew."

"I'm still not convinced the two of them didn't join up. Crow may've gone on ahead to the Forked S."

Joe shifted in his saddle. "I'll say it again: they didn't partner up. Crow hates MacKenzie with a vengeance for what he did to the Jakes, and I expect that's what he aims to get. He's tracking him, just like we are. But he's going to bide his time, make sure he doesn't miss again. Probably wants to make him suffer. Tell the truth, I think that wounding shot Crow gave to MacKenzie was purposeful. Crow's too good a shot. He wants to chase him down like a wounded animal. I think he was disappointed I missed that she-wolf, though."

"What's he to you? I know he's your cousin and all, but you said yourself he's no account. So did Wil. He didn't have a problem joining up with me to help find Crow."

Elkfoot chuckled, looked up at a wheeling hawk a ways off in the cobalt sky. "Wouldn't be too sure about Wil's actions, if I were you. He's always had a knack for making people think he's doing one thing when he's actually doing another."

"What're you talking about? Wil's never given me any reason to mistrust him."

141

A tight grin cracked Elkfoot's face. He studied the hawk. "Good," he said. "That's good."

☒

Venus—maybe ten, fifteen minutes behind the just set sun—shone brilliantly in the western sky when we entered the valley where the ranch house sat. Wil aroused some in the afternoon, protested having to ride the travois with Hector, although the dog had settled down. It appeared Elkfoot's medicine took hold and the dog slept. Wil wanted to get mounted, but we ignored him.

Nothing amiss at the ranch house. Smoke issued from the parlor and kitchen chimneys, lights came from windows—a couple downstairs, one up. Two cowboys guarded the front and back.

Turnbow rode out across the meadow to greet us. Came at a gallop, reined up ten feet to our front. "You git 'im?" he asked. No questions or surprise at Elkfoot's presence or the bundled travois.

"If you mean MacKenzie, yes and no," I said. "Crow Redhand shot him, but apparently not dead, like we thought. He ran off, him and his big black she-wolf."

"Crow Redhand shot MacKenzie?" He ignored my comment on the she-wolf, or it didn't register.

"You seen him?" I asked. "I was thinking he might head back this way."

"Ain't seen 'im," he said. "Looks like you been worked over some. Who's on the travois."

"Wil and Hector. They got the worst of it. We need to call the doc." I squeezed my heels into Clyde's flanks, nudging him into a walk, still stringing along Wil's horse and the travois. Elkfoot followed. Turnbow turned in step.

"What happened?"

"MacKenzie. Had a pack of wolves with him. They did most the damage."

"Wolves?" he said incredulously. "You sure they's wolves? Ain't never known a man with trained wolves."

"Yep. Big 'uns, too. Had a she-wolf black as coal and half again as big as Hector."

"I'll be damned," Turnbow said. We rode on toward the house in silence.

"What about the Major?" I asked. "The women okay?"

"Not much change in the Major, but he's still breathin. Asmita's hoverin over him like a mother hen, dosin him with her medicines. Won't hardly let the missus in there with him. Miz McDonald's awright. That other damn dog of hers makes sure of that. Lucky for you and Wil, Doc's comin out in the morning to check on the Major."

Wil sat up on the travois, bracing himself with an elbow. Hector stuck his head out from under the robe and bared his teeth, then disappeared back under it. "Maybe he can do something for this damn dog, too," he said, his voice still woozy.

Cait came out onto the porch as we approached bundled in her thick sheepskin over a navy-blue riding skirt, Athena at her side a little bristled. Long fingers separated the sheer curtains from the parlor window. I recognized the big ruby and diamond ring Miz Standback wore. Something about her from behind the curtains bothered me, but I didn't know why.

Cait didn't speak. Took in my wolf-bit hat and battered head, my disheveled clothes and bruised face.

Miz Standback walked out past Cait to the edge of the porch steps. "I hope you got him," she said.

"We did," I answered. "But he got away. Hurt bad, though. We figure he's dead by now."

Her lips pursed. "Who's injured?"

"It's Wil, ma'am," I said. "He's gonna need the doc."

She turned her eyes to Elkfoot. "Mister Elkfoot."

He touched his hat.

She turned to Husker—the house guard in the front. "Let's get Wil to a bed. I'll have Asmita tend to him." The big cowboy hauled up Wil, walking him to the bunkhouse.

Cait's voice roused Hector from under the buffalo robe, he howled, high and keening. Cait went straight to the travois and bent down to the stroke the dog's head.

"What's Hector doing here? I thought—" He tried to stand on his gnawed leg. "What happened to him?"

Hector whimpered, licked her hand.

"He's let out night afore last, but never come back," Turnbow said. "Reckon he met up with the deputy to help track down MacKenzie."

"Pretty much it," I said. "Big brute took on two of MacKenzie's wolves, probably saved Wil's life."

Cait stroked the dog, examining his leg and other wounds, new and old. "Don't know how he had the strength."

"Hard to figure what persuades some animals," Elkfoot said.

The evening star was a beacon in what was left of the daylight. "Well, it's getting colder," Missus Standback said. "You gentlemen come inside, get some hot food. Let's bring the dog, too. Poor thing." She considered me. "You could use some more of Asmita's fixing up, too, Deputy Smoak. I'll swear."

Hearing the talk, the cowboy Brooks came around from the back of the house. Elkfoot enlisted him to grab two corners of the buffalo robe upon which they carried Hector inside and deposited him by the kitchen stove per Miz Standback's instructions. All of us gathered there. I took a seat at the small table and removed my chewed hat. The cloth Elkfoot had wrapped around my head still showed blood splotches which I thought provoked a line of concern in Cait's brow, but she quickly turned her attention back to Hector. Weariness overtook me, my strength sapped.

Asmita came through the kitchen door from the dining room, stopped, muttered angrily at the gathered group. Her fierce eyes sparked with anger. I took it she was upset at the group dirtying up her kitchen. Her glare scared all of us a little, maybe not the missus. Brooks excused himself and hurried out the back door. Elkfoot spoke to her softly, I supposed it was Quapaw. She answered curtly, he said something back. They carried on about a half-minute. The anger in her voice turned to one of fear, her eyes widened some.

"Asmita," Miz Standback said. "Deputy Smoak needs attention until the doctor arrives. The man Wil Redhand, too. He's in the bunkhouse. And the dog . . . perhaps you can help Miss McDonald with anything for him."

The old Quapaw woman removed the bandage from my head, pressed my ripped-up scalp several places with a forefinger. She spread my shirt, not happy with my re-opened wounds there, either. Her expression reproachful on her weathered old face, said something in her tongue, then turned to the dog, squatting beside him. Hector, panting, licked the air in her direction, lowered his ears in submission. He squinted with pain, but he made no aggressive move toward the old woman, letting her touch him. He knew her, trusted her because she helped him in his earlier recovery.

Asmita pulled several jars and bowls out of a cabinet, mixed them with water and a portion of the Major's Kentucky bourbon. Part of the mixture was a liquid, part a thick paste. She brought one of the concoctions to me, motioned for me to drink it. I gagged and coughed, the whiskey its only redeeming quality as far as I could tell. She went to Hector, said something to Elkfoot, and he and Cait helped get some of the potion down the dog's throat. Hector didn't like it much, either, but within a couple minutes, he passed out. She went to work on his leg, the bones scraping as she set them back in place. She cleaned his bleeding wounds, plastered them with the other mixture, then splinted the leg.

I didn't pass out, felt light-headed, euphoric. The pain in my head, my body, seemed a long way off. Couldn't quite remember why we were all there. Cait stared at me with a look of . . . concern? Annoyance? Not sure. Occurred to me, hell, it overwhelmed me, that she was the most beautiful woman ever, more so even than what's-her-name back in Colorado. Felt compelled to tell her so. "Damned if you ain't the most beautiful woman I've ever seen." I think I grinned at her when I said it. Anyway, she grinned back. Think she even laughed some. That was beautiful, too, so I laughed with her. Then everybody else did.

I laughed it up until Asmita stuck that darning needle into my forehead and sewed up my pealed back flesh. It didn't hurt much, but it didn't feel good, either. It startled me, made me forget how good I felt. Heard Asmita say, "Hold head," and someone's big rough hands clamped over my ears. Had to be Husker's, I thought.

"Ahm like old shock," I said out of my forcibly pursed lips. Everybody laughed again, except Asmita. She sewed up all the tears on my head and neck that big she-wolf gave me, then swabbed them with her poultice. At least, I think so. Somewhere in there, I did pass out. Didn't remember a whole lot when I woke up the next morning.

⧗

My eyes focused on Cait at the side of my bed. That floating happiness in my head was gone. Felt like I had several railroad spikes in my skull. So much so, they out-pained the streak of fire across my chest, and the hot poker in my shoulder. I pushed down on the bed to sit up. "Son of a Bitch!" I fell back, hoping the wave of pain would pass.

"You're not ready to get up," she told me. "That wolf just about chewed your head off." She half-grinned, recognizing my frustration and agony. Wasn't a mean grin, though. Maybe a tinge of worry and concern. I kinda liked that. But my helplessness and that kinda mocking grin from her, I didn't. Sorta gave her power over me, I thought. "You ripped open those stitches I put in your chest." Her eyes shifted up to the fresh bandage on my left shoulder. "Guess you had an earlier wound, not completely healed. It started bleeding again, too." She lifted my shoulder, checking the status of the exit wound. "Who gave you that?" she asked.

"Gift from Crow Redhand," I said. "Second one." I rubbed the old scar on my neck from his first. Guess it'd have companions that the wolf bites would leave.

She clucked and shook her head. "I'd say that man dislikes you."

The memory of the fifty-caliber bore of that Sharps pointed six inches from my nose popped up, along with the thought of me living to tell about it. I thought about what Joe Elkfoot said. "Maybe," I said. "But not enough to kill me."

"Well." She brushed her hands down the front of her dress. "I'd better go see about Hector."

Doc Riley burst into the room, black leather medical case in hand along with that ever-present expression of weariness. Wore his usual rumpled vested suit, white shirt and string tie. The short salt and pepper beard. The wire-rim glasses perched low in his nose with thick lenses magnifying his eyes, gave him an owlish appearance, that air of wisdom and knowledge. He came straight to me, opened his bag and took out a stethoscope without so much as a howdy.

"How's Wil?" I asked. Guessed he'd checked on him before coming to me.

"He gave everybody fits in the bunkhouse last night," he answered. He listened to my heart and lungs. Slung the instrument around the back of his neck, searched my eyes intently with those owl eyes. I didn't get the feeling it was to make contact. "According to Turnbow, he woke up about midnight demanding to know why he was there, where he'd been, how he got those wolf bites. Claims he doesn't remember a thing since you all met Hector on that hill two days ago. Has a good concussion, big knot on his head, but I don't think he cracked it open. Not critical but needs to stay in bed another day or so. Least, until his headache and fuzzy vision goes away."

He lifted the bandages on my head and neck, moved to those on my chest and shoulder. "Missus Dromenko would want me to tell you she was right about telling you not to leave her care. You haven't done that bullet hole in your shoulder any good." He packed away his scope, buckled the medical bag. "On the other hand, looks like Asmita's witchery has done you more good than I could've." He fumbled through his coat pocket, pulled out a half-smoked cigar. "She's gonna put me outta business. Didn't need to bother with you."

"Did you look at Hector?" Cait asked.

"That dog?" He clamped the cigar in his teeth. "Well, I tried. Again, I wasn't needed with Asmita there. Besides, she's the only one he lets touch him. He's in good hands. He'll live if he stays outta any more fights for a while." He lit the stogie stub, blew smoke in my direction. "As should you."

Back at Cait. "Dog's leg probably never be quite the same, though."

"You see the Major yet?" I asked.

"Saw him first. Still in a coma, but his visible wounds are improving. His loss of blood was the main issue. He may never fully recover from that. Could be some brain damage."

His eyes peered over the top of his glasses, stern. "I'm going to tell you again, Deputy, you need to take it easy to give those wounds a chance to heal. Rest, as much as anything, helps fight infections. Wolf bites aren't anything to trifle with. Stay here and let these women take care of you, especially Asmita."

I smiled, then lied, "Yes sir, I will."

⏳

All that blood crusted in my hat had made it stiff. I sat on Clyde working it with my hands to soften it up before sticking it over the wrappings around my head. The places were still tender, despite Asmita's plasters. Only been a day since she sewed them up. Miz Standback told me to take one of the Major's hats, but they all came down around my ears. I have sort of a pinhead. My ragged and nasty old hat still fit.

"Take Athena," Cait said after I told her I'd track Crow alone. Wil was still a little goofy and disoriented, and Joe Elkfoot took off a couple nights back while Asmita sewed me up. Turnbow or any of the cowboys couldn't be spared.

"She doesn't need to get chewed up like Hector did. I'd feel better if she stayed here with you."

"You're not in any shape to take on Redhand or MacKenzie," she argued. "What if you meet up with both? What if they're working together as you suspect?"

Maybe it was a false sense of well-being following Asmita's *witchery*, as Doc Riley called it, and a few of her meals under my belt. Maybe it was bravado. I couldn't say. But I felt like this was something I had to do on my own. Wasn't sure I could bring either, or both, of them in alive. Hell, wasn't too sure I could bring myself back alive. My boots shook in the stirrups. Fought the fear in every fiber in my body. Good sense telling me Cait was right—I oughta have more men with me. But it was what the U.S. Marshal paid me to do, what I'd sworn to do. Believe that's what my Uncle Jubal would've said to me. I couldn't dishonor him.

"It's lawman's business, Cait. I can't endanger anyone else's life at this point. Besides, Wil's not able and the other boys are needed here. Be less noticed if I travel alone."

She started to say something but stopped. Think she read it in my face and understood. She was scared like me, only her heart wouldn't let her try to hold me back. Maybe she was raised like I was. I reined Clyde right, gently pushed my heels to put him into a trot.

CHAPTER 16

C old again that morning, clear but still. The ground and trees shone like silver. Warmed up enough the day before to melt some off the top of the snow, just to freeze back when the sun went down. Clyde's every step crunched through the crust. The big chestnut moved along slowly, not sure-footed on the re-frozen snow. In the silence, it sounded like cannon fire, or at least that Sharps of Crow's. Figured anybody within five miles could hear us coming. Slow-moving, we made easy targets. Made me edgy.

When you ride alone, and slow, about all you've got to do, is think. No one knew where Joe Elkfoot took off to. He just slipped off that night we were all in the kitchen. No one remembers him leaving, not even the hands outside. Most figured he headed back to his ranch. I kinda half-hoped he was trailing me, nervous as I was about meeting up with Crow and MacKenzie . . . and that big damn she-wolf. I thought more so about the wolf than the other two. Felt Crow wouldn't kill me, but not sure. Guess that's why I wanted Joe Elkfoot there, to talk Crow out of it again.

I headed back to the promontory where we all battled a few days back. Figured somewhere this side of it I'd pick up tracks of one man or the other. Could be both, if Crow was stalking MacKenzie . . . or helping him.

By noon the cold air couldn't hold back the raw rays of the sun, and the surface snow went from hard glaze to semi-slush. We moved faster but picked up no sign of my quarry. Made our way down a wide valley with gentle slopes to either side. Fairly dense timber flanked us on the left and right. From the center of the valley, each tree line was two, three hundred yards off. I kept Clyde out of the timber and in full sunlight to take advantage of the softer snow cover, and the sun's feeble

151

heat, but it left us more exposed. Didn't much like that but figured Crow would be the only one to take a shot from that distance and hoped like hell he still had that soft spot for me.

It was getting on mid-afternoon, the winter sun low in the southwest to my front. Clyde and I were maybe three, four miles from where Joe and I broke off from MacKenzie's trail that day past. Off in the timber to our left, something big paralleled us. Thought it was a black bear, but it didn't have that lumbering gait of a bear. Then it struck me like thunder: the she-wolf. Don't know why I didn't realize that when I first saw her, guess I didn't want to. A cold sweat broke from my body. I pulled the Winchester from its boot, cocked the hammer, and set the stock butt on my right thigh.

Smart enough beast to keep back in the woods so I couldn't get a clear shot. Several times I lost sight of her. She appeared like a wraith, faded back into the undergrowth knitting like a dark shadow between and through the denuded brush. The head-on sun obscured some of my vision, but I spotted the ghost creature sitting some fifty yards ahead, still back in the woods, watching us, waiting. Went on like that for a mile or so. Gave no indication she was going to come after us, even with the shadows lengthening.

After pacing each other more than a mile, I heard gunshots. The rapid fire of three pistol shots, followed by rifle fire. No mistaking that boom in the afternoon stillness. Heard it too many times in the past week. It came from Crow's Sharps. I pulled out my field glasses. About a mile away, the tree line to my right jagged off to a rock face, a back-slanting cliff jutted up about thirty feet on a hillside. At the base of the cliff, a dark hole stood out partially concealed by boulders. A serpentine cluster of juneberry trees flanked the far side of the downslope from the cave entrance to where a scatter of cedar trees roamed the near side. Out front of the cave opening, down some from the boulders, a figure stood over something or someone on the ground. Had to be Crow or MacKenzie, but I couldn't tell who was standing from that distance.

Back at the left tree line, the big wolf was gone. I kicked Clyde into a gallop, angling for the right-side woods. I feared more the man left standing was Crow with that Sharps. Once in the woods, I weaved through the dense bracken until I came to where the trees opened up to the cliff. Several frozen rivulets ran down the face of the rocky escarpment like milky snakes which ended in a burl of ice at the base. Thirty yards off, on the open decline from the cave, Crow stood. The body of a wolf lay sprawled at his feet unmoving, part of its head missing. Crow raised his gaze toward me, leveled the Sharps from his waist, pointed it in my direction. I raised the Winchester up to my shoulder, brought it to bear on him.

"You don't give up, do you, deputy?" He kept the big rifle leveled at me, the hammer cocked. Hoped Joe's words to him about the price of shooting a lawman had stayed with him. I breathed in deep and let it out, steadied the jumping barrel in my grip to keep a bead on him. Redhand could outshoot me in a heartbeat.

"My job, Crow," I said. "You broke the law, killed men. Hell, you shot me twice."

He laughed, stopped with a wince. I detected unsteadiness in his stance. "Didn't shoot those men. Fella rode with me, Mick Hallihan, did. You kilt him at that cabin up on the Neosho River."

"You're still culpable, Crow."

He weaved backward, took a small step that way. A dark blossom of blood above his waist glistened on his right side, another splotched thigh-high on a pant leg, the left. "What the hell's that mean?" he grumbled.

"Blameworthy. He rode with your gang. You put those men into those robberies, all actions committed during those crimes fall back on you, too."

"That don't seem right. I smacked Mick after he shot those fellas. Cussed him out good, too. If you hadn't've kilt him at that cabin, I's gonna cut him loose." The Sharps in his grip dipped some, but he raised it back to my eye level.

"Doesn't matter. You've gotta answer for them. It's the law."

He scoffed, placed the stock butt under his right arm, still pointed at me. He shifted off his left leg, hopped a little on the right. "White man's law."

I was apprehensive about the whereabouts of MacKenzie, glanced up at the cave. "You finish off MacKenzie?"

He didn't answer.

I raised my head from sighting down the barrel. "Believe you're shot, Crow. What happened here?"

He pointed with his chin at the bloody lump on the ground. "MacKenzie sent this wolf down to get me. I had to shoot it. I'd tracked him to here, he saw me coming, put a couple slugs in me. When the wolf came at me, MacKenzie took off. Don't understand why that man ain't dead after I shot his heart out."

"Reckon you missed his heart," I said, still with that uneasiness in my stomach. "He could be aiming to put us both down, right now."

"Naw, he's gone, or we'd be dead."

Worried about my chances in that stand-off, I edged closer to a clump of cedars huddled around a boulder. Thought I'd lay it out. "You working with MacKenzie?"

That pissed him off. "What t'hell you mean? Bastard killed my cousins, killed Sarah. Promised myself . . . and Sarah, I'd see him dead for that. Tracked him here."

We needed to end this, Crow and I, before he decided to go ahead and shoot me. Surprised he hadn't already. I stood only a foot away from the protection of the cedars. "You put down that rifle and come with me. I'll put in a word with the court, even about those other killings. Ask 'em to go easy on you."

"Indin don't get *easy* in a white man's court. I ain't going in with you, Smoak." He brought the rifle up to his shoulder, aimed down the barrel.

"Don't do it!" I shouted.

He squeezed, the hammer fell on the block with a loud click, the rifle didn't fire.

I fired, but the round thumped into the snow behind him. "Shit," I said and dove toward a cedar clump. Crow dropped the rifle and slapped up the pistol strapped to his side, cocked and fired in one smooth motion. The .45 slug burned a crease across the left sleeve of the Major's over-sized sheepskin. I hit hard on my right shoulder with a scream-inducing crunch; the same shoulder two days past into which Joe Elkfoot had popped my arm bone. The pain was so intense I could hardly get my breath. I hung onto consciousness, knowing Crow would surely finish me off this time if I passed out.

I scrunched behind the cedars, drawing in those parts of me still exposed. Crow fired again before I could chamber another round. The toe of my right boot disappeared in a stinging explosion. I drew what was left of the boot and my foot in behind me. Two more shots in rapid succession kept me pinned.

As I cringed behind the rock and brush, Crow shambled off down the slope. I levered in a round and fired, but that shot missed, too. He managed to reach a stand of juneberry trees and ducked into them. I got up to chase but found I couldn't run very well in my shot boot. It shoveled in a wad of snow with every step. And the pain in my shoulder staggered me.

Crow reached his horse in the trees and galloped away.

What I could see of his wounds looked bad. Wasn't sure how far he'd get, but Crow was one tough sumbitch. I didn't underestimate him. All my wounds hollered at me. I just didn't have the will or stamina to pursue him at that point.

It struck me that both Crow and MacKenzie were still on the loose, two wounded and dangerous animals likely primed to kill, and now I was in that loop.

Clyde, wise horse that he was, moved well away when the shooting started. I whistled him back to me. With night coming on, I needed a fire, needed rest and recuperation. The cave above me, MacKenzie's cave, was a likely shelter. With some effort and pain, I mounted Clyde and headed up the rise toward the black maw of the cavern.

As I rode up, the fading sun on the cliff face made the cave entrance more apparent. "You think MacKenzie has any more wolves in that cave?" I asked Clyde. His shying and head-tossing protests prompted the question.

"Well, we need to check it out, big fella. Don't think I can go on tonight. We'll have to give this one to Crow. Figure we'll be snug in there . . . if it's unoccupied."

Ten feet from it, Clyde intensified his objections, reared back his head and muttered anxiously. Easy, boy, easy," I coaxed. Pulled out the Winchester. "I'll go see if anybody's home," Crow said MacKenzie took off, but I wasn't so sure.

I tied the big chestnut off at a nearby juneberry and entered the cave. It had a big entrance: eight feet tall, about ten wide. The large entrance gave it a sense of depth, but darkness obscured how far. Twenty feet inside, near the center, a small depression glowed red: the coals of MacKenzie's last fire. The air ten feet inside was still relatively warm, guessing about twenty degrees better than outside. It had a feral, musky smell to it. I calmed my breathing, listened.

The cave was silent as a crypt. I crept toward the firepit, picked up an inch-thick piece of wood, one end of it at the edge of the coals still glowing. I blew on the ember end until a flame re-ignited. It wasn't much of a torch, but it'd do. Held it high above my head to let the flame's light reach as far into the cave as possible. The meager flare flickered against part of the back wall which angled deeper, fading into shadows. If wolves were there, or MacKenzie, they kept themselves well-hidden and quiet. Still a little spooked, I kept my guard up.

I found a kerosene lantern perched on a stool-sized rock near the firepit. I thumbed up the lamp's glass and touched the small torch to the wick. Once I adjusted the lantern flame, the cave lit up much better. A pile of firewood lay off against a wall, the angled back wall of the cave tapered to a rough black hole about a foot in diameter that led to deeper parts. Could hear a trickle of water coming from it. The wall to my left had piles of stores: beans, sugar, coffee, looked like jerked meat of some kind, other stuff in sacks. A coarse pad of dried vegetation, a horse blanket on top of it, lay spread some space off from the fire. Took it to be MacKenzie's bed.

No wolves, no MacKenzie, dead or alive, but plenty of evidence they'd been there. I leaned my rifle against the stool rock, threw some wood from the stash onto the coals in the firepit. Indeed, a good place to spend the night, I decided . . . if Clyde and I could stand the smell.

⌛

A sack of dried corn sat amongst MacKenzie's stores, so I coaxed Clyde in with that, plus a bucket of water dipped out of the cold stream that ran on the other side of that hole at the back of the cave. Clyde accepted the conditions after a bit; although, he was still nervous and muttered about it. The warmth inside helped him adjust.

My shoulder ached, but the pain stopped stabbing, and my other ailments were tolerable. Figured I wouldn't die in the night, or sleep much, for that matter. But that was a good thing. As much as I wanted to take some of Asmita's pain potions I brought, I couldn't afford sleep. Could be Crow or MacKenzie might double back.

I completely forgot about my shot boot. Wiggled my toes and felt for them. The big toe and the one next to it hurt some like they were sprung, but all of them were still there, none bled. The only shot-off toe was my boot's. I'd have to find some way to fix my boot as MacKenzie didn't appear to own a pair. I rummaged around his junk and came up with an old patch of buckskin. Alongside one of the walls lay a quiver of arrows and a bow. That piece of deerskin would do just fine to cover my open-toed boot, using the bowstring to cinch it up.

That chore kept me occupied until sundown. Once shed of all the excitement pumping through my veins, I noticed my hunger. I boiled up some of MacKenzie's beans and gathered some of the jerked venison to gnaw on. With the fire leaping in the pit, we were right cozy. Long as I kept it banked, didn't figure any wolves would wander in. I knew that big she-wolf was out there, too, but I never knew a wolf that wanted to be around a fire.

On the other hand, the firelight from the cave could be a beacon to any human having an interest. It still nagged at me that MacKenzie didn't work alone, that whoever hired him would send others. Now that I interfered with his task, they could come after me, too. That made me alert to the possibility. Hell, downright jumpy about it. The whole setup was spooky with MacKenzie and the cave and the wolves. But I couldn't forget Cait was the primary target, her and the Major. I hoped Crow, shot up as he was, continued in his pursuit of MacKenzie and would finally complete his revenge. I worried about Cait. MacKenzie was a madman besides being a hired killer. Even with Turnbow and his men on guard back at the Forked S, I didn't feel she was safe. The killer had an almost superhuman resilience to harm.

MacKenzie was the killer of the Jakes and the Major's attacker, the perpetrator of the events at Cait's, no doubt about it now. He confessed as much that night on the hill and remembering that dreadful clawed gauntlet raised above his head about to disembowel me made me a believer. I hated being delayed by the night and my own infirmities. I knew if Crow didn't catch MacKenzie he'd return to the ranch to complete his work. But it went deeper than just MacKenzie as a mad killer. Someone had sent him. Who and why were the biggest dangers to Cait and the Major.

Reclined against my saddle, the pain dulled, the fire warmed my aching bones. Couldn't keep my eyes from getting heavy-lidded. But I couldn't afford sleep.

I stood and rubbed my face with my hands. Removed my hat to scratch my head, but touching my tender bite wounds removed any veils of drowsiness in my brain. I swore some, picked up the Winchester and headed for the cave entrance.

Stepping to the edge, I moved into the rock shadows on the right to get out of the firelight. Old habits. A light breeze had sprung up after sundown, this one from the south with the promise of further snow melt if it continued into the next day. Not that night, though. With no clouds to hold in the heat, the meager heat from the daylight radiated out into the clear sky leaving the air still frigid. The moon, a couple of days from full, rose like a silver dollar in the indigo sky. It hung about thirty degrees above the horizon, so bright it cast a milky veil across the night sky obscuring all but the brightest pinpoints of starlight. The Dog Star and the Hunter stalked the sky. Over my right shoulder, the Dipper was in its perpetual spin around the North Star. The snow cover reflected the moonlight so brilliantly everything glowed in a ghostly blue light.

The night had a solemn and peaceful beauty, something that quieted my body and soul from all the chaos, pain, and violence of the past few weeks. I leaned back against the cliff face and took a deep breath, sucked in more of that peace, let it spread through me. Let it take out the slow burn of the bullet hole in my shoulder, the itch and sting of the slashes across my chest, the aching thump of those sewed-up rips in my neck and scalp, the throb of my bad knee. I rubbed my knee.

In my reverie, I thought again of Cait, her lightly freckled face, the one-sided curve of her resolute mouth, that chestnut hair and those eyes the color of a mountain meadow in May. Those thoughts and the moonlight worked on my state of being, easing down my fears, self-doubts, and anxiety.

A singular sound brought me crashing back into the cold night: A bass rumble rose to a long alto moan that pierced the night air like the wail of a tortured soul. Its song snatched me with cold terror. I gripped my rifle and searched the landscape for the howl's source. She sat on the ridge of a saddle raising the valley floor higher some three hundred yards to the north: the she-wolf. Even that far off, still huge. In the translucent light, she had no color: black as the ace of spades. She faced the cliff, the cave. Logic told me her eyes weren't visible from that distance, but I swear they blazed back at me, blue and cold and malevolent. How did this beast connect with MacKenzie? Old Long Walker's words came back to me, those of Wil and Asmita. Was this the demon of the Quapaw? The Dire Wolf?

We stood five minutes watching one another. A sound in the cave, a piece of firewood shifting in the flames, grabbed my attention. When I brought my eyes back to the wolf, she was gone. I rushed back into the cave and threw more wood onto the fire to build it high. I sat watching the cave entrance, checked my rifle to make sure a round was chambered. Clyde had heard it, too and danced with concern.

CHAPTER 17

Have to admit I nodded a few times during the night only to jerk back awake when my chin touched my chest or Clyde moved, my heart thumping with dread, my grip on the Winchester across my lap tightening vice-like. Daylight did come, eventually, starting with a dull gray beyond the cave entrance. The darkness lingered longer because thick clouds scudded in sometime in the night. I stirred the fire some, got water for another pot of coffee.

Clyde slept where he stood. I whistled softly to wake him. After a quick breakfast of hot coffee and left-over beans, I saddled him up. We headed out before sunup.

Hadn't gone for more than a mile when I noticed movement at the edge of the daylight. I reined back on Clyde. Stood in the stirrups and peered out across the valley floor. A small dot moved about a mile off, bigger than one man on a horse. I removed my field glasses from their case, adjusted the focus: Team of mules pulling a hay wagon, driven by someone I knew.

"Joe Elkfoot," I said aloud. "What the hell is he doing back out here, and with a wagon?"

I pulled the Winchester out of its boot and laid it across the saddle fork. Kicked Clyde to a trot.

When we got within twenty yards of one another, we both stopped. Elkfoot let the reins slack. I placed the butt of the rifle on my right thigh, the barrel pointed up, my hand gripping the waist, finger on the guard.

"What the hell are you doing out here, Joe?" I asked.

"Still mostly a free country, I hear. Believe I'm allowed to travel where I want, long as I keep in the Territory."

"Don't have a problem with where you go, Joe. Just the timing and why."

161

He laughed softly. "Come out here to collect bodies. Tell you the truth, figured you'd be one of them. Hoping MacKenzie'd be one. Wasn't sure about Crow."

"So, you're surprised I'm alive?" I asked.

"Kinda," he said.

"How'd you know I was out here?"

"Turnbow told me. But I figured you'd come back after Crow. That's why I went home and got my wagon."

He stretched to look back the way I came. "If you're left alive, where's the other two?"

"They got away," I said. "You might still put that wagon to use, though. Both are shot up. Might be dead somewhere by now."

He considered for a moment. "Don't reckon I need to look more past you, at present. You headed back to the Forked S?"

"Yep."

"If those two turn up anywhere, most likely it'd be there." He clucked, slapped the mules' backs with the straps and reined them in a right turn.

That promising wind from the past night continued into the day, building stronger. It blew from the southwest coming at a glance over my right shoulder. Those clouds that came with it pushed well off to the northeast. It wasn't exactly warm, but it was warmer than the day before, and with the wind and the sunshine the snow melted at a good pace. Patches of bare ground grew out of the ice and the trail we were on, not quite a road. It squished up mud beneath the horses' hooves and the wagon wheels. Another day of thawing and we'd slog through a black quagmire. Joe kept the mules at a steady pace, so we wouldn't get bogged down. We rode through the day without talking. The wind, the rattle and groan of the wagon the only noise.

Joe broke the silence. "How'd they get away?"

"Crow tracked MacKenzie to a cave he holed up in. Looked like MacKenzie had a lair for him and his wolves," I answered. "Anyway, they had a shootout. MacKenzie got some payback, put a couple slugs into Crow. I rode up right after it happened. MacKenzie sent one of his wolves after Crow, used that distraction to slip away."

"Sent a wolf after him?" Joe asked. "How bad's Crow hurt?"

"Took one in the side and a leg, his thigh. He brought the wolf down with that Sharps. Apparently, only round left in the buffalo gun; otherwise, I wouldn't be telling you all this. He did shoot the toe of my boot off, though."

Joe clucked, shook his head. "Hard to decide if you're the luckiest sumbitch alive or the unluckiest."

I shifted in the saddle, reached down and rubbed my knee. "I don't know about the luckiest alive but figure the fact that I'm still alive makes me pretty damn lucky."

We rode on. The wind gusted some, I pulled the collar up on the sheepskin. We made another mile before Joe spoke again. "You see any wolves around last night?"

The memory of that black wolf's howl made the wind sliding down the back of my coat feel colder. "Matter of fact, I did. T'was that big she-wolf." I said. "Why'd you ask?"

"Look yonder," he pointed his gloved rein-wrapped left hand to the front left. This side of the tree line, some hundred yards off in the long shadows of the timber, stood the she-wolf, her head lowered like she's sniffing the air. Close enough her blue eyes glowed like sapphires, despite the deep shadows.

"She's been pacing us off in the woods ever since we joined up," he said. "You reckon she's got a vendetta?"

"A what?"

"Vendetta. Means revenge, a blood feud. Learned it from a Sicilian guy I met during the Spanish War. Said it was a common thing where he came from. Seems like that she-wolf might have a reason."

I pulled the Winchester from its boot, sighted it on the wolf, eared back the hammer. Moved the front sight ten feet to her left, squeezed the trigger. A piece of ground erupted in mud and snow as the report from rifle fire rolled through the valley like thunder. The wolf took a sidestep to her right. Not a jump, just a casual step like my action merely annoyed her. I jacked in another round, fired that one off to her right. This time she didn't move, just turned her head towards the new crater the .44 slug left, then back at us. I chambered another round, leveled the gun at her chest. I applied pressure to the trigger, hesitated, then eased off. She trotted off into the woods behind her. She stood her ground, waited. Down the sights, her stare was almost one of arrogance coming back at me. It was like she knew I wouldn't shoot her.

"Did you miss her deliberate, or are you just a bad shot?" Joe asked.

"Both," I said.

"Why's that?"

I kept the rifle at port arms, scanning the woods for any sight of the wolf, knowing that was futile. "Something told me not to."

I immediately felt my answer was weak, foolish. I had lots of reasons to kill that wolf, but something in my gut held me back. Maybe it was the sound of old Long Walker's voice in my head, a visceral fear of my own I couldn't explain.

"Well, don't believe she'd hesitate to kill you," Joe said. "You had your shot, better hope it's not your last. Can't turn your back on a she-wolf. They're crafty, more devious than your male. Likely, she'll be back, and when you least expect it."

I knew he was right.

Clyde tossed his head, stamped his front hooves to the left trying to tell me he was tired of standing there, restless, wanted to move on. Figured he must've caught scent of that she-wolf. Something nagged at me, too. Something in Joe's words. Couldn't put my finger on it, but a surge of dread raced through my veins, sent a tremble down my legs.

"Figure we got more'n four hours or so back to the Forked S," Joe said. "Only a couple hours or so of sun left. We should camp, give the animals a rest. Hate to travel in the dark with that big black wolf lurking around. She might've rounded up some more friends."

Joe's idea to stop for the night was best, but panic kept rising inside me. Cait was still in danger, with MacKenzie still out there. All of them back at the ranch house were, even with Crow Redhand still after him. Especially with Crow Redhand still after him. I decided to go on alone. Reason told me I shouldn't, that I should stay behind with Elkfoot, but reason had left me, overcome by a sheer flood of trepidation.

"You camp. I've got to get back to the Forked S."

"Why you in such a fright?" Joe asked.

I couldn't be sure Joe Elkfoot wasn't a part of the whole conspiracy forming in my head. Hell, that kind of thinking may've only been wild speculation on my part built more on reaction than cause. Big gaps in the whole scheme lay void of facts. All I knew for sure at that moment was a loud whisper in my head to get back to Cait.

"Not sure," I answered. "Just a gut feeling that something back at the ranch isn't right. I gotta go on. You'll come on back tomorrow?"

Joe raised his eyes from under the brim of his hat, had a slight smile. "Why, you think I wouldn't?"

"To be honest, Joe, I'm not so sure you and Crow aren't a part of all this. Believe you're out here to help him. Just a lot of questions left unanswered. Tell you this: you find Crow and help him escape, you'll get prison time for aiding and abetting a felon."

I dug my heels hard into Clyde's flanks. Knew I probably couldn't count on Elkfoot showing up back at the Forked S. Hell, him and Crow were cousins. Blood amongst the Indians was thicker than water, especially when it came to carrying water for a white man.

CHAPTER 18

he remainder of the day moved into a clear night, the moon coming up with it. That milky ribbon of stars the Cherokees called the Dog Trail; the Choctaw, the Spirit Road, arced across the dome of the sky from horizon to horizon, clear even through the moonlight. The south wind stopped, and what heat blew up with it escaped into the skydome, turning the snowmelt to a re-frozen crusty terrain.

I pushed Clyde harder than I should've, but he bowed his neck and kept after it, not complaining. We glided through the darkness at a lope, his breathing rhythmic and unlabored. Expected to come in sight of the ranch before midnight, that sense of urgency still clinging to me. The persistent nag in my mind set off my preservation sense, that intuitive instinct, whatever you wanted to call it. Only this time it wasn't about me, it was about Cait and the others.

Thoughts rolled on during that steady lope through the night. They tumbled through my brain like a rock slide down a twisting slope: Cait's trouble with those dubious partners of her late husband and the killing of him. The way Emily Standback described her father. They both seemed connected—crime bosses back in Chicago. Emily's dad wanted the Major's land, and when he couldn't buy it from him, must've finagled Standback into marrying his daughter. Not a hard thing to accomplish considering her beauty and charms. Hard to figure why the Major was attacked unless it was just angry vengeance on MacKenzie's part. That didn't make sense, though, even if he was crazy. Pro killers don't usually act on emotion, it's bad for business. But MacKenzie was crazy like a fox. He liked to kill, no doubt about that, but his method played into the minds of the locals. He stirred up a great deal of fear in the Quapaw, which also created a distraction. I think that's more the reason he killed the Jakes the way he did. He may've had some incentive, sure. On the other hand, maybe that was part of the plan, too. Appeared to me the man who tried to kill Cait was also the man sent to kill the Major, and that one of Cait's husband's partners was Emily's father. But I kept coming back to why he'd want his son-in-law killed. He already had the land, or at least, his daughter did. Why did it suddenly become more important to get it now than wait for his daughter to inherit it?

The house was mostly dark. Light shone from the parlor windows, and a dimmer one lit an upstairs window, that of the Major's bedroom. Hard to tell who, if anyone, was up. I rode Clyde to the barn.

The barn door rattled when I pushed it across the ice-crusted rails it hung on. As I hurriedly led Clyde into the dark maw and turned to pull the door closed behind us, lamp light reflected off the wood. Behind me, Bennie held a lantern high with his left hand, a shotgun pointed at my direction in the other.

"Bennie, it's Deputy Smoak," I called to him.

He lowered the shotgun's barrel. "Sorry, Mistuh Smoak. I's a bit nervous. Been some strange goins on here tonight." He walked toward us, holding the lantern out to inspect Clyde. "Yo hoss needs tendin." He said it as a statement, not a question.

"What kind of strange things?" I asked. My unease for Cait deepened.

"Well, for one thing, that Quapaw woman, Asmita, she come out here last night, built her a fire right here in the barn, right over there." He pointed to a black spot in the middle of the dirt floor. "She started mumblin things, tossin stuff into that fire. I don't know what they was, suppose t'was some of her witch fixins. I says to her, 'Look here, woman, you goin burn this place down.' But she ignored me, went on with it.

Smelled sumpin awful. Upset all the stock." He got quiet, shook his head, eyes downcast.

"What else?" I asked.

"Well, suh, long about dark, hosses started getting agitated out in the corral, like they do on the trail when they smells a bear or something. I takes my Greener outside for look-see, and sho' nuf, out on that pasture ridge sits a wolf in the moonlight plain as day. Not no ordinary wolf, but a big black one. Thought it was a bear at first, then I could see it was a wolf. Just stood there watchin me. So, I walk out past the barn and corral, maybe a hundred yards away from that wolf, and fire off one barrel of that ten gauge. Too far off to hit it, but thinkin to scare it off. Didn't work, though. Just kept standing there lookin at me.

"Mistuh Turnbow, he come out t'bunkhouse, hollered over askin why's I shootin. Wolf was still out there, so I pointed. He called to Husker to bring their rifles. They saddled up and rode after that wolf, but it had took off. Big wolf like that could take down a cow by itself. An' y'got one wolf, they's probly mo'. Anyway, they rode off after it, ain't come back. Be hard to hunt a black wolf in the dark."

I sucked in air and blew it out, thunderstruck. Had that she-wolf outpaced me by several hours? How was that even possible? And why'd she show up back here? Could there possibly be two of them?

"Take care of Clyde, Bennie."

I left the barn, walking fast, almost at a run, to get inside the house. I hoped to hell no harm had yet come to Cait. Strange goings on by Asmita, but then, she was a strange woman. Suppose she went to the barn to perform her ritual to both get out of the cold and get out of the sight of Emily Standback. Thinking back on Asmita's behavior, suppose there was no love lost between them. Asmita had been with the Major long before he brought home his bride.

169

I crept onto the porch. No guard posted, maybe they set up inside to get in out of the cold. Grabbed the knob to enter unannounced, thought better of it and knocked softly. Didn't want to stop a load of buckshot if that guard was sitting inside. I got no response. Knocked again, this time a little firmer. Waited a quarter minute, but still nothing. Took a deep breath and turned the knob, put my shoulder to the door.

Athena greeted me, tensed at the base of the stairs, teeth bared, and a threatening rumble coming from her throat, giving me no uncertain terms.

"Easy, girl, easy," I said, my hand extended palm-down in a gesture of—I hoped—peace and friendship. She slacked off a bit when she heard my voice but kept her wariness.

"It's me, your old friend Jubal." I held my fingers out for her to sniff, which she did. That mollified her some, but she stayed on guard. I knew not to make any sudden moves.

"Where's Cait?" I asked the dog. Didn't really expect an answer but hoped the sound of my voice continued to work on her. No one in the parlor, dining room, up the staircase.

"Cait?" I called. No answer. "Emily?"

Asmita came to the railing at the top of the stairs the long barrel of her shotgun pointed down at me.

"Asmita, it's Deputy Smoak." She greeted me with indifference. "Where's Miz McDonald, Miz Standback?"

"Out back," she answered. "Hear noise, go to check."

"That where your guard is, too?"

"Yes. They all go. Leave big dog here to guard front door, me to shoot."

"How's the Major?"

"Same."

I went through the house to the kitchen's back door. Athena followed. "You stay," I said to her. "Stay at the front door." I gestured in that direction. She cocked her head, didn't advance as I slipped outside, closing the door behind me.

The moon, then past its zenith, gave the patchy snow-covered ground a pearly cast cutting the shadows with sharp lines, deep and dark. I drew my Colt there in the gloom of the back porch. The back of the barn and the horse corral were off to my right, some fifty, sixty yards out. A smoke trail drifted from the bunkhouse chimney another thirty yards beyond that. Two other structures were spaced off to my left: a smokehouse and a carriage shed. Nothing moved anywhere.

From the half-open door of the smokehouse, a dim light flicked on from inside. There almost immediately followed a clatter as something heavy fell against wood and metal. I ran to the building's door, flattening myself against the outside wall. "Cait?" I called out.

"In here," came the reply. It was Emily Standback.

I pushed the door open the rest of the way, entering cautiously, my gun at the ready. An electric light bulb, dangling from the center rafter beam by a single cord, cast a stark light across the room. Its sway created shifting shadows in its wake. The lump of a man lay on the floor, an overturned table and a clutter of various tools spread around and on him. The two women stood apart from him, each pointing a firearm at the other—Emily held a pistol, Cait her Henry.

The scene confused me. "What the hell's going on?"

Cait spoke first. "Glad you showed up. Emily's about to kill me."

"Other way around, Deputy Smoak," Emily said. Her eyes shifted to the man on the floor. "She butted Brooks there in the back of the head with her rifle. Then turned on me. She was ready to pull the trigger until you showed up."

"The Standbacks hired MacKenzie," Cait said. "They're part of those who had my husband killed."

That fit part of my suspicions, but something didn't seem right. I moved a little closer to Cait, my gun hand wavering between the two women. Emily sensed my bias. "Ask her who attacked Justice," she said.

"MacKenzie did," Cait cut in. "Deal gone bad. You know yourself he's a madman."

"MacKenzie didn't attack my husband," Emily said. She gestured towards Cait with the barrel of her .38. "It was her and her pack of dogs. She thinks Justice and I were part of those behind her husband's death."

Turnbow slipped in through the door behind the women and stood listening in the shadows. He dipped his head to acknowledge me.

"I don't *think* it, I *know* it," Cait said. "You and that bunch back in Chicago and your daddy, want my land back. Probably because you want to mine the zinc on it."

"Hold it, hold it," I said. "You've found zinc?"

"Big deposits. Lead, too. Bigger than the Colemans'. She didn't know that when the Major sold us that parcel. Now she wants it back."

The pieces of this puzzle were getting scattered in my head. "Cait, there were dog tracks all around where those cows were killed."

Her eyes bore hard into mine, then back to her adversary. "Don't buy into her story. Yes, my dogs and I were there, but it was after those cattle were attacked. We headed back to the cabin. I was afraid whoever or whatever killed those cows might still be out there somewhere."

"You mean MacKenzie and his wolves. I believe yours was the deal gone bad," Emily said. "That's why he cut up your animals with that claw of his like he did those cows. Maybe you reneged on his fee."

That surprised me. "How'd you know about MacKenzie's claw?"

Her pause only lasted a second, but it was long enough. "Mister Turnbow told me," she said.

172

"That right, Cole?" I asked the man in the shadows.

He stepped into the light, moved slightly behind me. "Don't believe I did." Emily's expression didn't show surprised to see him.

Her eyes shifted to him then back to me with uncertainty. "Why you must have." Her half-smile twisted one corner of her mouth. "Well, somebody did. In all the confusion, I—"

"None of us said anything about a claw," I said. "Because nobody knew about it at the time. You know anything about a claw, Cole?"

"First I heard of it," he said.

"I only knew of it was a few days ago, when he tried to use it to kill me," I said.

"That night on the roof," she said. "He cut your chest with it. That's when I knew about it."

"I didn't see it. I thought it was a knife."

She grew quiet. "Guess you've figured it out, Deputy. Too bad." She smirked at Cait and me.

"So why don't you put down that pistol," I said. "We'll get this all sorted out. I'm sure your father has a good lawyer."

"Nothing to sort out," she said. "Mister Turnbow, please shoot Deputy Smoak."

I heard the pull of the pistol against leather and the cock of the hammer. I twisted to my left and fell backward, swinging my Colt toward the top hand. He fired first. The slug burned a grazing path across the front of the sheepskin, chest-high. I returned fire, my shot striking Turnbow high on the right side of his chest sending his pistol flying from his hand. He crumpled to the floor, and I jacked the hammer of my Colt back ready to fire again. He writhed in pain.

Almost simultaneously, a volley of shots exploded in the confines of the smokehouse. Not sure how many—three, four. When I turned my attention away from the foreman, Emily Standback lay slumped against the back wall as if flung there,

Cait lay on her back at my feet, and Wil walked toward us, smoke coming from his pistol barrel. The cowboy Brooks still lay face-down, but his right arm was now extended, a pistol in his lifeless hand.

"You awright?" Wil asked, counting the fallen.

I scrambled on my knees to Cait. A patch of red spread from her left side at her ribs. I put my hand on it to stem the flow, lifted her head in my other hand. Her eyes were opened, semi-focused. "Cait?" I said.

Wil toed Emily and Brooks with his boot. "These are dead," he said. Went over to where Turnbow sat cussing and moaning, picked up his discarded gun, squatted next to him and checked him for any other weapons. "Don't believe he's got any more fight in him."

"Go to the house and call the doc," I said. "Tell Asmita to get out here, fast."

He left at a trot.

CHAPTER 19

he lines around Asmita's eyes deepened when she saw Cait's wound, her wrinkled old lips pursed with concern. She gave Cait a quick examination, her dark eyes darted amongst the others. Couldn't tell if she was upset or pleased about the demise of her mistress. Turning back to Cait, she said, "Take to house, lay on table in kitchen." She went over to Turnbow. "You later," she told him then added matter-of-factly, "You live."

"Wil," I said. "Keep an eye on Cole, till Doc gets here."

"Doc'll be here in about an hour," he said.

I carried Cait into the house and laid her on the kitchen table per Asmita's orders. She stopped most of the bleeding once we got her inside.

Cait was conscious and in a lot of pain when Doc Riley arrived, though not totally coherent. Asmita had done what she could, but the wound was serious beyond her abilities. After his initial exam, Doc said, "No exit wound. Bullet hit a rib and glanced down inside her abdomen. No telling what kind of damage it did there. If it fragmented, could be worse. Looks to be some internal bleeding."

He sighed, wiped his bloody hands on a towel Asmita handed him. "I'm gonna have to open her up and explore, try to get that bullet . . . or its pieces, out of her." He searched in his bag, pulled out a bottle of chloroform.

I headed for the smokehouse to check on my scout and his prisoner. Wil was pressing a bandana to the wound, most of the bleeding had stopped. My bullet hit Turnbow square on the right collarbone, deflected down into his right arm where it impacted and broke the two lower bones. The cowboy was in a lot of pain but in no danger of dying. Asmita sent some of her pain potion along with me. Turnbow sat leaning against a wall, sweating a lot and gritting his teeth; a tough ole cowboy not given to admitting pain. Still, he didn't argue about the potion, swallowing the whole vial in one gulp. Didn't even choke at the smell and taste.

Squatting next to Turnbow, I surveyed the room – Emily Standback still lay splattered against the back wall. Brooks face-down in a pool of his own blood. Wil removed the pistol from Brook's loose hand and sat it atop the righted table. He caught my look, must've known my question, spoke before I asked.

"Just as I come in the door, Brooks there was raising his gun to shoot. Didn't know what was going on in here, so it surprised me. Not sure he's going for me or Miz McDonald. Anyway, he fired, missed us both. I'd already drawn before I came in, so I fired back at him. As you can see, I didn't miss."

"Guess you're feeling better," I said.

He scratched an ear. "Not too bad." Gave a chin point toward the bloody back wall. "Cait shot her, she shot Cait. Guess when the shooting started, it set 'em off." Shook his head. "Miz McDonald gonna live?"

"Doc's working on her. Wound's bad."

Asmita's brew started to work on Turnbow. The tightness of his face loosened some, he breathed easier, and his eyelids drooped.

"What's this all about, Cole?"

He lifted his lids a little, half-focused eyes finding me. Might've been the start of a grin on his face, but it turned into a grimace. He cursed. "It was the Missus," he said. "It's like the McDonald woman said, but she's only partly right. Miz Standback's daddy sent MacKenzie to kill McDonald, only the missus wanted more, wanted to get rid of the Major, too. He didn't have nothing to do with tryin to kill Miz McDonald."

"What'd she gain by doing that?"

"Control of the whole ranch, I guess. Ain't sure what all but I think it was something more, someone else."

"What, the Major has a mistress?"

"Other way around. Missus had a lover."

"What? Who?"

"Ain't someone you'd expect."

"Hell, I didn't expect *any*." I waited.

"Joe Elkfoot," he said.

"Ho-ly crap," I said. "Are you sure about this?"

"Sure as I'm sittin here with a bullet hole in me. She figured, long as MacKenzie was here to do one killin, he could do another, that'un bein the Major. It 'uz convenient. Course, MacKenzie didn't want no two for one deal, she had to pay him exter."

I was stunned, never expected this at all. "What's your part in all this, Cole? And Brooks?"

He chewed on the inside of one cheek. "I come up from Texas, cowboyed for some outfits down there. Had to leave after I killed a man in Denton, son of a senator. Wouldn't've made no difference had I known that beforehand, though. He's a smart-assed little prick who offered up one too many insults to me in a bar one Saturday night, so I killed him. Wasn't no fair-fight, I just cut him open, spilled his guts out onto the bar floor sawdust.

"Anyway, I's drunk but sober enough to know I'd hang quick. I took off, headed up here to Indin Territory. Ended up working cow pens at a sale barn in McAlester. That's where I met the Major. He's just getting started out, needin hands, so I talked him into taking me on. I's his first. Told him about my troubles back in Texas. Told me, give him an honest day's work, not steal from him, he didn't care 'bout m'history. Ever'thin seemed to work out fine until he brought the missus back to the ranch."

Turnbow, in his woozy state, slumped some to his right. The pain from that movement brought him back around with a few choice cuss words. I nudged him to continue where he left off. "Go on," I said.

"Couple years went by when I started noticing things with her and Joe Elkfoot. Don't know how long they'd been carryin on before I took notice. I thought, sure as I'd seen what was goin on, the Major would, but it appeared he didn't. Think Asmita knew, too. She feared the Missus too much to say anything. I never said nothin neither, but I's thinkin about it. She noticed my noticin and called me out on it. Told her it weren't none of my business, but she didn't trust me. Figured with my loyalty to the Major, I'd spill the beans sooner or later. Told me she knew I's wanted man in Texas, and that she had the means to send me back there, or worse. After this MacKenzie thing come up, the Jakes' killins, the Major, I believed her. Then she paid me a bonus. Said there's more where that came from if I lined up with her."

He sighed and fell silent. His eyes appeared a little glassed-over, his face muscles fell slack. I thought he died until he suddenly sucked in some air and spoke up again.

"Brooks there was just stupid. Stupider than me, anyways. Weren't nothin wrong with Brooks she could blackmail him with. He's just a simple cowhand. A cowhand without much smarts. Fifty dollars looked pretty shiny to him. That's what she bought him off with. Dumb sumbitch died for fifty dollars."

"Husker and Wiley in on this, too?"

"Naw. Husker's a good man." His words started coming out in a slur. "Wiley's an asshole, but he don't have no dealings with the Missus."

Turnbow faded fast at that point, his eyes rolled back, his head drooped. I slapped him a couple times on the cheek.

"Hey! Hey! What about Elkfoot? Was he in on the Major's attack?"

He roused some, eyes unfocused. "He's . . . He's . . ." He drifted off for good.

I needed to get to Elkfoot but just wasn't up to the ride back to them that night. Besides, I didn't want to leave Cait, until I knew she's out of the woods. Daylight would be soon enough to go back after Elkfoot.

I picked up the foreman's hat and put it on his head so it covered his eyes. Spoke to Wil. "Did you know any of this about your cousin?"

"Which one?"

"Joe," I said with exasperation. "That he was carrying on with Emily."

He shrugged. "Yeah, I guess a little. Joe's always been kind of a skirt chaser. Never knew Miz Standback was out to get rid of the Major, though. Doubt Joe was involved with that."

"Maybe, maybe not," I said. "Doesn't look good for him though."

Wil turned his head and spit.

"Let's get Turnbow outta here. We can move him into the big house for the time being. Get Doc and Asmita to look at him after they finish up with Cait. He's gonna be out for a few hours, anyway."

We got him head and foot, turned him to his left side so's not to grab his wounds. At the house, Asmita pointed us to the dining room table. Doc ignored us, intent with his surgery on Cait.

"How is she, Doc?" I asked.

"Got the internal bleeding stopped, part of her liver was damaged. Bullet didn't fragment much, so I think I got the pieces out. She's alive, but not by much. Lost a lot of blood. That's my biggest concern right now. Sepsis is next in line.

Next twenty-four to forty-eight hours are critical. We'll just have to wait."

"Move her my bed," Asmita said. Pointed to a room off the kitchen.

"Let her body settle down from the surgery for about an hour first," Doc said. "I'll keep an eye on her, let you know when we can move her."

⏳

She made it through the night. Some of her color returned, and Doc was cautiously optimistic—his words—but still called her critical. Nothing I could do, so I saddled up Clyde to head back to where I left Joe on the trail. Wil wanted to join me. But first, we went out to the bunkhouse. Curious that Wiley or Husker didn't show their faces after all the noise of the previous night.

Wiley was cooking up breakfast for the crew when Wil and I walked in, said Husker was in the barn doing morning chores when I asked. "You didn't hear anything last night?" I asked the cook.

"Hear what?" He kept at scrambling eggs, turning bacon.

"Gunshots."

Wiley turned to us, Husker came in through the cook room outside door. He was ashen, out of breath.

He paused, unsure what to say, how to begin. "Missus is dead," he finally spit out. "Brooks, too. In the smokehouse, I seen 'em when I went in there to get—" His wide-eyes searched mine, Wil's, Wiley's. Pulled off his hat and laid it on the table, sat down. "They been shot dead."

"The hell you say," Wiley said. His expression confused. "Where's Turnbow?"

"Up at the ranch house. He's been shot, too," Wil said.

I still didn't know if Emily's corruption extended to Wiley and Husker even with Turnbow vouching for them. I suspected not. "He's gonna live. That's the good news. Bad news is he and Brooks worked for the Missus. She's the one tried to have the Major killed, hired MacKenzie to do it."

"Well, I'll be damned," the cook said. He turned back to his eggs and bacon, which were starting to burn. I filled them in on the rest of the story concerning Elkfoot and all. Wiley snorted at that news, Husker shook his head.

"I need you boys to go up to the house and help Doc and Asmita with whatever they need. Miz McDonald was shot and is in bad shape. Mainly, I need you to keep an eye on Turnbow."

"What're you gonna do?" Wiley asked.

"Wil and I are going back out to get Joe Elkfoot." I didn't mention Crow.

"What about them bodies?" Husker asked.

"Leave them, they're not going anywhere. Go to the house, ask Doc to call the Sheriff in Miami and the undertaker, too."

⧗

As Wil and I rode off, snow was already picking up its melt from the day before. Wind held steady out of the southwest, the sun was bright. If Joe started out at sun-up, we'd meet up in a couple hours.

It occurred to me I was a lone white man about to meet up with two men both related, both Quapaw. Three, if Crow showed up at Joe's wagon in the night. Never any problems or issues with any Indians, never tried to interfere with their ways. Still, it remained, and probably always would remain, Indian versus whites. Not necessarily in an open hostile sense, but somewhat suspicious and apprehensive, especially with lawmen. Human races moved along in the world inclined to distrust one another, despite any good faith actions on either side. Suppose that'd been true about any conquered people throughout human history. The conquerors expected the conquered to become one of them. Sometimes that was a good thing in the long run, sometimes not.

About an hour into our ride, my trepidations spilled out. "What'm I riding into, Wil?"

I wanted his eyes to meet mine, he spit to his left. "You wondering whose side I'm gonna be on?" he asked.

"Reckon I am."

"We've ridden together a few weeks now. Been through a few things. Major vouched for me. That still not enough?"

All true but didn't erase my doubts. "I'm a white man; you and Joe and Crow are Quapaw cousins. I know what that means."

He grew quiet, kept his eyes on the horizon to the front of us. I held my tongue, waited for his answer.

"Coming yonder," he said. Pointed with his chin.

I saw movement in the distance. Took out my field glasses. Still too far to make out many details, but it was Elkfoot alright.

⧖

We stopped ten yards apart. Wil and I stayed mounted, A saddled horse was in tow tied to a back rail. Crow's. There was blood on the saddle.

Joe kept to the wagon seat. "You feeling better, Wil?" he asked.

"I'll live a while longer," his cousin answered.

"Surprised to see you boys out here this morning."

No one in the wagon bed, at least not visible. I pulled my Colt, laid my wrist across the horn. "You pick up an extra horse since I left you?"

"Yep," Joe answered. "It's Crow's. He's under that buffalo blanket in the bed. Believe he's passed out. Come into my camp about midnight, shot full of holes, near bled to death and froze. Might be by now."

From the wagon bed, Crow cussed a blue string, most directed at and about me. He ended it with a single statement: "I ain't dead."

"Guess I's wrong," Joe said. "Seems to be doing better."

"I'd hate to hear how you'd feel about me if I was the one who shot you," I yelled toward the wagon bed.

"You did, you sumbitch," he called back.

I raised my pistol, cocked the hammer.

Joe put up a hand. "Not armed," he said. "I took his weapons. Afraid he'd wake up in a delirium and shoot me."

I swung off Clyde, walked to the side of the wagon and threw back the buffalo hide, my gun aimed at his face. Joe had patched him up some. "Yeah, well I believe you're one up on me with who shot who."

He grumbled, but let it go, too weak to argue. "Did you catch up with MacKenzie, finish him off?" I asked.

He shook his head.

I re-holstered and turned back to Joe. "Had trouble back at the ranch," I said.

He waited.

"There was a shooting," I continued. "Brooks was killed, Turnbow shot, Miz McDonald and Miz Standback . . . Miz McDonald's hurt bad, may not live." I cleared my throat. "Miz Standback is dead."

Joe's jaw set firm. His eyes came down to mine, cold and black. "Who shot who?"

"Looks like Emily tried to set Cait up. She lured Cait out to the smokehouse aiming do away with her. Seems she had some confederates—Brooks and Turnbow. Apparently, had Brooks along to do her dirty work, but Cait was on to them. She cold-cocked Brooks and confronted Emily. They had a stand-off. That's when I came in, then Turnbow, then Wil behind him. It came out Emily and her father hired MacKenzie to kill Cait. Then Emily hired MacKenzie to kill her husband, but he botched both. I may've gotten in the way some."

I filled Joe in on the rest of it. "Cait come out the better of the two, but not by much," I said. "Cait may not live."

Joe let all that settle in. Kept his gaze on the mules' backs, his expression stone.

"Something else came up," I said. "Word is you and Emily . . . Well, you were mixed up with her."

He lifted his eyes off the mules to Wil, then down at me. "You think I'm in on all this?"

I scratched the side of my face, reset my hat. "Well, thought had crossed my mind. It doesn't look good, Joe."

"Yeah." He rubbed a gloved forefinger under his nose, sniffed. "S'pose that's true."

I headed back towards Clyde, said over my shoulder to Joe, "Let's get on back to the Forked S, get all this sorted out."

I caught a flicker of motion from Wil, heard the click-back of the hammer on his Scofield. "Put it down, Joe," he said.

Elkfoot leveled his double-barrel at me, the web of his left thumb laid across the hammers. If I drew, I'd be a dead man.

"You ear those back, I'll have to shoot you," Wil said.

Elkfoot hesitated, his grip tightened on the shotgun. He moved his index finger inside the triggers guard.

Wil extended his arm, pointing straight at Elkfoot's heart. "Dammit to hell, I ain't fooling, Joe."

I hooked my quivering thumbs into my belt. "This ain't helping you, Joe."

He shifted his eyes between me and Wil, breathed heavier. Weighed his options. I hoped Wil wasn't doing the same.

"You'd shoot your kin, Wil?"

"Ain't my first choice, Joe, but you killing this deputy would just be cold murder. Kin or not . . ." He glanced quickly at me. "White man or not, that just ain't right. Besides . . . the

Major, Sara and Sam and Elam, young Zeb, there's been enough."

A tense few moments passed while we all considered. Joe lowered the shotgun, laying it across his thighs. "This ain't the way she wanted it, but it'll end up the same."

He shook his head slowly, side-to-side. "Took me a while to see her scheme, I's blinded by her wiles. Time I finally caught on, it was too late. Sucked us all in. Me, Turnbow, Brooks."

Wil lowered his pistol, too, resting his wrist on the saddle horn while Elkfoot talked.

"Wanted me to kill the Major and Miz McDonald but told her I wouldn't do it. I saw what she's doing. Get an Indian to do the killing, wouldn't nobody blame her. She'd just have to deny everything. Indian don't stand a chance with the law. If it's choosing between a pretty, rich white woman and an Indian, Indian's gonna lose.

"Emily did all this. I never wanted to be a part of it. But that woman has . . . had a way about her, almost magical. She's a hard woman to resist."

He paused as if to give us time to reflect on it. The face of the general's daughter back in Colorado flipped up in my mind.

"She wanted me to do the killing, but that was one thing she couldn't talk me into. That was her first plan. When I wouldn't go along, she got in contact with her father. He sent MacKenzie. Think that's what the old man wanted to do all along but went along with her logic. Getting me to do it would've saved them all a lot of trouble . . . and expense."

"What talked you out of it?" I asked.

He stared off to the woods. "I liked the Major. Even though I's messing with his woman, considered him a friend. Always felt guilty about what I's doing, tried to break it off several times but like I say, she's a hard woman to resist.

"Then MacKenzie showed up and I knew what he was. And I knew I's probably on the list, too. I's no longer any use to Emily or her dad, and I knew too much. But the Jakes killings threw them off-guard, created more investigation than they wanted, like you showing up. It complicated things."

He tapped the barrel of the shotgun with fingernails, sorting thoughts. "They got lucky, though, when that old Quapaw tribal story of the Dire Wolf popped up, Asmita's reactions and all, Emily decided to use it to her advantage. Didn't matter how many killings they had, they could be blamed on an insane killer who thought he was the Indians' legendary monster come to life."

He fell silent at that point. We all did.

Crow was the first to break the hush. "You'uns just gonna let me die out here? I need to get to a doc."

CHAPTER 20

MacKenzie could feel the bones grinding when he moved his left arm. Not totally useless, but the bullet broke something up inside. Using the arm with the claw was doable only with blinding pain. And it multiplied his rage.

That Quapaw Redhand, who he'd worked with on the ranch, hunted him. Must have something to do with that Quapaw woman he killed. MacKenzie hadn't figured on that, most were too afraid to come after him. He misjudged, and it nearly cost him his life, maybe it would his arm.

Redhand persisted, tracking him to his lair. But MacKenzie put two bullets in him, and with the help of *Makade-ma'iingan,* who sent one of her nephews to attack Redhand, he escaped the Quapaw again.

He managed to make it to his alternate dwelling, a place not as comfortable and large as the other, but more secure, secluded. He hoped the bullets he put in Redhand would eventually kill him, but just in case, he covered his tracks.

The wound worsened and sent him in and out of consciousness. He couldn't recall what time had passed. At one point he realized, if he was going to survive, he needed to burn the wounds, seal the holes front and back.

He built a fire, and with his knife blade golden-hot, pressed it to the round cavity in his back. Agony seared into him, the smoke from his blackened hide filling his nostrils like the stench of burning death. Sweat poured from him like drops of blood, yet he did not cry out. Gasping for air, he reheated the blade and pressed it to the crater in his chest. Pain swirled through him like a whirlwind of fire, but rather than scream, he let the choke from his burning flesh sweep him into blackness.

Makade-ma'iingan walked slowly toward him out of the gloom. She circled him, her head low, her cerulean eyes lancing into him like arrows. Her voice spoke in his grandmother's tongue. "Myeengun, you must rise and finish your work, rip out the throats of the whites who oppress and pursue us. The spirit of your grandmother, the spirits of all your people, demand it. I am Otshee monetoo, and I command it."

She lunged, sinking her yellow teeth deep into his chest where he'd pressed the knife. The flash of pain struck him like a sudden bolt from angry clouds. It reached so much beyond his level to endure, that this time he did cry out. His feral howl screaming out into the cold night, rolling through the valley like a keening from the damned.

He awakened shivering, quaking so violently that all his bones ached, not just those crunching in his shoulder. The cave was dark, the fire reduced to a few dim red embers. The night cold swept in through the cave opening to grip him like the clutch of *Gitchi-gami*'s waters that day as a boy he'd fallen through the ice. He could not stop his trembling. Since that day, cold had never challenged him, but this night his sweat-soaked buckskins hung on him like those sheets of ice. He didn't know how long he lay unconscious, but long enough for the raging fire, without and within him, to die and the cold air to encase him.

His hands shook so severely he could barely place the wood to rebuild the fire. Crawling close to blow on the embers, nausea overwhelmed him, and he retched black blood. But he feebly blew, then again and again. One small flame burst out of an ember alighting some bark. He eagerly blew more, and the flame grew igniting twig branches. The fire sustained, the warmth increased degree by slow degree. He lay in its growing embrace waiting for his shivering to slow. Thirst overpowered him, and he fumbled for his canteen, mercifully finding it within reach. He slept. Hunger awakened him . . . and pain. Bright daylight entered the cave, warm sunlight touching him where the dying fire left off. In his pack, he found venison jerky and gnawed it down.

He didn't know how many days passed, several. There were some provisions in the cave and water. He gained strength, forced himself to stand and move about, gather firewood. The pain lessened enough to at least become ignorable. Enough to where he could concentrate on his rage and hatred. The rancher would die and the McDonald woman, but first, the lawman. MacKenzie figured, where the woman would be, the lawman would be. He would go to the ranch and wait for him, give him a long and torturous death as a sacrifice to *Otshee monetoo*.

⌛

No one saw him slip into the orchard near to the ranch house. The twilight helped, but the activity at the front of the house drew the attention of everyone who may have noticed his slouch toward the trees. The constant pain scattered his concentration and blurred his vision. The scene outside the house confused him: they loaded a woman into a funeral carriage who wasn't dead. Men talked to her and she answered. Other men scattered about, cowhands. Was it Emily Standback or the McDonald woman on the stretcher? Something happened here.

Three men rode off with the hearse. MacKenzie tried to focus. The lawman? Yes, it was the lawman and his partner, the one he thought *Makade-ma'iingan's* nephews had killed. And the third man . . . the Quapaw Redhand.

His head swam. *"Follow them,"* her voice said to him. *"Find an opportunity in the night to kill them all."*

He skulked after them, keeping well-hidden in the woods. The sound of their talk filtered in through the trees as he crept along, but most of it he couldn't make out. They traveled on for some time, deeper into the darkness. He was anxious to attack; however, his injury made him unsure, less confident. He could not find the right spot to make his strike. The lawman and the other were vigilant and edgy. They held their guns at the ready. He heard the lawman say something about Emily Standback being shot. He surmised that was the woman in the carriage. They were taking her to the hospital. That meant the McDonald woman was back at the ranch house with the Major.

Lights of the town ahead made him halt his stalking, letting the group proceed toward the lights. His plan became suddenly clear: he would return to the ranch and kill the rancher and the woman, then wait for the lawman to return, as he knew he surely would.

He breathed rapidly, sweating. The exertion from his long day had left him weak, and despite the pain and hatred that boiled within him, weariness overtook him. He would return to the ranch to kill them all, but first a little rest to regain his strength, to regain his rage for the tasks ahead.

He slept.

oc called the undertaker, Ted Freeman, to take the bodies back to be boxed up. Brooks was planted in the "undesirables" corner of the Baptist Cemetery away from the graves of decent folks. Wiley, Husker, and Turnbow came to see Brooks off, but not much was said. I went along to make sure Cole didn't take off. Not that there was much chance of that. Doc had put him in a sling and a wrap that held his right arm tight to his body. I turned him over to the Ottawa County Sheriff after Brooks's burying. Turnbow's crimes in cahoots with Emily Standback would be under local jurisdiction. But he also faced extradition to Texas for that murder charge. Sheriff Dunbar could hold him until such time I was most likely the one sent to haul him down there.

Freeman took Emily's body back to his mortuary, too. With the Major near dead, her only other next-of-kin was Frank Veneto. It fell on me to send a telegram informing him of his daughter's death. He sent word back he was coming to take his daughter's body back to Chicago. He didn't ask why a U.S. marshal was sending the telegram instead of his son-in-law. My guess is he knew why, knew her death probably wasn't an accident. I hoped retrieving her remains was all he intended to do, but I wasn't sure. He might want to finish the job where MacKenzie failed plus get his daughter's killer. With men like Veneto, business is one thing, revenge another. They carried vengeance like a sword, ready to strike swiftly and silently, especially when it involved retribution for the death of a daughter.

It took eight days, but between Doc Evans and Asmita, Crow pulled through. Although, I believe Asmita was more inclined toward euthanasia than healing when it came to

Crow. Doc didn't totally disagree with the old witch, but his loyalty to his oath prevailed.

Crow lost a lot of blood, but his wounds proved not life-threatening. Still, it took that week before he was well enough to haul off to Tulsa. I parked him in the bunkhouse with Wil and Hector guarding him.

I didn't press anything with Joe Elkfoot. He was just at the wrong place at the wrong time and weak of flesh. But that's a man thing, especially with a good-looking woman who can take advantage of it. Some more'n others.

Cait's fever broke at sunup during my shift to sit up with her. She had more color than the evening before, so I reached over and felt her forehead which was cool. "It's a good sign, but she's not out of the woods," Doc said. She smiled at my touch, blinked drowsily, and went back to sleep. She awoke fully later that morning telling Asmita she was hungry.

"I'd like to get her to the hospital," Doc said. "Missus Dromenko's not as good a caregiver as Asmita, but pretty close. Certainly stronger. Plus, I'll have more time to keep an eye on Cait. I think she's strong enough to make the ambulance ride. I'll call Ted."

Seeing the need and opportunity, Ted Freeman had converted one of his funeral hearses into an ambulance.

"It'll be a slow ride back to town," Doc said. "But a sight more comfortable than one of the ranch wagons. Ted installed a fancy suspension he ordered from a French coach outfit, which softens a lot of the jarring, and his old horses aren't given to spooking . . . no pun intended."

I cared about Cait's comfort, but with Frank Veneto's coming arrival it was more about her safety.

"Wil and I better escort the ambulance, Doc. With MacKenzie still out there, Cait's in danger. And I'm uneasy about what Emily's father might do. If he finds out Cait shot

Emily, he'll want her dead more than ever, and not just for her land and oil shares."

Asmita burst into the room, came straight to Doc. "The Major, he is wake. He ask for Missus."

"Awake?" Doc said as he hurried past her. I stayed in the room with Cait.

⏳

Due to funerals scheduled, Ted couldn't get his ambulance out to the Forked S for two days. That gave Cait more time to strengthen, which she did admirably. Asmita's aromatic soups no doubt helped. None of us inquired about the ingredients.

The Major advanced, too, taking in Asmita's liquid diet.

The morning of the third day, Doc came into Cait's room after looking in on Standback. "Major wants to see you," he said to me.

"You tell him about Emily yet?"

Doc removed his glasses and pinched the bridge of his nose. "Yes. Just that she died, none of the details. Told him you'd fill him in."

I let out a long breath. "Thanks."

"Curious," Doc said. "Major didn't appear to be all that grieved."

I found the same thing when I stood by his bed, holding my hat. His lower lip trembled some, he swiped a forefinger across his nostrils and sniffed when I told him the whole story . . . not including the part about Joe Elkfoot.

"I got no grudge against Cait McDonald," he said. "Disappointed in my men, though, especially Turnbow. Thought I could trust him." He fell silent.

Directly, he coughed into his hand and spoke. "I knew what Veneto was up to, just never thought Emily would take it this far. Didn't even dawn on me that MacKenzie was their hired killer, even when he attacked me. Just thought he was a crazy man."

"He is that," I said.

"You say Redhand saved you from MacKenzie's claw? Wonder if he's still alive?"

"MacKenzie? Was the last time I saw him. Man has superhuman strength. Best we keep guards around the house. Wouldn't hurt to put those dogs of Cait's inside here, too."

"Asmita and I'll be ready for him." He pointed to the old Indian woman sitting in a corner with her shotgun. "Veneto probably won't stop, either. Especially knowing how Emily died. If MacKenzie doesn't finish it, Veneto'll keep sending someone until they do. Has anyone told Veneto?"

"Not that I know of. Only thing I've said, is that Emily was dead. I'm sure the question'll come up. All he's gotta do is ask the undertaker how she died."

"What about Emily shooting Cait?"

"Didn't bring that up."

Asmita slipped out of the room like a midnight owl on the wing. I spun my hat, holding the brim in my fingers, searching for the words to bring up the next subject. Something I didn't think he'd want to hear.

"Did Doc tell you Veneto is coming to take Emily's body back to Chicago?"

The Major coughed, cleared the phlegm. "Probably just as well."

Not the reaction I expected. Asmita came back into the room with a bowl of soup on a tray along with some other edibles I couldn't identify. She promptly ran me out.

⧗

Dread and unease gnawed at my gut all the way back to Miami. It was near the end of daylight before Ted Freeman rolled his ambulance up to the ranch house. Sun was down by the time we loaded up Cait and started back to town. The twilight made the deep woodlands gloomier as we moved along the road. Felt like someone out there was trailing us. Something off the road, a dark shadow moving through the woods. Nothing ever truly visible, though, except maybe by my own apprehension. Just jumpy about that big black she-wolf of MacKenzie's . . . and MacKenzie himself. More imagination than reality, I suppose. Been no indication of the killer for over a week. Besides, more than an even chance Crow's shot with that Sharps had eventually killed MacKenzie.

Despite Ted's fancy French suspension, the ambulance ride wasn't comfortable for Cait, but she endured it with no complaint. Crow probably should've been in the ambulance, too, but I put him a-horse. He complained the whole way. Too bad. No way I was letting him ride in there with Cait.

Sheriff Dunbar sat on a bench outside his office when we came down Main Street. A burly man stood next to him, leaning against the jailhouse wall. He wore a badge, too. Dunbar introduced him as Thomas Hobart. I called the sheriff from the ranch to let him know about when to expect us. Crow went in easily with the deputy. He was eager to get into a cell and lie down. Wil elected to stay at the jail, too.

Cait's ashen face and pain-filled eyes spoke of her weariness when we arrived at the hospital. I followed as the attendants carried her into Dromenko's women's ward. The big Cossack waited, hands-on sturdy hips. She gruffly directed the two terrified men to a bed, all the while accusing and admonishing them for their ham-fisted handling of her patient. Only other patients in the room were a couple of new mothers. They got Cait situated in the bed and beat a fast retreat. Dromenko turned to me. "You lookink worser than when I am last sceink you," she said. I heard disapproval in her voice, some disgust.

"Been a rough few weeks." My tone was sheepish.

"Hmmph," she said.

Cait, despite her discomfort, was trying not to laugh. "You take good care of this lady, Missus Dromenko."

"Bah," she said with a wave of her hand. "Always takink care, even for bad patient. But she beink not bad patient like you, I bet. Now, go."

"Okay." I bent at the bedside, put my hand on Cait's shoulder. "I'll be back to check on you. You're in good hands."

That got a smile from her. Dromenko a little, maybe. Cait whispered, "Thanks."

I headed back to Sheriff Dunbar's jail. Wil was probably ready for some supper. I wanted to get to a hotel room, find a hot bath. When I walked in, Wil sat in a chair, the back of it leaned against the wall over near the heat stove. He held a mug of coffee, smoked a cigar. Sheriff Dunbar sat at his desk leafing through some papers, a lit stogie wedged between two fingers. The small room was thick with the acrid smoke. Next to the gun rack, a telephone box hung from the wall behind the sheriff's desk. They both raised their heads when I came through the door.

I peered down the short hall to the holding cells. "Where's your deputy?"

"Went to get some supper," Dunbar said. "He's gonna take the night shift. About to come get you. Got something you'll wanna know."

He held up his coffee mug. "Mind pouring me another cup?" I took his mug, turned to the pot on the stove. "Get yourself some, too, if you like." I grabbed a mug off the shelf, poured two. Wil held his cup up for a refill. I returned to the desk. The sheriff motioned to the chair opposite.

"Have a seat. Care for a cee-gar?"

I coughed into a hand. "No thanks. What's the news?"

Elbows on the desk, he drew in on the cigar, slowly puffed out a small blue cloud. "Been goin to the train depot every day, see who's coming into town. Three men today, an older man with two apes. Apes wearing suits and bowlers, though. The old man the same, only he had a diamond stickpin through his tie, big as an acorn. Didn't look like your usual folks getting off the train."

He smiled when I raised my eyebrows, but it was a grim smile. "I checked with Otis at the hotel. It's Veneto."

When we brought Brooks in for burying, Turnbow to the Jail, I filled the sheriff in on the situation with Emily and her dad and Major Standback and Cait. The land grab deal, the whole shooting match . . . literally. Don't remember if I told him who shot who. Didn't think I did. He didn't ask. I told him about the pursuit of MacKenzie, mine and Crow's, the latter's bizarre behavior. Didn't get into anything about him and the wolves, though. Not sure why. Guess it just sounded too crazy. Don't think Wil said anything about it, either.

"When did they get here?" I asked.

"Not more than an hour before you did."

So much for assassins in the woods on the way in. That meant the wolf was stalking us. I swallowed some coffee. It tasted like hot tar smelled. "Veneto's here sooner than I thought," I said. "Just looking for the old man, though. Didn't figure on the apes."

"Man like him probably has 'em with him ever'where he goes," Dunbar said. "Could be he figures to see the job finished this time."

We both thought about that a few seconds. I rubbed my knee. "What's the plan?" I asked.

"About to ask you the same thing."

"Don't think this is in my jurisdiction."

"Hell, deputy, stopping killers is in any lawman's jurisdiction."

I half-grinned. "Didn't mean the stopping, only the planning. My plan's simple: try to talk him and his goons into going back to Chicago. Failing that, shoot 'em."

"Kinda what I had in mind, too, only backwards. Think it'd be smarter to shoot 'em first."

I reset my hat, looked at the half-open wooden door leading to the jail cells. "Something else," I said.

"What?" Dunbar took another drag from the cigar, watched the cloud he blew out.

"It's, uh . . . it's . . . well, this is gonna sound kinda strange."

He flicked cigar ashes on the floor. "Strange how?"

"Have you had any reports of wolves?" I glanced over at Wil. He eyed the floor.

"Wolves?" The sheriff smirked at my question. "Whadda you mean?"

"Well, wolves." My voice rose an octave. I shrugged, cleared my throat. "Anybody seen wolves around, especially a big black one?"

Dunbar showed annoyance. "I know about what old Long Walker said about the Jakes, and that old Indin legend, but ain't been no talk of wolves in town outside of from them Quapaw. Said yourself MacKenzie admitted to the Jakes' murders and that attempt on the Major, and how he did it. There's your wolf. Sounds to me you're just spooked by old Long Walker's tale."

Embarrassment scrunched my face. I half-heartedly smiled, nodded. "Could be." I hesitated. "But a black wolf has been stalking . . . well, definitely trailing me. It's a big she-wolf. MacKenzie had a pack running with him when he attacked me. She was the leader. Thing is, she's bigger than any wolf I've ever seen. So, yeah, I'm spooked."

I removed my hat. "These are bite marks, wolf bite marks."

Dunbar sat silently considering what I was telling him. He bit into his cigar, drew in some more smoke. I turned to Wil for corroboration. He cleared his throat before he spoke.

"That day we went after MacKenzie, I don't remember being attacked. Don't remember much of anything until waking up in the bunkhouse a couple days later. Never saw wolves, but the boys in the bunkhouse did. Said that black one was prowling around the ranch house and barn. Turnbow and Husker even rode out after it, said it looked big enough to take down a steer or cow. Now, the legend among my people about the Dire Wolf is a powerful one, heard it all my life. This business with MacKenzie and that black wolf plays in strong with it. And we did find wolf sign where the Major was attacked, and his cows killed. Tracking MacKenzie, too."

"That's all interestin," the sheriff said. "But what's it got to do with Veneto?"

I chanced another swallow of coffee. "Nothing, I guess. Just been on my mind. Figured I'd lay it out for you, in case . . . dunno. I'm gonna go get a hotel room. If I run into Veneto and his boys, I'll tell him you're looking for 'em." Dunbar laughed without humor.

"Talk to Otis at the desk. He's kind of a snooty sumbitch, but he's a useful source for info. Keeps up with everyone's comin's and goin's. Tell him I sent ya. Old Joseph, too. He's the bellman and elevator man. Friendlier than Otis."

"Wil, you coming with me?"

"Think I'll stay here with these outlaws. Thomas Hobart n'me are old friends. We got some catching up to do. Besides, you tend to attract lead."

"Suit yourself. I'm sure Chuck has an extra cell you can sleep in."

"Soon as Hobart gets back, I'm heading home," Dunbar said. "Got a telephone there, too, if you need to get aholt of me."

I took Clyde to the livery behind the hotel. After getting him squared away, I slung my saddlebags over my shoulders, headed around the corner to the front entry. The Coleman Hotel took up a prominent corner on Main Street. Outside of the grain elevator, it was the biggest structure in town, and a sight more elegant. Coleman was a prominent name in these parts. Two brother well-diggers, George and Alfred Coleman, discovered huge deposits of lead and zinc in the area, most of it under Quapaw land. They went from well-digging to mining to millionaires. Lead makes bullets, zinc makes brass.

One man sat in the hotel lobby reading a newspaper when I came through the front doors. Off to the right, through a set of French doors, staff was setting up the dining room for their evening customers. From the looks of all of it, a lot fancier place than most where I'd stayed. A tall skinny man with thinning slicked back hair stood behind the check-in counter as I approached. He wore a shiny dark blue vest over a white shirt and tie. Gave me a cool look. "Good evening, sir," he greeted me without a smile.

"You Otis?"

"Yes sir, I am. How may I help you?"

I pulled back my coat front to reveal my badge. He glanced at it with cold indifference. "Sheriff Dunbar told me you might be helpful in an investigation I'm doing." He raised his eyebrows.

"But right now, I need a room. Looking for a bathhouse, too. You got one here?"

"All our rooms have tubs, *with* running water." I thought his smile was a little condescending. He turned the registration book toward me. "How many nights will you be staying with us?"

"Not sure, yet. At least one." I filled out the register, pulled my letter of credit from my shirt pocket, handed it to Otis. "You take this?"

He took it and read it, frowning. "Certainly, Deputy, ah .. . Smoak." He wrote something in a ledger, handed me back the letter without looking up.

"You had some men check in earlier today from Chicago, man named Veneto."

"Yes." He laid a key on the counter. "You'll be in Room two-oh-three."

"What rooms are they in?"

He considered me further. Didn't think he was going to answer. "They're in the Coleman Suite, top floor." He pointed to an old black man sitting on a stool inside a metal cage. "You can take the elevator if you wish. It's perfectly safe." He eyed my saddlebags. "Do you have any *more* luggage?"

"Everything's here." I patted the leather. "What time do they start serving supper?" I asked.

"*Dinner* service begins at five, sir."

"Dinner, huh? Anywhere in this town, I can get supper?"

He peered down his nose. "Several places, none I'd heartily recommend."

"No, I expect not."

I grabbed the key off the counter and walked to the big staircase next to the elevator, gave the old man a salute. He grinned back, kept his seat on the stool.

I wanted that bath before I went up to see Veneto. Didn't figure they'd do anything in the next hour or so.

CHAPTER 22

I rung the elevator up to the second floor after my bath and change of clothes. "Need to get to the Coleman Suite," I said to the old man as I stepped into the contraption.

He noticed my unease. "First time in an elevator?" he asked as we whined and swayed slowly upward.

"Naw, I rode one in New York City a few years back, and in Denver. Didn't like those ones, either."

"This is the second elevator in the state," he'd said. "Since we been a state. Mistuh Coleman put it in when he built the hotel back in aught-three. I been the onliest operator since. M'name's Joseph."

"Nice to meet you, Joseph," I said, tensing my legs against the slight sway.

I knocked and waited, knocked and waited . . . three times. The Coleman Suite took up the whole fifth floor. Only one door in a short hall when I got off the elevator. Old Joseph said he'd wait in case nobody answered the door.

I returned to the elevator and Joseph. "The men in that suite, they leave recently?"

"Yessuh, took 'em down 'bout n'hour ago. They ain't come back."

"Why didn't you tell me that before you took me up there?"

"You didn't ask about it, suh. Ain't my place t'tell you, you didn't ask."

Guess I had to respect that. "You know where they were headed?"

"Yessuh, believes you'll find 'em in the dinin room. That's where they went when I brung 'em down. Ain't seen 'em leave, but I ain't been in the lobby the whole time, neither."

"Thanks, Joseph." I stepped out of the elevator, pulled two bits out of my pocket and handed it to him before I headed for the front desk. He took it, smiled and tipped his hat.

Otis, hands folded on the counter, watched the lobby. Reminded me of a crow on a fence searching for carrion. He frowned when he saw me walking toward him. "Everything to your liking, Deputy?"

"Couldn't be better, Otis." I put an elbow on the counter and gestured with my head toward the double doors leading to the dining room. "Is Veneto in the dining room?" I asked.

"He is." Otis pointed with his chin. "The older gentleman sitting in the corner."

I figured as much but wanted to confirm it. Only one of his attack dogs sat at the table with him.

"One of his party got up and left about fifteen minutes ago," Otis said. "Went out the front entrance."

A telephone sat at one end of the desk. "Need a favor, Otis. Call Sheriff Dunbar and tell him one of Veneto's men is on the street."

He raised an eyebrow. "Are these men dangerous?"

"As a pit of rattlesnakes."

His eyes widened. He opened his mouth to speak but didn't, grabbed the phone. I headed for the dining room.

Thought Veneto would be bigger. Apparently, his henchmen helped compensate for his stature. The man sitting to Veneto's left had thick black hair slicked back atop a square head. Had a single dark eyebrow above small eyes, a roman nose, small mouth, and broad jaw. Hard to tell how tall he was, the tweed coat he wore fit tight. Even sitting he was much bigger than me.

Frank Veneto, on the other hand, appeared small sitting next to the other man. It was an illusion, making him seem smaller than he was. Sitting or not, he was still short, I'd guess fix six or so. Had broad shoulders, though, and a wide chest.

He wore a thick black beard and mustache cut in the Van Dyck style, the whiskers covering all his chin, but kept short. Eyes were dark, hair a wavy salt and pepper. He didn't notice my approach, chewing on a piece of steak just forked into his mouth. The big fella stopped eating, tensed, his eyes hard on me as he slipped a hand inside his coat. I stopped a yard from the table, regarded the heavy as coolly as I could muster, then smiled at the other.

"Mister Veneto?"

He chewed, looking up at me with indifference. Made a slight gesture with his hand to stay his bodyguard who started to stand. He didn't answer my query.

"I'm Deputy Smoak from the U.S. Marshal's office in Tulsa." I pulled back my coat to reveal the badge. "I heard you were coming to town to retrieve your daughter's remains. I'm sorry for your loss, sir."

He put a napkin to his lips, took a sip of wine. "You come all the way from Tulsa to tell me that?"

"No, sir, I was here on other business when things started happening at the Forked S."

"Then you're here because of my daughter's murder." He didn't bother introducing me to his table mate.

"Well, sir, I was there when it happened."

"I'm told she was killed by Cait McDonald."

"You know Cait McDonald?"

"My daughter mentioned she's a neighbor. I think my firm had some business dealings with her late husband some years back."

"Your daughter shot Miz McDonald. Cait returned fire. It was self-defense."

He dipped his chin almost imperceptibly, spread his lips slightly with half-lidded eyes, took another drink of wine. "What is it I can do for you, deputy?" Dunbar was right about that stickpin, it was huge.

"First, I wanted to pay my respects." I glanced over at big nameless, his eyes on me like those of a stalking cougar, his expression more like a rhino.

"Okay, you've done that." He snapped his fingers at the passing wine steward, held up his glass. "What else?"

The dining room got suddenly warm. I could feel sweat under the band of my hat, a trickle from an armpit ran down across my ribs. Told myself to slow down my talking, not go on so fast. Needed to get my point across without sounding as scared as I felt.

"I don't mean to be insensitive to your grief, Mister Veneto, but I'm hoping you'll gather your daughter's remains and be on the train back to Chicago tomorrow."

He eyed me closely, but I couldn't tell if he was reading my insides. "My son-in-law, Justice, has been badly injured, too, Deputy. But you probably know that. I plan on riding out there tomorrow to look in on him, see if I can get a handle on all these tragedies." The wine steward refilled his glass, Veneto sniffed it and took a swallow, let out a sigh of satisfaction. "And I don't plan on going back to Chicago until I do."

He sat spinning his wine glass by the stem, his mouth hard and tight. Nameless leaned back in his chair, hooked his thumbs in his vest letting his coat spread. A pistol hung holstered under his arm.

I turned to a table behind me where some laughter erupted, hoping that would conceal my swallow, then faced the gangster again. "The thing is, Mister Veneto, I've already got a handle on it." I swallowed again without trying to conceal it. "I know you're involved. I know you hired MacKenzie. I know how you and your daughter planned to eliminate Major Standback and Cait McDonald to get his ranch and her land. I know you're after the minerals there. Colemans tried to buy them out but couldn't."

I shut up, waiting for his reaction. His eyes took on the look of a rattler coiled to strike, his mouth curved in that same deadly smile. Nameless stood, waiting for his boss to give him the word. I stepped back, pulled my coat behind the butt of my Colt, rested my hand on it just in case. Nameless and I traded steely-eyes. The laughing table behind me stopped, the room quieted.

"Sit down, Carlo," Veneto said to his bull. Now he had a name. I let my hand slide from the pistol grip. Tension in the room lessened, folks went back to their meals and conversations, albeit a bit whispered.

"So, you know all these things," Veneto said. It came out as a statement, not a question. He was unconcerned. "What proof?" That snake smile came on him again, but without the eyes. He had me there. Everything I knew was circumstantial, hearsay, even his deceased daughter's confession. Nothing I could arrest him on.

"None," I said. "But it's all true. I know it and you know it. I'll be watching you closely until you leave."

He shrugged, drank some more wine. The snake smile vanished. "Probably a good idea on your part, Deputy. If I was you, I'd want to watch my back, too."

"That a threat?"

He laughed. Carlo laughed. "Nah, just friendly advice."

I walked out of the dining room. Headed to the hospital to check on Cait. Something bothered me: where was thug number two?

The hospital sat two blocks off Main Street. I hurried toward it as fast as my bum leg would carry me, that bad feeling in my stomach increasing with every step. Someone ran toward me, calling my name. Didn't recognize him at first and drew my gun. Within thirty yards, under the dim street lights, I saw it was Wil, out of breath, excited.

"Smoak, they got Turnbow. Broke him out."

206

"What? Who did?"

He bent at the waist, hands on knees, breathing hard. "I dunno." He took in a couple more gulps of air. "I'd gone out to the privy. Got back, Hobart's on the floor, bullet hole through his forehead. I didn't hear a gunshot. Cell was open. Turnbow's gone."

"Crow, too?"

"He's coming out as I's going in." He straightened. "Said it was a fancy-dressed white man, big, tough-lookin. Said Turnbow told the guy about Cait in the hospital, would take him there. Man threw the keys in Crow's cell and they left. That's when I come for you."

I pointed to the hotel. "Go tell the man at the desk to call the sheriff, meet us at the hospital." I broke at a stiff-legged dead run. Turned at Second Street, headed up it toward the hospital two blocks away. Pain in my leg screamed at me, but I ignored it. It was my discomfort or Cait's life.

Half a block from the hospital, within sight of it, a body lay sprawled in the middle of the dark street. I knelt beside it. Turnbow. Dead. Shot in the back of the head. Once Number Two caught sight of the hospital, must've decided he didn't need the cowboy anymore. I heard running footsteps coming up behind me. Spun in a crouch and threw out my Colt. "It's me, deputy." I recognized Wil's voice. He stopped beside me, looked down at Turnbow's body. "Sheriff's on his way," he said.

The building was a two-story brick structure, fifty yards long, half that wide. The main entrance faced Second Avenue, emergency entrance at the back. I figured the killer went in the front like any other visitor.

"Go to the back entrance," I said to Wil. "Cait's on the second floor. Come up the back stairs." He took off. I went to the front entrance. Didn't bother trying to conceal my drawn gun. The first flight of stairs ascended right off the lobby.

Swinging through the door, I took two steps at a time up the stairs. A startled nurse at the reception desk stood and yelled, "Hey!"

The women's ward was an eight-bed room off the central hallway about halfway down. At the second-floor landing, I edged my head around the door frame. The killer was nearing the doorway to the ward. Stepping out into the hall, I raised my Colt in a two-hand grip. "U.S. Marshal. Stop right there!" I yelled.

He turned my way, raised his pistol—a strange thing with a long fat barrel. It chirped, and a chunk of the door frame inches from my right ear blew off, pieces of it stabbing into my neck and cheek. The Colt boomed as I returned fire, but I missed. He aimed for his next shot. I dove to my left and fired, this time the bullet caught him in the knee. The momentum of my dive slid me across the hallway floor, my head and shoulder slamming into the wall, my gun clattering out of my hand. The assassin staggered forward a couple steps, bringing his gun up to finish me off when something whanged into the back of his head. The impact had the hollow sound of a church bell. He crashed to the floor, his pistol rattled onto the tile, spinning away from his grip. At the entrance to the ward, Mrs. Dromenko stood over him, clutching a stainless-steel bedpan in her meaty hand, but he didn't move.

I moved toward the laid-out thug, picked up his weapon. It had one of those suppressor devices attached to the barrel. Heard about those but never seen one in person, just pictures. Guy who invented them thought they'd be useful for city folks who wanted to target practice without disturbing the neighbors. The killer's knee wound spread a small pool of blood on the tile floor, but Missus Dromenko's bedpan bludgeoning had knocked him out cold.

"You're bleedink again, Deputy Smock," Dromenko said. She yanked a sliver of wood from my neck.

I winced, muttered, "Ow."

"Is Missus McDonald okay?" I craned my head around the massive nurse to see into the ward, down near the other end where Cait's bed was.

I moved to go into the ward, but Missus Dromenko put a firm hand on my chest. "Is good. But you cannot go see. Viztink hours ofer."

Wil came up the stairs, stood over Number Two. "I heard shots. Is he dead?"

I holstered my Colt. "I caught him in the leg, but Missus Dromenko laid him out with a bedpan. Dead? I don't know."

Wil squatted next to the thug. "Believe he's breathing."

"Get something to tie him up with," I said. "Need to check on Cait."

Others started arriving on the scene—an attendant, a janitor, floor nurses, that nurse from the lobby. Sheriff Dunbar came up the back stairs, pushed through the gathering. He eyed the thug, turned to Wil. "Where's Hobart?"

Wil turned his eyes to the wall for a couple seconds, then back to Dunbar. "Back at the jail, dead. This man come in, shot him, took Turnbow. Musta shot him, too. He's laying dead back on Second Street."

Furrows creased the sheriff's brow. He sighed big. His eyes came to mine. "You find Veneto?"

"In the dining room at the hotel." I gestured to Number Two. "Veneto and the other guard dog. Told him just what I said I would: load up and get out of town. Didn't seem inclined to do that."

"Didn't expect he would." He turned toward the ward. "Miz McDonald okay?"

"Yep." I stepped around Missus Dromenko and her hand. She moved with me, pressed back. "Missus Dromenko, under the circumstances, surely you can make an exception."

She grunted, removed her hand from my chest reluctantly. "Hokay. Five minute." She followed, Dunbar trailed us. The two terrified young mothers clutched their swaddled infants close to them as we passed. I touched my hat. "Everything is okay, now, ladies." I hoped I sounded convincing.

Cait was awake but drowsy. "I heard noises, a gun, I think." Her words came out sleepily, a little slurred.

"Nothing to worry about," I soothed. "Go on back to sleep."

She smiled a little and drifted off, still under the influence of her last dose of morphine. I turned to the nurse, whispered, "Sheriff's deputy is dead, another man, too. That man in the hall came to kill Miz McDonald. There are others. Is there someplace we can move her where it'll be safer," I looked back at the mothers with their babies. "For everyone, until we can get this settled?"

"There is room," Dromenko said. "Special for Coleman family, but we can use." She faced the sheriff. "Need protection, more men."

Dunbar stuck out his lip. "Yep. I'll find some help for that." Sadness clouded his eyes. "Let's get that slug out in the hall back to the jail, then go to the hotel for the other two."

"Missus Dromenko, if you'll make arrangements to get Cait, uh, Miz McDonald moved to that room, I'll leave Wil here as a guard."

"Hokay."

We all went back to the hall. Number Two was still out. Dunbar spoke first. "I'll use the phone downstairs to get Ted Freeman over here with his meat wagon to haul this heap of manure to jail. We'll stop and pick up Turnbow, too. Can't leave bodies layin around on the streets." That sadness came back to his eyes. "Take care of Thomas, too."

CHAPTER 23

he light of the gibbous moon helped the ride. At our breakneck pace, we and the horses could better see where we were going, what might be ahead. Veneto and Carlo got at least an hour's head start.

Once we squared everything away back at the jail, we discovered Frank Veneto and his man had hired a rig from the livery and left town. Not hard to figure where they were headed. The attempt on Cait had a dual purpose: not only to eliminate her but to create a diversion.

I didn't figure Veneto to be a stupid man, but these blatant actions weren't smart. He knew the attempt on Cait's life would point straight back to him. I guess his grief and bent for revenge blinded him to the obvious. On the other hand, maybe he hadn't counted on me interfering. When Dunbar and I got to the hotel, Otis told us the two Chicago men left the dining room and hotel shortly after I had earlier. My guess, they upped their schedule to go to the Forked S.

The buggy was pulling up to the front porch of the ranch house when we entered the valley. I ran Clyde hard the five miles out there but gave him an extra kick to make that final two-hundred-yard sprint. Veneto's man, Carlo, took a stance behind the thick oak in the front yard, his boss entered the house. I could hear Athena's loud challenge and growl, a pop, then silence.

Husker came around the corner of the house to Carlo's left. The thug took him down with one shot. He swung his pistol back to us and spat out three shots in quick succession. Two of the three slugs cratered holes in the dirt in front of us. The third found our range, though, catching Dunbar's horse in the chest. The horse screamed and tumbled, throwing its rider headlong to the ground. I reined left to head for the orchard

211

just off one side of the house, hoping Clyde or I didn't catch the next one. Heard two more pops from the pistol, bark splinter off an apple tree in front of me. I slid from the saddle and slapped Clyde's rump to send him away from the line of fire, moved at a crouch deeper into the woods of the apple grove. Dunbar lay in a heap where he'd fallen, no movement.

No part of Carlo stuck out from behind the oak. He either hunkered behind it reloading or had moved. Hoped it was the former. I took off through the cover of the grove to the edge closest to the wide porch which swung around the side of the house from the front. It was about a thirty-yard dash in full moonlight between the apple grove and side of the porch elevated about three feet above the ground. Most of the snow was gone. A small icy hump remained next to the porch where it'd been shoveled off. Still no movement in or around the oak tree, or on the porch. Used the deep shadow of the wide porch to conceal me as I tried to flank him.

I made it to the snow pile and crouched, listening. Hearing nothing and seeing nothing, I slid under the porch railing and crawled to the side of the house. I stood, felt almost safe in the shade of the porch roof. I edged along the clapboard siding, waited at the corner. If Carlo was on the other side, I feared my pounding heartbeat would give me away. I rounded the corner, anyway, crouching, pointing my Colt into the darkness with both hands.

The front porch was empty, no Carlo behind the oak tree. That beforehand sense kicked in, something wasn't right, so I turned. I heard a click behind me, then swearing. He charged, swinging with intent to clobber me in the ear with his misfired pistol, but I crouched and pulled the trigger just as the brute slammed a knee into my shoulder sending my Colt flying from my hand. His body somersaulted over me. I heard him grunt in pain. We both rolled with the collision. Each of us came back to our feet facing one another. He charged again, but slower. I sidestepped and swung a right with all my weight behind it. My fist connected to the side of his jaw with a solid crack. He grunted and fell.

I searched the porch for my pistol, knowing it would be the only equalizer I'd have against the big thug if he got back up.

Carlo got back up. With a stagger. Rubbed his jaw but winced. He bent slightly and pulled a blade from his boot top. A small glint of moonlight caught the edge. The eight-inch blade had a curve to it, his fingers held the knife through four knuckles at the hilt, not dissimilar from the blade MacKenzie used, just smaller. Its appearance changed the balance of power to his side. I really needed to locate my Colt.

He came at me slow and deliberate with a look of malice aforethought. I backed. He growled and swung the blade, but I avoided it. The swing was just to put the fear in me. It worked. No doubt in my mind the next one would be for real.

I backed into the porch rail, the foot of my bad leg slipping on some leftover ice. Carlo swung the blade again, but I grabbed his arm with both hands as the blade slashed down toward my neck. A punch to the side of the head with his free fist sent me to my knees, but I held onto the arm with the knife. Thrown onto my back, his considerable weight came down totally atop me. His left hand encircled my throat in a crushing grip as he pushed the tip of the blade in the other hand ever closer toward my jugular. All the strength in my two arms barely kept the dagger away and I was flagging. Carlo slowly but surely began to overpower me.

From far away I heard two booms come from inside the house. The thought crawled around to me, almost in serene disappointment, that Veneto finished his job.

Something wet and warm soaked through the side of my coat. I thought Carlo finally slit my jugular, but I never felt the stick. The brute suddenly slumped fully down upon me, his left hand released its grip on my throat, the other arm in my two hands went limp.

When I got air back in my lungs, blood back in my brain, I pushed the dead weight off me. Dead was right. Be damned if my one shot hadn't put the bullet in his chest.

I sat there for a few seconds trying to re-focus and figure out what was going on.

"You awright, deputy?" someone asked.

Husker sat on the top step of the porch his back against a rail post. He held his pistol in his right hand laying across his thigh, fresh blood covered most of the front of his coat.

"Husker." I crawled over to the cowboy. "How bad you hit?"

He wheezed. "Aw, I've had worser. Mustang throwed me onest broke three ribs believe hurt more'n this. Saw you two goin at it, so figured I wasn't dead enough I couldn't help you out, but that bastard keeled over before I could get a shot off. Reckon you killed him, but it musta took him a while to figure it out."

"Yeah." I laughed without humor. "Almost too long awhile."

Wiley came running up, carrying a shotgun. "What the hell's goin on up here? That damn dog of yours was raisin hell in the bunkhouse, heard the gunshots." As if on cue, Hector came limping out of the darkness, sniffed Husker, me. He stepped up on the front porch and whined. Guess he picked up Athena's death smell.

"Look after Husker," I said. Took Wiley's shotgun and entered the front door.

Athena's limp body lay in the entry, a bloody bullet hole in her neck. No one downstairs, but I figured that. I took the stairs a step at a time, slowly, the shotgun cocked and held to my shoulder. Feared the worst: the Major and Asmita dead. Veneto lurking in the shadows.

214

The Major's bedroom door was ajar, weak light filtered through the crack. I could detect no movement. I eased the door open with the shotgun barrel keeping myself against the wall outside.

"Veneto!"

"Deputy Smoak, it's safe." I recognized the Major's voice. It sounded stronger than when I last heard it. I turned into the room, gun still at the ready.

Standback still lay in bed his pistol in his hand resting atop the bedcovers. Asmita sat across the room cross-legged on the floor, the butt of her shotgun on the oriental rug that covered most of the oak plank floor. The barrel pointed to the ceiling. Veneto's body was sprawled on the floor, a pool of his own gore beneath him, some—his, I supposed—splattered on the footboard and bedcovers.

"Heard the door open downstairs," Standback said. "Thought I recognized Frank's voice talking to his man. Suspected he shot the dog. I was ready for him. Been expecting him. He came into the room. Shot him in the stomach. Didn't stop him, though. He raised his gun to shoot me.

"Asmita," he motioned with his gun-free hand to a chair in the corner, "sitting over there in the dark, blew him half in two with that twelve-gauge."

Asmita returned my stare but said nothing. "Reckon it's over then," I said.

iley brought Husker into the parlor, set him to half-recline on the settee. The cowboy wouldn't die. With his toughness, and between Wiley and Asmita, I knew they'd get him back to cowpunching. Men like him don't stay down long if there's a chance to live on, whether it's after falling off a horse or taking a bullet. My guess, he'd be back stringing fence within a week.

I went out to check on the sheriff. The carcass of his horse lay where it tumbled. Shot through the heart. Found Dunbar sitting on the spot where he landed, legs splayed in front of him. Mud soaked half his face and all the front of his vest and pants. Dunbar turned his head in a slow swivel, searching, confused. "Where's my hat?" he asked. I retrieved it, handed it to him. He examined it front and back, crown and sweatband like he wasn't sure it was his. He stuck it on his head and asked, "Where's Hobart?"

I chewed my upper lip. "Back in town, Chuck. Remember? Veneto's man shot him."

His eyes cleared a little. "Oh, yeah." He paused, wiped some of the mud from his face, off his vest. Turned his gaze to his dead horse. "Dammit. Samson was a good horse." Back at me. "Did you get 'em?"

"Yeah, they're got. Veneto's dead, so's his man. Major and Asmita are okay. Gonna have to call Freeman again to collect the bodies," I said.

Dunbar got to his knees, swung to a stand with a stagger. "You sure been a boon to Ted's bidness, Deputy," he said.

The dead horse reminded me. Put thumb and forefinger into the corners of my mouth and gave a whistle. Clyde didn't appear, so I gave another whistle. Waited a full fifteen seconds expecting the horse to come trotting out of the apple orchard.

When he didn't, uneasiness filled me. I feared he caught a bullet during all the gunplay, so I entered the orchard to find him.

The high gibbous moon splintered the darkness around and between the rows of apple trees, making even the slightest movement in the light breeze suspicious. The bare-limbed trees were spaced about ten feet apart, their trunks six to eight inches in diameter, heights to ten feet or so with bottom limbs three-four feet off the ground. There were maybe eight rows spaced about ten yards apart, each thirty yards long. Hard to tell in the dark. Not a real good density for hiding, but Clyde was nowhere in sight. I called out, whistled again.

The silence in the night and in the moonlight-speckled orchard was disquieting. Unreasoned fear crept through me. I thought of MacKenzie, remembered seeing him escape his encounter with Redhand. Reason said he had to be dead by now, given the wounds he received from that fifty-caliber bullet. On the other hand, dread told me he was no ordinary man. I couldn't shake the feeling he still stalked his prey, would come here to the Forked S to complete his work. I couldn't count on him being dead until I saw him so.

I crouched, gun drawn, swiveling on the balls of my feet to see what I could out in the dark around me. My burn leg didn't let me get as small as I wanted. I would be easy to spot if MacKenzie was out there. Only hoped I'd spot him first.

I saw the flash of the claw in the moonlight, or maybe thought I did. I spun and jumped back a split second before it would rip into my back, but it caught my raised pistol at the cylinder, flinging it from my hand. His backswing raked into the lower limbs of an apple tree as I rolled behind it. MacKenzie roared in pain and rage. I scrambled away into the maze of the apple orchard before he could recover.

In my flight to get away, I lost my bearings. The orchard rolled over a small hill where I found myself at its bottom.

Couldn't see the house nor find its lights. Didn't think I stood a chance against MacKenzie unarmed, even in his wounded state. Now he was a madman made more insane with pain. Besides, after my earlier bout with Carlo, I was spent.

He didn't use stealth in his approach. I could hear him crashing through the trees, his breathing loud and ragged, amplified by a growl. He came relentlessly toward me as if he could see me in the dark.

My rifle was still in its boot on my saddle. I had to find Clyde. Or I had to find my way back to the ranch house. I took off perpendicular to MacKenzie's charge running almost blindly through the orchard. My right foot wedged under something and stuck as the rest of my body lunged forward. My ankle bent at an awkward angle and something popped. Pain shot up my leg and into my hip. I went down in a heap. I tried to stand but fell again.

The killer still crashed towards me, a hint of furious glee mixed into his growl as he saw me trying to crawl away. He stood above me, ready to make his kill. He attempted to raise his gauntleted claw high but couldn't. I flailed around on the ground, my hands desperately searching for anything to use as a weapon. He gripped me by the ankle with his good hand and yanked me toward him, swung the clawed gauntlet in a low arc. I raised my arm to block the blow and the claw raked into my coat sleeve, the blade ripped into the thick leather and wool of the sheepskin but didn't find flesh. He drew back to strike again. My hand closed around a length of wood, a fallen limb about three inches thick which I brought up to foil the blow.

I kicked the boot on my sprained ankle squarely into his crotch, mustering as much force as my fear-charged body would give me. I bellowed, partly from pain, partly from my own rage. He grunted and staggered backward.

I came to all fours and scrabbled to the nearest apple tree and behind it. He sagged, his strength withered. My kick had taken some of the fight out of him. He moaned and gasped for air, bent at the waist. But he was still enraged and dangerous.

I stood, having to put my weight on my bad leg as the right ankle wouldn't hold. Still had that wood club in my hand, its length some five feet. I lunged toward the assassin swinging the limb double-handed toward him. The branch struck the side of his head like an ax into an oak. He staggered sideways and went to his knees, but managed another swipe with the claw, this one catching my bum knee. I heard the rip of my pant leg and felt the warmth spreading there. I went down, almost all my strength sapped, breathing hard.

MacKenzie collapsed face-down. He pushed himself up on one elbow, dazed, shaking his head to clear it. We lay only a few feet apart, both exhausted from our combat. He started to crawl toward me, I skittered away on my back, my crippled legs not much help in the attempt. He was gaining on me. He came to all fours, lunged and chopped the claw toward my face. I dodged in a half-roll and the claw hacked into the wet earth. My left hand found a rock slightly bigger than my hand. Clutching it, I swung it hard connecting just behind his right ear. He roared and raised the gauntlet claw again, this time close enough upon me to give a fatal blow.

The night exploded and flashed. MacKenzie sucked in air and his upper body shunted sideways. He turned and stood to face his new attacker. The gun roared again. MacKenzie bellowed and leaped upon its bearer, growling and slavering like the wild beast he was. Both men fell in a twisting rolling brawl. Another gunshot. MacKenzie moved to the top. He paused, breathing raggedly, his victim well under his control. Whoever it was that attacked MacKenzie, had saved my hide, put three bullets into him, but it wasn't enough. He sat atop the gunman like a triumphant predator, letting his prey behold him before he delivered death.

I somehow got to my feet and lunged at the duo. I struck the back of MacKenzie's head with the jagged rock still in my hand. I pounded again and again. I felt the blood splatter around my hand and onto my face. He toppled and lay still, his breathing tortured and shallow. Then it stopped.

I fell backward scrabbling feebly a few feet until I found the trunk of an apple tree. I sat up against it. Still holding the bloody rock in my bloody hand, gasping for air, I stayed there watching the heap of the two bodies until I was sure MacKenzie wouldn't rise again. But the other did. He got to his knee, then to his feet. He still held his pistol in his right hand. Crow Redhand raised the gun, pointed it at my head. He held it there for a long time. I was too exhausted to fight anymore, even to try to talk him out of it.

"Third time's the charm, Crow," was all I could think to say. Then I waited.

Musta been a minute before he lowered that pistol. Felt like a couple hours.

"We're even now," he said. "Don't come after me." He holstered his gun, turned and walked out of the orchard.

I stayed where I was, too drained to move. After about ten minutes, Clyde walked up to me out of the gloom. Touched his nose to my forehead and snuffled.

CHAPTER 25

I couldn't mount up. It wasn't easy to limp on two legs, but with Clyde's help, I managed to get back to the Ranch house. I got as far as the porch steps. Wiley heard me and came out. Took one look and said, "I'll fetch Asmita."

She took off my boot and examined my ankle. "Not broke," she said and pulled on my instep and heel. I screamed, and something popped again. To my wonderment, it didn't hurt as much after that. I could walk on it, even swollen. She cleaned up the cut across my knee and bandaged it, declaring it didn't need sewing up. Plastered it and my ankle up with some of her snake oil. Didn't offer me anything for the pain, though. I think all my wounds over the past couple weeks had depleted her stores.

Sheriff Dunbar couldn't locate Freeman, who was no doubt already busy with what we left in town, so we commandeered a ranch wagon to haul the bodies in ourselves. By the time we headed back—Dunbar manning the wagon—the moon hung well past its zenith, but still high and bright. A few wisps of clouds passed briefly in front of it now and then. Once again, riding along the cold night road through the dark woods, I got that skin-crawling feel, hair on my neck standing up. Couldn't help but wonder what was out there looking back at us. Of course, I didn't see anything, only felt it creeping along just out of our sight in the dark trees. Didn't hear anything, either, except what my mind made me think I heard. I knew it wasn't MacKenzie. He was under a tarp in the wagon. But the she-wolf was out there, paralleling our ride. That's what pounded in one side of my brain, the other side telling me it was damn foolishness to think that.

We got back to town well after the moon set and the sun about to come up, our breath frosty in the cold indigo of the dawn light. I turned off toward the hospital, Dunbar kept along Main Street to make his delivery to Ted Freeman. A few lights were on at the hospital with morning stirrings taking place. It was near shift change. One of the orderlies who helped with Cait exited from the ambulance entrance and came in my direction. It was the one whose dark eyes didn't quite look at you when he looked at you. Young man named Monroe, about twenty.

"Mornin," I said.

He smiled, eyes pointed somewhere off my left shoulder. "Mornin, Deputy."

"Headed home?"

"Yep. Long night?" My tattered appearance not unnoticeable.

"Yep," I said. "Which way's home?"

He pointed toward Main, in the general direction of the Coleman Hotel.

"Wonder if we could do each other a favor?" I reached into my front pocket, fishing. He kept his eyes on that spot off my shoulder waiting for me to explain.

"Would you mind taking Clyde here to the livery behind the hotel? Maybe that'd give you a ride partway home." I reached out to hand him a half dollar piece. "Tell the man to feed him, brush him down good."

He considered my hand offering the coin but didn't take it. "Be glad to, Deputy. But I don't want nothing for it."

"Appreciate it," I said, re-pocketing the coin.

He mounted and rode off. I knocked the heels of my boots against the outside brick wall, despite my bad ankle, to knock what mud off I could and limped into the hospital. Wil sat in a chair leaned against the wall next to the Coleman Suite's door. His head was bowed, hat pulled down over his eyes. I pounded the wall with the heel of my fist as I gimped down the hall toward him, but he didn't rouse.

"Hey!" I said. He pushed his hat up.

"Some guard," I said.

"Thanks." Rubbed his face and eyes with both hands. "Nobody got past me all night."

Just as I prepared to give a soft knock on the door, it opened. Missus Dromenko came out.

"You been here all night, too?" I asked.

"Da. Miss Bremer come take my place. I leaf now." She brushed by me, then stopped and turned. "Is danger gone for her? You catch bad men?"

"Yep. How's she doing this morning?"

"Some better, I tink. Slept night. Is waking now."

"Can I go in?"

"I check for you." She re-entered the room, closed the door behind her. I waited in the hallway, holding my hat by the brim turning it in a circle.

"Long as you're here, believe I'll go get me some breakfast," Wil said and sauntered off down the hall, not the least bit curious about what had happened.

"I'll meet you back at the sheriff's office," I called after him.

It took a few minutes for Dromenko to return. "Is okay, now. You go in."

With her and Miss Bremer's help, Cait managed to prop herself up. Her sallow skin hung on gaunt cheeks, but she had put her hair up some.

"Hello, Jubal," she said. Her smile was warm, but her eyes still held pain. I dreaded giving her more, telling her about Athena.

"It's over, Cait. Veneto's dead. So's MacKenzie."

Her expression echoed relief. "The Major?"

"He's okay. So's Asmita."

I studied the water pitcher on the stand beside her bed, trying to come up with a gentle way to give her the next bit of news.

"And Athena? Hector?"

She was a keen woman. Read my expression like an open scroll.

"Athena . . . she . . . Veneto shot her." I shook my head. "Hector's okay, though. Well, he's still bunged up and crippled, but he's alive. Didn't get into the fight."

Her eyes welled, a tear rolled down her cheek. She wiped it away with a finger. "Well, I suppose I can take what's left, take Hector, and try to put things back together at my place. When I get out of here."

After a bit, the question just popped out. It'd been niggling at me. "How'd you know about Emily Standback and MacKenzie, all of it?"

Miss Bremer made herself busy around Cait, fluffing her pillow, pouring her a glass of water, taking the chart off the hook at the foot of the bed as if to read it. She pretended not to notice us as she fussed around Cait's bed.

Cait watched her, I turned to her. "Miss, could you excuse us?"

The girl did sort of a curtsy. "Of course. I'll go get your breakfast, ma'am."

Cait waited for the nurse to exit before she spoke.

"It was the subtle but increasing hostility toward me when I was in her home. She never did really like me, so I just tried to ignore it, make the best of the situation. Then Turnbow kept coming around and Brooks, they'd have whispering conversations away from me, stop talking when I came into the room. It made me distrustful, I guess with good reason. I started sneaking around trying to listen in. Caught them a couple times. Once she was talking with Turnbow about MacKenzie and finishing off the Major. The other time was the day they wanted to kill me. I knew what they were up to when they lured me out to the smokehouse, but I played along, figuring it was them or me. It was my only chance. Good luck that you came along when you did or Turnbow would've got me. Believe that was part of the plan."

She got quiet, turned her eyes to the window.

"You found lead and zinc on your land?" I asked.

She nodded. "Major had discovered some, too. But he's like me, didn't want to disturb the land to get at it. He'd seen what it'd done to the Quapaw land up around Picher and over at Joplin. Didn't want his ranch turned into that. He loves it too much. Told me he's a cattleman, not a miner. He admires George Coleman but didn't want the trouble that came with the wealth, that he was content with what he had. I think Mister Coleman respected him for that. Guess I felt the same way. My husband's leases have left me comfortable. I love those woods and hills the way they are. Don't care to have the invasion of men and machinery and the denudement that comes with mining. It'll always be there. Maybe someday I won't want to live there anymore, but right now I'm content to live the way I do."

I watched my hands spinning my hat. "Sounds like you got it figured out."

We shared a long awkward silence. "What're you going to do now?" she asked.

Quit spinning the hat and put it on my head. "Thought I'd go get some breakfast."

She laughed, then stopped from the pain it caused, still grinning, though. "No, I mean now that everything's settled. Are you heading back to Tulsa?"

"Oh." I grinned back, maybe a little sheepish. Felt some heat on my cheeks. "Well, things aren't settled. Two of my prisoners are dead and one got away."

"Which one." Her eyes got bigger.

"Crow Redhand. Still, need to bring him in. That's what I was originally sent out here to do."

☒

First place I went to was Joe Elkfoot's. Sure enough, Crow'd been there, but took off. Joe said Crow told him about all the doings with Veneto and his men, our death match with MacKenzie. To Joe's credit, he tried to talk Crow into turning himself in, but Redhand was too afraid he'd hang.

Sheriff Dunbar was holding a telegram for me when I returned from Elkfoot's. Tulsa office wanted me back there. I protested, but my boss said Crow Redhand would have to wait. Something more pressing came up. Not sure what'd be more pressing than the likes of Crow Redhand, but I'm not one to disobey orders. Still, I was conflicted. Crow shot me twice, I shot him once. He saved my life twice, I'd saved his once. But the settling between us would have to wait for another day.

About a week went by before I could tie everything up with the Major and Sheriff Dunbar. The sheriff was short a deputy, so Wil signed on with him. Told Wil I sure did appreciate his help and companionship, that I'd be proud to have him ride with me anytime. Guess he considered it a job offer as he said he'd consider it, but at that moment he preferred to town deputy for Sheriff Dunbar.

Made one last trip to the hospital to check on Cait, say goodbye. She could walk some by then, sit for periods. Doc said she was gonna come out fine. I didn't know what my parting words would be, after all we'd been through. I'd developed strong feelings but didn't know how to express them. Only way I knew to deal with them was to take off. Anyway, didn't figure she had as much shine on me as I did her.

"Hector followed me in from the Forked S," is how I started out after I asked how she was doing. She knew why I was there. "He's found him a place over at the sheriff's office to bed down, get some food and water. Reckon he'll be fine there until you're ready to get back to your place."

She had a sad face. "No, I doubt he'll want to come back with me, not back there."

I shifted my feet. "Aw, Heck's kind of grumpy, but he won't leave you. He . . . he loves you."

She smiled in that sad way but didn't say anything else about it.

I cleared my throat, getting ready to open my mouth to say something, something that took a considerable amount of screwing up my courage to do when Mrs. Dromenko plowed into the room.

"Is time for bath," she said. I stepped back to let her wedge by in front of me to the bedside. "You go. Comink back later." She busied herself fussing with Cait.

I looked at Cait, she looked at me. Guess we both knew there wouldn't be any coming back later.

Walking down the hall, Mrs. Dromenko called after me at the hospital room door. I turned, she came into the hall, closing the door behind her, I walked back to her. Her eyes creased at the corners with gravity, had some fright in them.

"You hear about boy?"

In all the excitement I completely forgot about him, the Jakes boy. She licked her lips, swallowed. I figured it was not good news. "Zeb Jakes? He die?"

"Nyet." She shook her head. "He is come to, but . . ." Put her hand to her mouth. "Is gone. Walk out of hospital."

"Gone? Somebody come take him?"

"Walk out his own. But someone wait for him outside."

"How can that be? He's blind."

"When he come to, is not blind. Is miracle, I tink. Only . . . walk out of hospital."

"What? Didn't anyone try to stop him?"

"Monroe, me, but he is strong, and . . ." Now genuinely afraid, wringing her hands.

"And what?"

"Look in eyes wild, fierce. And, and . . . blue. It scare me. I back off. Monroe, too."

I didn't quite know what to make of this story. "When did this happen?"

"Last night. Monroe follow him outside, watch him go to meet old man near woods. Monroe said old Indin man. They go together into woods, not town."

"Long Walker," I whispered to myself. Might be a good thing. Old Long Walker may be the closest the boy has to family . . . except for his dad.

I rode out around noon. Said so long to Wil and Dunbar. Crouched down next to Hector sprawled next to the stove. Gave him a piece of jerky I had in my coat. It was gonna be a part of my lunch, but I decided it'd serve better as a parting gift to the beast who saved my life. He took it and chewed while I scratched the back of his thick neck.

A mile out of town Clyde jerked the reins, grunted, turned sideways a bit. I spun the horse around to see if I could find what jumped him. A hundred yards back, Hector came limping toward us. We waited till he got close. He looked up at me, panting easily, sat, licked his chops, looked away like I wasn't all that important to him.

"Guess Cait was right about you. You ain't wanting to stick around here, are ya?"

He glanced up at me when I spoke, but his eyes went back to the yonder, still panting. He didn't really give a damn what I had to say.

"Well, you can come with me if you want. Guess there's enough room on the trail for another crippled-up old dog. We got that much in common."

I headed on. Heck stood and followed. Doubt my invitation would've mattered to him, anyway.

We passed on through Quapaw land, passed near the cold ghostly cabin of the Jakes, past the thick woods near the river where Long Walker's lodge stood nearly hidden. A curl of smoke from the treetops was the only indication of its whereabouts. Most likely Crow would be there, with his boy. I considered for a long minute going in there to see about Crow, the old man, see for myself the blind boy who now had sight. But something told me not to. Something about sleeping dogs . . . or wolves. Crow had, after all, saved my life.

Not far past there, Hector stiffened and growled. We stopped in our tracks. His head was erect, ears perked forward, back bristled, a growing rumble came from his throat. I followed to where his nose pointed above those curled lips. Took out my pilfered Army field glasses. A quarter-mile off stood the big form of the she-wolf, black like a shadow in the sunlight. Her lips curled in a momentary snarl as if she could see and hear Hector's challenge, me looking back at her. It struck me as a malevolent grin, an evil ancient grimace that spoke of a primordial hunger. She stood un-cowed at any human presence, a daunting beast who would tear into your soul as easily as your flesh, just as the Downstream People feared. We stood and watched one another for a few minutes before she turned and trotted away.

Hector was content to stand, bristle, and growl. He didn't appear inclined to go after the wolf.

I didn't argue with the big dog.

A Personal Note from the Author

Thank you for taking time to read *Dire Wolf of the Quapaw*. If you enjoyed it, please consider posting a short review on Amazon and telling your friends. Word of mouth is an author's best friend and much appreciated.

Would you consider being in my Readers Group? As a member, you'll receive periodic emails from me (no spam) about new releases, promotions, giveaways, blog posts, etc. No more than about twice a month. I would love to have you in the group. Please visit my website to sign-up and receive a free ebook:

www.philtrumanink.com

Thanks again – Phil Truman

About the Author

Phil Truman is a native Oklahoman. A graduate of Tulsa University, he's a former teacher, coach, businessman, and Vietnam Era veteran. Phil is the author of six Oklahoma/Indian Territory-based novels, in genres of mystery, adventure, and historical American Western. He and his wife Darlene have lived in the Tulsa suburban city of Broken Arrow for more than 40 years. Phil's website is at www.PhilTruman.com. He can be contacted at Phil@PhilTruman.com.

Made in the USA
Coppell, TX
08 September 2020

37269355R00139